PLEASURE CRUISE

What Reviewers Say About
Yolanda Wallace's Work

The War Within

"*The War Within* has a masterpiece quality to it. It's a story of the heart told with heart—a story to be savored—and proof that you're never too old to find (or rediscover) true love."—*Lambda Literary*

Rum Spring

"The writing was possibly the best I've seen for the modern lesfic genre, and the premise and setting was intriguing. I would recommend this one."—*The Lesbrary*

Murphy's Law

"Prepare to be thrilled by a love story filled with high adventure as they move toward an ending as turbulent as the weather on a Himalayan peak."—*Lambda Literary*

Lucky Loser

"Yolanda Wallace is a great writer. Her character work is strong, the story is compelling, and the pacing is so good that I found myself tearing through the book within a day and a half."—*The Lesbian Review*

Visit us at www.boldstrokesbooks.com

By the Author

In Medias Res

Rum Spring

Lucky Loser

Month of Sundays

Murphy's Law

The War Within

Love's Bounty

Break Point

24/7

Divided Nation, United Hearts

True Colors

Tailor-Made

Pleasure Cruise

Written as Mason Dixon:

Date With Destiny

Charm City

21 Questions

PLEASURE CRUISE

by
Yolanda Wallace

2018

PLEASURE CRUISE
© 2018 By Yolanda Wallace. All Rights Reserved.

ISBN 13: 978-1-63555-219-5

This Trade Paperback Original Is Published By
Bold Strokes Books, Inc.
P.O. Box 249
Valley Falls, NY 12185

First Edition: July 2018

Credits
Editor: Cindy Cresap
Production Design: Susan Ramundo
Cover Design By Melody Pond

Acknowledgments

This book was incredibly fun to write for two reasons: it not only gave me a chance to take a virtual tour of some of the countries I have always longed to visit, it also afforded me the opportunity to catch up with some of the characters from my previous books.

Like readers, I often wonder what some of my favorite characters' lives are like now that they've found their respective happily-ever-afters. With *Pleasure Cruise*, I was able to revisit them and, in some cases, bring them a bit more turmoil along the way. I hope you enjoy the journey as much as I did.

As always, I would like to thank Radclyffe, Sandy, Cindy, and the rest of the Bold Strokes Books team for providing the fantastic support system that allows me to continue indulging my favorite hobby.

I would also like to thank the readers for their continued support. You rock!

Finally, I would like to thank Dita for continuing to put up with me and all the characters in my head. I couldn't do any of this without you.

Dedication

To Dita,
Every day with you is a pleasure.

ALL ABOARD

Amy Donovan loved her job. On most days. Today wasn't one of those days.

Keeping a tight grip on the walkie-talkie that would be her constant companion during the next eight days and seven nights, she watched anxiously as a steady stream of passengers laden with carry-ons made their way from the cruise terminal to the *Majestic Dream*. Most carried one or two small suitcases, while some had five or six pieces of luggage in tow. And that wasn't counting the larger bags they had been required to hand over to a porter stationed outside the terminal. By the time the guests made it to their staterooms, their bags would be waiting for them outside their doors. Theoretically. With so many guests and pieces of luggage in play, there were guaranteed to be a few mix-ups. Amy expected to be fielding calls regarding lost and/or misplaced items for the next few hours—if not days.

She had always envied travelers who packed light, but she had only recently become a convert. Her personal high was the five bags she had taken on a luxury cruise to Tahiti, but she had managed to cram all her belongings into one suitcase this trip because she would be too busy to wear much more than shorts, comfortable shoes, and a string of brightly colored SOS Tours T-shirts and tank tops. She planned to get dressed up for the formal captain's dinner on the last night of the trip, but her more eye-catching outfits would have to wait until she wasn't on call twenty-four hours a day. If someone's toilet flooded their stateroom while they were lounging around one of the two pools, or a passenger had a medical emergency in the middle of the night, she needed to make sure she was wearing something sensible instead of sexy while she supervised the repairs or waited for the Coast Guard helicopter to arrive.

This was work, not a pleasure cruise. For her and the rest of the staff, anyway. The passengers who had forked over thousands of dollars for one of several vacation packages her company offered might beg to differ.

Amy was pleased to see that, despite the large influx of new arrivals, check-in was going relatively smoothly. According to a team member keeping an eye on things in the cruise terminal, the lines were moving quickly, and no one seemed to be objecting to the thorough security screenings. Apparently, everyone was already in vacation mode, even though their vacations had barely begun. She hoped the good vibes would continue after the ship left port and set sail for Turks and Caicos, the first of four scheduled stops along a route that would lead from Fort Lauderdale to three islands in the Caribbean and back again. If not, she and everyone else on board could be in for rough seas in the days ahead.

Modern cruise ships were so big they were often referred to as floating cities. If that was the case, this particular town was smaller than some, and it had a distinctly lesbian feel. Amy wouldn't have it any other way.

She had been working for SOS Tours since the company went into business three years before, slowly working her way up from unpaid intern to salaried employee. When she first started working for the company, she had been a lowly gofer whose main responsibilities were making sure she kept the coffee pots full of fresh brew and didn't screw up the daily lunch orders. Now she was an assistant vice president tasked with making sure two thousand paying clients' "trip of a lifetime" didn't turn into a collective nightmare.

"No pressure," she said under her breath, even though she was already tempted to gnaw at what remained of her fingernails.

After the passengers turned over their passports to the purser for safekeeping and posed for a photograph the ship's crew would use to identify them when they presented their ID cards during the voyage, they were allowed to board the ship and make their way to their staterooms on one of the ten decks. A few people balked at having to part with their passports—until seasoned travelers assured them it was standard procedure.

The control freak in Amy understood their reluctance. She had been equally hesitant on her first cruise until the free spirit in her had convinced her that giving up a little bit of control was a fair tradeoff for the exciting adventure looming before her. The trip itself hadn't been especially memorable, but it had sparked her love of travel and stoked her interest in seeking out a career in the industry.

The disparate parts of her personality made her good at her job. Her organizational skills helped her keep each member of the team focused on providing their clients with the best possible experience, while her ability to go with the flow came in handy when the inevitable moment arrived that their carefully laid plans went awry.

She had learned the hard way that no matter how many contingency plans she made, there was always at least one scenario she hadn't expected. Things would be different this time, though. They had to. Because the alternative was unthinkable. If even one thing went wrong during this trip, it could prove disastrous. Not only for her, but her employers as well. The company's reputation had already been damaged. Another bad outing could ruin it completely. Then where would she be? Most likely sitting on a barstool nursing a lemon drop martini while she decided what she wanted to do with the rest of her life after she had allowed the best job she ever had to slip through her fingers.

"I can't let that happen," she told herself as the boarding process continued. "No way. No how." Even though it was much too soon for a status report, she raised her two-way radio to her mouth and hailed Breanna Lafaele, her trusted second-in-command for the week. "Talk to me, Bree. How's it going down there?"

In addition to talking Amy off the ledge not if but when she got overwhelmed, Breanna was in charge of the Indies, SOS Tours-speak for clients who had chosen to travel on their own instead of with a life partner or a group of friends. Her twin sister, Leanna, also worked for SOS. Leanna spearheaded Wahines on Water, a program geared toward enhancing the vacation experiences of clients of color. The moniker reflected Leanna and Breanna's Hawaiian heritage, but the group was inclusive of other minorities and their allies. In other words, WOW wasn't a private party. Everyone was welcome to attend its get-togethers if they chose to accept the invitation.

Breanna and Leanna looked and sounded so much alike Amy often had to refer to their name tags to tell who was who. There was no confusing their personalities, though. Breanna was the life of the party, while Leanna was more reserved. Relatively speaking, of course. On trips like these, when everyone left their day jobs behind and concentrated on giving the clients a vacation they wouldn't soon forget, both twins turned into whirlwinds. One of many reasons Amy was grateful to have them on her team.

"Everything's as smooth as a set of silk sheets," Breanna said with an earthy laugh that went a long way toward settling Amy's jangled nerves. "Relax, girl. We've got this. What happened on the Cancún trip isn't going to happen this time around. Not on our watch."

"From your mouth to God's ears." Amy wished she felt a fraction of Breanna's confidence. She wasn't normally wracked with self-doubt, but this situation was as far from normal as it could get. Perhaps she should stick to scouting potential vacation destinations instead of supervising the trips themselves. Too late for that. Even though the anchor had not yet been raised, for all intents and purposes, the ship had already sailed. "Let me know if anything changes."

"Will do."

Amy, Breanna, and the other members of the SOS Tours staff onsite had inspected every inch of the ship in the days leading up to embarkation. Not once, but twice. The administrators of the cruise line SOS had partnered with for this voyage had assured Amy everything was fine, but she didn't want to take any chances. She couldn't afford to. Not when so much was at stake. Not only was her name on the line. So was the company's.

SOS Tours was one of the most well known organizations focusing on women-only travel. The company specialized in cruises, though it had recently started adding resort trips to its brand. Amy was in favor of diversifying SOS Tours' travel portfolio, but she had heard whispers from industry insiders and even some clients that they considered the move a very expensive mistake. Now the whispers were getting louder as the number of SOS Tours' critics started to mount.

SOS Tours was still trying to recover from the public relations disaster that had occurred during its inaugural land-based trip six months ago. After armed members of the infamous Jaguars drug cartel had stormed the swanky Mariposa Resort in Cancún, Mexico, the ensuing hostage situation had resulted in the death of one SOS Tours staffer, hundreds of traumatized guests, and numerous skittish customers.

Amy had stopped trying to keep up with all the cancellations that had come rolling in once SOS Tours resumed normal business operations after the ill-fated Cancún trip. Clients weren't the only ones who were nervous. Wary of a possible repeat incident, several SOS Tours employees had turned in their notices. Some had defected to rival companies, but most had chosen to enter another line of work altogether in case SOS's bad karma followed them to their next travel-related gig.

Amy couldn't blame them for being anxious. Even though she hadn't witnessed the events in Mexico firsthand, her friends' accounting of what had taken place made her feel like she had been in the room with them while they cowered in fear.

She had shed buckets of tears and tossed and turned through countless sleepless nights while she tried to decide if she should remain with the company or join the exodus out the door. In the end, she had decided to stay put. SOS Tours was her dream job, and her co-workers were like family to her. Now her loyalty was being rewarded.

She had been granted the opportunity to serve as cruise director for SOS Tours' first scheduled trip since the nightmare in Cancún. A great deal was riding on the outcome of the journey— possibly even the company's survival.

A successful voyage marked by thousands of smiling customers and even more fond memories would go a long way toward erasing the recent past. But if the trip went sideways— from bad weather to unexpected mechanical problems to a dreaded norovirus outbreak—it could mean the final nail in the coffin.

Amy felt confident she could find another job if she had to, but she knew she wouldn't enjoy her next position nearly as much as she did her current one. Where else could she get paid to help women plan the vacation of their dreams, then be granted the privilege of watching those dreams come true?

Travel agencies had once been on the verge of becoming obsolete, thanks to the dozen or so websites that allowed potential travelers to book their own flights and accommodations, but business across the industry was on the upswing. Amy was happy to assist clients who had grown weary of trying to stay abreast of the latest travel restrictions and would rather leave the groundwork to professionals who were paid to keep up with the ever-changing list of sanctioned countries. Instead of jumping ship like her former co-workers had, Amy was determined to not only help SOS Tours maintain its standing in the niche market it served but improve upon it.

"But first, I have to survive the next eight days."

❖

Spencer Collins showed her boarding pass and driver's license to the security agent in the cruise terminal lobby. After the agent returned her documents and waved her through, her ears began to ring from the cacophony inside the cavernous building.

"Look out," someone said. "Coming through."

Heeding the warning, Spencer took a step to her left to avoid getting run over by a family of four, a couple in color-coordinated outfits and two teenagers paying more attention to the text messages on their cell phones than where they were going.

"Whose idea was this again?" she asked herself after her close encounter with the harried nuclear family.

Definitely not hers. The trip was her mother's idea. Her parents booked a cruise for their anniversary each year. They always returned home raving about what a good time they had and asking Spencer to tag along on their next trip, but she always found a reason to beg off. This time, they didn't give her a choice. They had taken her to dinner for her birthday and made a big show of presenting her with a card while they waited for dessert to arrive. Instead of the gift certificate to her favorite electronics store she had asked for, they had surprised her with an all-expenses paid Caribbean cruise.

"Doesn't the itinerary look amazing?" her mother had asked, barely able to sit still.

"Yes," Spencer had said hesitantly, "but I don't know if I'll be able to go."

"Nonsense," her father had said. "You have more vacation hours built up than some people have regular ones. I'm sure that company you work for can live without you for a week or two. It's time you got out of the house and let loose for a change."

Her idea of fun was going fishing on a quiet lake or playing a video game on her couch, not spending a week with two thousand random strangers.

"Since it's a women-only cruise," her mother had said as the server placed an oversized double-chocolate brownie on the table, "maybe you can finally meet someone."

Spencer had been mortified by her mother's oh-so-public mention of her nonexistent love life. She had felt like digging a hole and crawling into it. The server had caught her eye after she set three dessert spoons on the table. Spencer had expected sympathy, but the expression on the server's face had been anything but compassionate. Not altogether surprising, given the server was a member of the group of mean girls that had made her life miserable—both in high school and beyond—but Spencer had been surprised to find herself agreeing with the server's bleak assessment of her chances at finding true love.

With frenemies like these, she had thought as she'd blown out the candles on her birthday brownie, who needs enemies?

She had accepted her parents' well-intentioned gift with a smile and promised to try to have a good time on the cruise, but her resolve hadn't lasted long. In fact, she had spent most of today's six-and-a-half-hour drive from Pipkinville, Georgia, to Fort Lauderdale, Florida, trying to convince herself to keep going instead of turning around. She was still doing the same thing now.

"You've made it this far," she said as she joined the long line snaking through the screening machines at the security checkpoint. "You might as well keep going."

Geena Davis's character had said something similar at the end of *Thelma and Louise*. What had that gotten her? A slow-motion drop into the Grand Canyon, that's what. Spencer wasn't looking to repeat the feat. But what was she looking for exactly? A change of pace, a change of scenery, or a chance to prove she wasn't the lost cause everyone seemed to think she was?

"All that and then some."

After she finally made it through the line at security, she joined the line in front of the check-in counter for the next round of hurry up and wait. When she finally reached the front of the queue, she presented her passport, boarding pass, and ship card application to the Centennial Cruises employee manning the desk.

She peered at the screen as the employee—the small rectangular name tag affixed to his crisp white uniform said his name was Ian—entered the information on her application into his computer.

"There we go," he said after he tapped the *Enter* key with a flourish. "If you'd like to open an expense account, I can take care of that for you now. All I need is the credit card you'd like to use to make the purchases."

Spencer didn't plan to buy anything in the next week since most of the food and drinks were all-inclusive, but she handed over her credit card just in case. "Better safe than sorry."

Ian punched a few more buttons and double-checked the data he had entered. "You're all set." He returned her credit card, but handed her passport to the purser. "Don't worry," he said with a practiced laugh as she fought down a wave of separation anxiety. "You can ask for your passport back if you decide to leave the ship for any reason. Just give us fair warning so we'll have enough lead time to retrieve it for you. We wouldn't want you to miss any of the exciting excursions we have available."

Spencer was scheduled to take several excursions during the cruise, but she hadn't had a hand in choosing any of them. Her mother had assigned herself those chores and hadn't asked for any input. Spencer's only task had been getting herself to the ship on time. In her work life, she was used to calling her own shots. This time, she was forced to follow someone else's lead for a change. Even though the ship had yet to leave port, she could already tell she was in a much different world.

"This is your cruise card." Ian handed her a small plastic card listing her name, the name of the cruise line, the dates of the voyage, and the name of the ship. "Please keep it on or near you at all times. The card is multipurpose. Its primary function is as a cabin door key, but it also provides access to the ship. You'll need to present it to a member of our security team each time you attempt to disembark or board. The information contained on it includes your dining assignment and muster station. You'll use one every day. The other, hopefully, not at all." He glanced at his computer monitor and scanned it until he located the information he sought. "You have an early dining assignment. Table forty-six in the main ballroom on the upper promenade deck. Second seating begins each night at six, which will give you plenty of time to enjoy a leisurely meal before the first of our two nightly shows."

When she had gotten home from her birthday celebration, Spencer had ventured to SOS Tours website to take a peek at the list of entertainers scheduled to make appearances during the week. If she remembered correctly, a pop star who had just won the Grammy for Best New Artist would be giving a kickoff concert before the ship set sail in a few hours. Once they were underway, a slew of comedians, musicians, athletes, and celebrity chefs would take turns performing, giving how-to demonstrations, or sitting down for fan-friendly question-and-answer sessions. Unlike her parents, who attended practically every event offered on their cruises, Spencer didn't want to spend her vacation running from one deck to another in the hopes she wouldn't miss out on something. That would be almost as stressful as being at work. On the other hand, she didn't want to spend the entire week holed up in her room either. What was the point of coming on this trip if she didn't allow herself to take part in the spectacle?

"Since the *Majestic Dream* operates on a cashless system, you'll need to present your ID card each time you choose to dine in one of the specialty restaurants or make a purchase in any of the dozens of shops we have on board." Ian's voice drew Spencer out of her reverie. "You'll be given a receipt after each transaction, and you'll have a chance to review your final bill on the last night of your voyage so we can make any corrections or adjustments before you close your account."

His speech sounded rehearsed—as if he had delivered the lines hundreds of times before—but his obvious enthusiasm was so infectious Spencer wondered if she should have gotten booster shots before she left home.

She adjusted her grip on her rolling carry-on. Her palms were sweating. And not because of the warm Florida sun beaming through the terminal windows. Having grown up in the South, she was used to the heat and humidity. The weather wasn't what had her so at odds. It was everything else.

Since she worked from home—her desk was her dining room table and her usual work uniform consisted of a T-shirt and a pair of baggy shorts—she was used to doing most things remotely. All this external stimulation was almost too much to take. But wasn't that the reason she was here in the first place? To prove she could connect to someone without a computer, monitor, mouse, or router involved?

"Do you have any questions?" Ian asked when he finally finished delivering his spiel.

"Just one. What do I do next?"

Ian nodded as if he had been expecting the question. "You have only two more stops left before you can officially start your vacation. The ship's photo staff is waiting to take a welcome photo you can purchase after you board. When that's done, stop by the I-Pass kiosk for a security photo. That picture will be entered into the ship's computer database and linked to your ID card, allowing the staff to positively identify you each time you make a purchase or attempt to exit or board the ship."

Spencer bypassed the optional welcome photo because she had an aversion to kitschy souvenirs. Especially those involving green screens and digitally superimposed images of frolicking sea creatures. After she posed for the mandatory security photo, she headed down the walkway that led to the *Majestic Dream*.

The ship teemed with activity. Spencer stood in the middle of the maelstrom, uncertain where she was supposed to go. Her ID card listed what deck her room was on, but she had no idea how to find it.

She looked around for someone to ask, but all the stewards seemed to be busy helping other passengers. If she had a map of the ship, she could find her own way. But she had been doing just that for as long as she could remember. This week, she was supposed to be trying something different.

It had been years since she'd drifted this far outside her comfort zone. Ten, to be exact. She hadn't been on an honest-to-God vacation since high school when her senior class had taken a five-day cruise to Cozumel, Mexico. She had looked forward to the trip for months, but it had turned out to be the worst week of her life. After they boarded the ship in Miami, she had spent the first two days upchucking in her room before she finally managed to get her sea legs under her. Then everything had gone from bad to worse.

She closed her eyes as she tried to forget the night she had earned the unfortunate nickname that had stuck with her to this day: Kamikaze Collins. The night she—

"Do you need some help?"

Spencer opened her eyes to find a vision standing in front of her. The label sounded corny, even in her head, but she didn't know how else to describe a woman as drop-dead gorgeous as this one.

The woman was tall, tan, and blond. She was like Bo Derek in *10*—minus the cheesy, only-on-vacation cornrows and the slow-motion jog on the beach. With the right amount of persuasion, however, perhaps she would be willing to try her hand at both.

Spencer didn't normally go for blondes, but something about this one made her want to flip the script. Was it the way the woman filled out her tight red tank top and skimpy khaki shorts? Was it the perfect posture that accentuated her broad shoulders and narrow waist? Or was it the sunny smile that lit up her face, making her look even more beautiful than she did when her features were at rest? Perhaps it was all three. Whatever the reason, Spencer wanted to move closer instead of shying away.

The woman extended her hand, her grip strong and sure. "I'm Amy Donovan. I'll be your cruise director this week."

"Spencer Collins. It's nice to meet you."

Amy reached up and removed her sunglasses, revealing eyes as blue as the cloudless sky above. "Is this your first trip with SOS Tours?" she asked, tucking the folded handle of her sunglasses inside the neck of her tank top.

Spencer dragged her gaze away from the sight of Amy's glorious cleavage. "Yes, does it show?"

"No, you look like a seasoned veteran," Amy said with a laugh. The sound was like music to Spencer's ears. She wanted to hear the melody again. Preferably on a continuous loop. "But I'm pretty good with faces, and I don't remember seeing yours before."

Amy rested her fingers on Spencer's forearm in a gesture that was probably supposed to be reassuring. Instead of calming her down, the contact got Spencer's pulse racing. When was the last time she had been touched by someone other than herself?

"If you don't mind my asking," Amy said, "how did you hear about us? Since we don't run commercials, and our print budget isn't as high as the mainstream tour companies, I'm always interested to know how potential travelers discover SOS Tours exists."

"My parents bought the trip for me as a birthday present. My mother's a real coupon queen. She's constantly scouring the internet for deals. After the incident in Cancún, she said she was able to find the ticket for a song. I think she found it on a resale website after the original owner decided not to use it." After Amy's face fell, Spencer felt like kicking herself. She had never been very good at making small talk, and she had apparently gotten worse at it over the years instead of better. She wished she had given a short reply instead of feeling compelled to run off at the mouth, but it was too late now. Some things never changed.

"That wasn't the company's proudest moment," Amy said as the light seemed to go out of her eyes. She shook herself as if she were setting aside a bad memory. When she spoke again, the perkiness she had exuded earlier had returned. "I'm glad you decided to take a chance on us anyway. Did you come with someone, or are you flying solo?"

Spencer didn't want to launch into a sob story. Not here. Not now. And especially not with someone she had just met. "It's just me," she said simply.

"Then I need to introduce you to Breanna. She's in charge of our independent travelers this week. She has some really exciting activities planned for you. Let me see if she's available."

Amy raised a walkie-talkie to her lips, but Spencer stopped her before she could call for reinforcements.

"Don't," she said more forcefully than she had intended. Amy arched an eyebrow in response, prompting Spencer to temper her tone. "I'm sure I'll run into Breanna sooner or later. Right now, all I want to do is find my room, unpack my bag, and try to unwind."

"I hear you. I'm looking forward to relaxing with a glass of wine myself, but work comes first. Would you like me to show you to your room?"

"Just tell me where to go. I'll take it from there."

"Sure. No problem." Amy looked at the room assignment printed on Spencer's boarding pass. "You're on the navigation deck. That's two floors above this one. It's where the bridge is located. You'll know where we're going almost as soon as the captain does." She returned the boarding pass but didn't let go. "Are you sure you don't want me to show you the way?"

Spencer would have preferred to have Amy help test how soundproof the walls were in her cabin, but Amy's comments about work had changed the dynamic. She had thought they were establishing a bond, however tenuous, but the truth was Amy wasn't flirting with her. She was simply trying to please a client. Spencer had confused friendliness for interest before, but never again. She was done repeating past mistakes.

"No, thanks. I can manage. See you around."

Amy watched Spencer walk away. What had just happened? One minute, she and Spencer were chatting like they were old friends. The next, Spencer seemed like she couldn't get away fast enough.

Amy felt compelled to apologize, even though she didn't know what she had done or said to set Spencer off. Their conversation had been filled with the usual banal pleasantries two strangers trotted out when they first encountered each other, but their all-too-brief chat had offered enough glimpses into Spencer's personality to prompt Amy to want to get to know her better. She decided to seek Spencer out in the next day or two in order to smooth things over and check in on how her trip was going. But it was probably a good idea if they didn't get too close.

SOS Tours staffers were urged to be friendly and engaging when they interacted with customers, especially while they were onsite for a trip, but it was against company policy for them to sleep with clients during vacations. They could flirt until the cows came home, but they couldn't hook up with anyone until the outing they were assigned to came to an end.

Amy had never been tempted to break the rules before, but there was a first time for everything.

As she headed to the theater to observe the final sound check for the kickoff concert that was supposed to take place an hour before the scheduled four o'clock departure, she tried to convince herself she had been doing nothing more than demonstrating good customer service by abandoning her post and offering to show Spencer to her room. Deep down, though, she knew better. That admission could get her in a world of trouble.

Even though they had just met, Amy was entranced. The vulnerability in Spencer's body language had drawn her attention; Spencer's quick wit had captured her imagination. Their abrupt parting only piqued Amy's curiosity.

She wanted to unlock the secrets hidden in Spencer's hooded brown eyes. Dance with her under a moonlit sky. Hear whispered secrets spill from her lush, full lips. Feel the warmth of her lightly freckled skin. Taste the sweetness of her kiss.

But she couldn't do any of those things until the ship returned to port a little over a week from now. By then, it could be too late. By then, Spencer could have met someone else. Someone who was free to fan a flicker of interest into a flame instead of someone who was duty-bound to lower the heat.

"It's for the best," she said, trying to sell herself on the idea. "I've got a job to do."

And a company to save.

Jessica Hart was in over her head. She had known it for a while now, but today was the first time she had dared to admit it to herself.

The security lines in the cruise ship terminal were long as usual, filled with tourists anxious to get the tedious screening process over with so they could board their vessels and begin their vacations in earnest.

Jessica would be on board with them as soon as she cleared security, but her experience was bound to be vastly different from theirs. While the passengers soaked up the sun by the pool, headed to some exotic port for an optional excursion, downed half their body weight in high-end seafood, or bellied up to the bar to drown themselves in umbrella drinks, she'd be helping them work off their week's worth of overindulgences as she toiled as a fitness pro in the ship's gym.

Skipping the lines reserved for guests, she joined the one set aside for ship employees and waited her turn. How many times had she done this? Ten? Twenty? A hundred? It didn't matter at this point because she had decided this time would be the last.

She set her pair of carry-on bags on the conveyor belt and slipped the security screener a fifty-dollar bill not to look too closely at what was inside them in case she was selected for one of the random security checks to which ship employees were occasionally subjected. She was well aware of every item that had been crammed into her *Star Wars*-themed carry-on, but she had no clue what was inside the black duffel bag she had picked up from the storage locker she had paid a visit to a few hours ago. After the first few voyages, she had stopped looking inside the packages she was ordered to smuggle on board the ship she was assigned to. When she received a text on her burner phone, she paid a visit to the storage locker and retrieved the bag and cash left behind. She deposited the cash and handed off the bag to someone else. No harm, no foul. She doubted her explanation would go over well in a court of law, but it was the best thing she had been able to come up with.

It was easier not knowing. That way, she could tell herself she wasn't doing anything wrong. She was simply doing her job while earning some much-needed extra money in the process. She knew it wasn't true, but the lie helped her be able to sleep at night instead of being held hostage by a guilty conscience. If she wanted to run her own gym one day instead of spending her whole life working for someone else, she needed to come up with the cash for the down payment. Her credit wasn't good enough for her to convince any reputable bank's loan officer to lend her the money, and her salary from Centennial Cruises was enough to pay her bills, but it would never come close to being able to finance her dreams.

Money wasn't the reason she had said yes when Pilar Obregon asked her to sneak a few bottles of her favorite Scotch on board because none of the ship's restaurants or bars featured it on the menu, and passengers weren't allowed to bring bottles of hard liquor on the ship. Lust was. But the five hundred bucks Pilar had slipped her had proved to be more satisfying than the sex they'd never gotten around to having.

Pilar, a former beauty queen from Mexico City now based in Cozumel, was involved with some rich dude who was always too tied up with work to accompany her on the cruise she took from Miami to Jamaica each fall. Jessica didn't know whether Pilar was the man's wife, girlfriend, or mistress because Pilar changed her story as often as she did her lavish wardrobe. Not that Jessica minded. She wasn't big on details, especially when the subject was other people's relationships. As far as she was concerned, ignorance was bliss. But that was before Pilar changed the rules without consulting with her first.

Jessica had told Pilar time and again they needed to make sure their arrangement remained strictly hush-hush, but Pilar obviously didn't get the memo because the next thing Jessica knew, people identifying themselves as Pilar's friends started asking her to perform similar favors for them as well.

Thanks to Pilar's obvious popularity, granting favors was practically a full-time job. Jessica knew she should have said no the first time Pilar batted her big brown eyes and asked if she could help her out, but the amount of money Pilar offered her to perform a few minutes of work had simply been too good to turn down. That was three years and countless trips ago. Now Jessica was into something she wasn't sure she could find her way out of. The price would be steep if she did manage to figure things out, but it was one she was more than willing to pay. Though freedom wasn't free, it was definitely worth the expense.

Even though her nest egg wasn't large enough for her to start shopping for prime real estate, she couldn't keep putting herself through this. The money was still tempting, but the risk no longer held the same appeal. Instead of wondering how much scratch she could earn by providing the means for adventurous passengers to chemically enhance their time at sea, she was starting to wonder what would happen if she got caught. Would she be able to explain her motives to her parents, or would they be too traumatized by seeing her behind bars to bring themselves to care why she had agreed to become a drug mule?

Jessica sighed as she stepped into the body scanner. She felt like a puppet, but she had no idea who was pulling her strings. She communicated with only a handful of people about her extracurricular activities, and none of them had ever said who was ultimately responsible for forking over the cash and product she picked up before each trip. Pilar had gotten the ball rolling by providing her name to a friend of a friend of a friend, but—a few bottles of smuggled whiskey aside—Jessica doubted Pilar would ever do anything to get her manicured nails dirty. Beauty queens and prison clashed as badly as plaids and stripes.

Jessica's luck had held out so far, but she didn't want to push it any further. Although she liked taking risks, she wasn't willing to keep gambling on her freedom. But would walking away also mean risking her life? If so, it was a chance she had to take. It was time to start living the better life she had been working so hard to achieve.

After she exited the body scanner, she waited for her bags to pop out of the X-ray machine. The screening process usually took only a few minutes. What was the holdup today?

She glanced at Corey Holmes, the screener she had bribed, but he wouldn't meet her eye. Corey frowned as he stared at the monitor displaying black-and-white images of the luggage being X-rayed.

Jessica's heart raced as Corey halted the conveyor belt and called for a supervisor. She was tempted to bolt for the nearest exit, but realizing running would only confirm her guilt, she somehow managed to convince herself to remain where she was. Perhaps she was overreacting. Perhaps she could still wiggle her way out of this mess. And perhaps getting caught was no longer an unwanted possibility but an unfortunate reality.

"What's going on?" Joseph Patterson, Corey's supervisor, asked when he arrived.

Corey pointed to the monitor. "Looks like we have some contraband in one of these bags."

"Yep, I see it."

Jessica tried not to panic when Joseph reached for the black duffel bag and began to unzip it, but she could already see a bright orange jumpsuit in her future and she was starting to imagine spending the next ten to twenty years of her life behind bars.

"Not that bag," Corey said quickly. "The one with Darth Vader's face on it."

Jessica watched as Joseph unzipped her carry-on, rummaged through it, and removed two large bottles of mineral water.

"You know the rules as well as I do, Jess," Joseph said. "All guests and employees are limited to one unopened bottle of wine or champagne, and nonalcoholic beverages packaged in bottles are prohibited."

"Sorry." Jessica struggled to keep her voice steady. "I forgot those were in there."

"No problem. I'll hold on to them for you until you get back." Joseph tucked the bottles under his arm. "Drop by my office when you're ready to pick them up."

"I'll do that. Thanks."

"No problem. Have a good trip."

"Sure thing." After Joseph walked away, Jessica grabbed her bags off the conveyor belt and caught Corey's eye. "Thanks for the heart attack, asshole."

"If you turn that fifty into a hundred next time," he said with an avaricious grin, "I'll make sure it won't happen again."

"If I have anything to say about it, there won't be a next time."

"Tell me something I haven't heard a thousand times before from other people in your line of work. Didn't you see *Godfather III?*"

"I've got news for you," she said before Corey could trot out his terrible impression of Al Pacino. "Neither of us is Michael Corleone."

"If you don't want to end up like Fredo," Corey said, lowering his voice, "don't rock the boat."

Jessica decided to ignore rather than heed Corey's warning. After she exited the terminal, she handed the duffel bag to a steward who would be responsible for moving much more than luggage after they boarded the ship. "This is my last drop-off. Tell them I'm out."

"I don't pass messages. I move weight." Brandon Gould added the duffel to the pile of suitcases neatly stacked on the luggage cart he was leaning against. He took a drag on his cigarette and blew out a plume of smoke before he tossed the spent butt aside. The thick muscles in his forearm flexed as the discarded cigarette flew through the air. The oversized wristband on his left arm covered the tattoo he hid from passengers who might be less inclined to tip someone who was inked up. "If you want out," he said as he began to push the heavy cart toward the long gangplank that led from the dock to the ship, "spread the news yourself."

As soon as the trip ended, Jessica intended to do just that. If, that was, she could figure out how. Neither a text nor an email would do. A breakup like this one required the personal touch. And she had eight days to find the courage to do it.

DAY ONE

S pencer chose to take the stairs instead of the elevator in an effort to burn off some of her nervous energy. By the time she finally found her room, she felt like she had been walking for hours instead of only a few minutes. She waved her key card in front of the reader affixed to her stateroom door, waited for the light to turn green, and let herself in after she heard the lock slide open.

When her mother had expressed her excitement about snagging the ticket to a deluxe suite, Spencer had feigned the appropriate amount of enthusiasm. Now she didn't have to pretend.

By cruise ship standards, the room was huge. Almost six hundred square feet, by Spencer's estimate. The high-end suite down the hall was more than twice that size, but it was probably more than twice the price, too. She was glad her parents had taken the time to buy her such a thoughtful gift, but she was glad they hadn't gone all-out on the expense, especially when her chances of fulfilling the mission her mother had assigned her were somewhere between slim and none. She knew how badly her mother wanted her to be in a relationship—to find someone, settle down, and be happy—but she didn't see how it was possible. It was incredibly difficult to say much more than hello and good-bye to someone when you and your partner were seldom if ever on the same schedule.

Even though Spencer lived on the East Coast, the tech company she worked for was located in Seattle. She was able to work remotely, but thanks to the three-hour time difference, her workdays began and ended well after those of her family and friends. The time they spent together was limited to the weekends, when she tried to cram in all the experiences she wasn't able to share with them during the week. If she ever met someone she connected with, they might be able to make a go of it for a while, but she suspected they would eventually drift apart as she lived one life and her partner lived another.

"Have fun," her father had said when he and Spencer's mother had come to see her off before she began her drive to Fort Lauderdale.

"You deserve this," her mother had said, tears welling in her eyes. "Go and have the time of your life."

All she had to do was get out of her own way long enough to let it happen. Something that had thus far proven impossible to do. More often than not, she had turned out to be her own worst enemy. For her, software programs were far easier to create and maintain than relationships. Even the buggiest program could be saved if you applied the right patches. Some relationships couldn't be saved no matter how many fixes you tried, especially if you weren't sure you actually wanted them to work in the first place.

Spencer wanted happily ever after and everything that went along with it. She'd be lying if she said she didn't. She simply wasn't sure she knew how to go about it—or had the energy to learn.

She tossed her suitcase on the bed and looked around the room. The suite featured two divans that could be easily converted into one king-sized bed. She tested the mattress on one of them. It didn't seem lumpy or hard, but she wouldn't truly know how comfortable it was until she crawled under the covers and turned in for the night. She was tempted to do so now. The long drive from Pipkinville had worn her out, but she didn't want to waste the first day of her vacation drooling on her pillow. There would be plenty of time for that in the days and nights to come. She had decided to proceed with this trip so she could let her hair down for the first time in years, and she was determined to do just that. Even if she had to fake her way through it.

She walked over to the sofa bed, which looked roomy enough to accommodate two people. Not that she knew what that felt like anymore. She hadn't shared a bed—or her life—with someone since college. When, for a few blissful years anyway, she had been able to slip the shackles that had always kept her from being fully, freely herself. Graduation had brought about much more than the end of school. It had also brought about the end of her first and only relationship. Would it also be her last?

Every once in a while—usually when she'd had a few too many shots of whiskey—she missed having someone to hold. Sleeping with a pillow cradled in her arms wasn't the same as spooning someone who could return the favor. If she wanted to move on—if she wanted to try again, for real this time—she needed to figure out how. And soon.

Before she set out on the drive to Fort Lauderdale, she had almost managed to convince herself that a temporary hookup might be what she needed. The perfect elixir to make her feel like she was part of the world instead of hiding from it. It hadn't taken long for reality to shoot that theory all to hell. The rollercoaster of emotions she had experienced during her brief conversation with Amy a few minutes earlier made her realize a shipboard romance wasn't what she needed. In fact, it could end up doing more harm than good. It was painfully obvious she wasn't ready to embark on a relationship, temporary or otherwise. Perhaps she should settle for making a few new friends instead.

An itinerary of the day's events lay on the nightstand next to the bed. Spencer picked it up and gave it the once-over. Reagan Carter's kick-off concert was supposed to start in a few minutes.

The rest of the schedule consisted of various meetings designed to welcome everyone on board. Those with dietary and/or special medical needs were supposed to meet in one room. First-time travelers with SOS Tours were supposed to meet in another. Spencer was used to eating whatever was placed in front of her, and she wasn't in the mood to sit through either a loud concert or a boring orientation speech. The Happy Hour event scheduled to take place in one of the five bars on board piqued her interest. The itinerary said the event was limited to Indies, passengers who were traveling alone. She definitely fit into that category. She was even wearing the designated ball-and-chain necklace to prove it. Perhaps she could find a kindred spirit or two while she sipped on some distilled ones.

She dug through her welcome packet, located a map of the ship, and charted her course to the appropriate bar. She was a couple of hours early, but it couldn't hurt to get an early start.

Taking a deep breath, she stepped into the hall and closed her stateroom door behind her.

"Here goes nothing."

❖

As she waited to go onstage and address the crowd, Amy could feel the energy start to build. It happened before each trip—a goose bump-inducing surge of excitement, anticipation, and sisterhood—but the sensation was far more intense on a relatively small cruise ship than it was on a sprawling resort. Clients were in closer proximity on a ship, giving them more chances to interact with the staff and each other.

Amy loved these moments, when hundreds of women realized they were free to be themselves for the duration of their trip and could openly show affection to their partners without having to check to see who might be watching. In far too many areas of the countries they called home, that option wasn't available. For the next eight days and seven nights, the *Majestic Dream* would be a giant floating safe space.

Amy loved being able to provide an opportunity for women to be able to be completely themselves. Sure, she had heard a few complaints about SOS Tours' pricing. Even with discounts for booking early, the per person rates were higher than determined bargain-hunters could find on their own. Repeat travelers, however, seemed more than willing to accept the tradeoff, shelling out a few extra bucks in exchange for a week of feeling like a member of the majority instead of a pigeonholed minority. All-inclusive food and drinks didn't hurt. Amy was already dreaming about the glass of champagne and large slice of strawberry cheesecake she was going to treat herself to after her day's official duties were finally done.

Check-in day was always hectic. Once guests started arriving, the onslaught didn't stop until hours later. If you were blessed by the check-in gods, only a few guests showed up at the same time. More often than not, dozens came spilling out of the complimentary charter buses at once, testing staffers' ability to keep guests happy without anyone losing their patience—or their tempers—in the process.

The boat was scheduled to set sail in a little over an hour, so the check-in process for this trip was nearly complete. Amy had been fortunate to this point. She had been in close contact with her staff and the ship's crew all day, but with no reports of lost luggage or upset clients, she hadn't been called into action.

"So far, so good."

"Relax," Breanna said, giving Amy's shoulder a reassuring squeeze. She pulled the velvet curtain aside and took a peek at the hundreds of women settling into their seats in the spacious performance venue. "There are only about a thousand women waiting to hang on to your every word. No pressure."

Pressure was Amy's constant companion. She not only thrived on it, she practically needed it in order to survive. When she was in school, she had always waited until the last moment to complete her assignments because her creative juices didn't start flowing until whatever deadline she was up against began to approach. Work was no different. The more hectic the situation became, the calmer she felt.

"Is Reagan ready?" she asked.

"Almost. She's doing vocal exercises to warm up. I told her to expect to go on in five minutes. Or are you feeling especially chatty today? If so, I could go back to her dressing room and tell her to aim for ten."

"I plan to make this short and quick." Amy jerked her thumb at the crowd on the other side of the curtain. "They're waiting to see Reagan, not me."

"Are you sure about that?" Breanna arched an eyebrow as she looked Amy up and down. "Your legs look a mile long in those shorts. Every passenger on this boat would love to do you. If I didn't know about the stash of gas station junk food in your desk, I might feel the same way. Have you finished those pork rinds yet, or are you saving them for the zombie apocalypse?"

"We can't all live on salad, tofu, and veggie burgers."

"Stuff that has some actual nutritional value and contains less sodium than a salt lick, you mean?"

"Yeah, that." Amy took the ribbing with the good nature with which it was intended. She knew Breanna was only trying to keep her from psyching herself out, and she loved her for it. "Now pass me the microphone so I can get this show on the road."

"You're the boss. This week, anyway. Next time, it'll be someone else's turn."

"If this week doesn't go well, there might not be a next time."

Breanna's smile didn't falter. "With the two of us in charge, what could possibly go wrong?"

Amy hoped neither of them would get the chance to find out. For their sake as well as the company's.

The crowd, already buzzing with excitement, whooped when the stage manager dimmed the lights. Amy expected the cheers to subside when she walked onstage, but they only grew in intensity.

She held her hand against her ear, egging the crowd on. She knew the cheers weren't for her but what she represented: the true beginning of a trip some of the women smiling back at her had waited weeks, months, or a lifetime to take. She applauded along with them as the SOS Tours theme song blasted from the speakers.

"Welcome, Sisters of Sappho," she said when the song ended and the members of the crowd settled back into their seats. "My name is Amy Donovan and I'll be your cruise director this week. I talked with some of you today and I hope to spend time with the rest of you in the days and nights to come."

She held a hand over her eyes to shield them from the glare of the spotlight shining on her as she peered into the crowd. She saw several familiar faces from previous trips and spotted a few new ones she had met during that afternoon's check-in process, but she didn't see the face she was hoping to see the most: Spencer's. Had Spencer decided to skip the show in order to avoid having another awkward run-in with her or had she found entertainment elsewhere? She made a mental note to check with Breanna later to see if Spencer dropped in on the Indies networking event in the Reverie bar on the lido deck. Or maybe she'd cut out the middleman and attend the event herself. The more, the merrier. Wasn't that how the old saying went?

"I won't stay out here too long. I know you're looking forward to watching Reagan Carter perform just as much as I am." The young singer was known for her soulful voice as well as the complex melodies that showcased her powerful pipes. Today, however, she would be performing a stripped-down acoustic set for a highly-anticipated change of pace.

"Right now, I'm enjoying watching you," someone called out.

Amy laughed as a series of wolf whistles made their way around the room. "Let's see if you still feel that way after I go over the housekeeping items on my list."

Returning travelers groaned because they knew what was about to come next: the usual announcements about respecting each other's personal boundaries as well as the daily reminder of the importance of smokers confining themselves to designated areas so the fumes from their cigarettes, cigars, or pipes wouldn't disturb those who didn't partake. No matter how many times she made the plea, someone always chose to ignore it, necessitating yet another admonishment the following night. Amy hated that part of her job, but she was willing to put up with it in order to continue experiencing the give-and-take with the audience.

"Thank you for choosing to travel with SOS Tours. Returnees, welcome back. Newbies, welcome to the family. This is going to be a great week, so let's get it started. Sisters of Sappho, please welcome Reagan Carter!"

She ceded the stage to the night's headliner and watched from the wings as Reagan began to perform. Reagan was dressed in jeans and a T-shirt, her casual outfit mirroring her no-frills setup. She sat on a stool in the center of the stage, an acoustic guitarist on one side and a bongo player on the other. She closed her eyes and began to sing. The crowd hung on every soaring note—and begged for more when the forty-minute set came to an end. Reagan obliged with one encore, a spirited rendition of the Tracy Chapman cover that had first launched her into the public eye.

Amy applauded with everyone else as Reagan took her final bows. Forcing herself to become a professional again instead of a fan, she escorted Reagan and her entourage off the ship so the captain could weigh anchor.

"That crowd had some serious energy," Reagan said as she and her girlfriend prepared to disembark. "I'll have to do one of these trips again sometime as a passenger instead of a performer."

"We look forward to having you back."

Amy watched them go, then joined the dozens of women lining the railing as they prepared for the ship to head out to sea. The ship's horn let out two long, loud blasts, forcing everyone to cover their ears. Amy felt her adrenaline race as the large craft slowly began to move. The trip was officially underway.

Her ears were still ringing from the cheers of the concertgoers in the theater as well as the roar of the crowd on deck so she almost missed the distinctive crackle as her walkie-talkie came to life.

"Houston," Breanna said, "we have a problem."

Spencer claimed an empty stool in front of the bar and took a look around the room. The walls of the Reverie were painted various shades of electric blue, the traditional bar seats had been replaced by comfy chaise lounges or even comfier daybeds, and the light fixtures overhead looked like clouds forming in a dusky sky. Paintings and illustrations that seemed more like Salvador Dali fever dreams were interspersed throughout. The place could have doubled as the backdrop for a Cirque du Soleil performance instead of a spot to grab a quick drink or spark up a conversation. Spencer half-expected to see a sad-faced clown or a scantily clad acrobat appear at any moment.

"Would you like something to drink?"

The question drew Spencer out of her trance. She was disappointed to see the bartender who had posed it, a perky brunette with an accent that screamed New England, was dressed in a polo shirt and shorts instead of one of the more elaborate outfits she had been imagining. She reached for one of the drink menus scattered across the bar top and examined the list of specials. The names were almost as colorful as the drinks themselves. Tangerine Dream. Neon Nightmare Negroni. Pomegranate Delusion. Fairytale Fantasy.

Spencer wanted to order something festive to celebrate the start of the first vacation she'd had in years, but she didn't want to wander around with what looked like a glass of windshield wiper fluid in her hands. She opted to go with something traditional instead of something trendy.

"I'll have a dry martini."

"Shaken, not stirred, right?"

The question didn't come from the bartender but from someone to Spencer's left. Spencer turned to see a woman with close-cropped platinum hair, dancing gray eyes, and a mischievous smile standing next to her. The laugh lines around the woman's eyes and mouth said she was a good fifteen to twenty years older than Spencer, but her gym-toned body and stylized haircut made her exact age as hard to determine as her motives. Was she simply making conversation, or was she on the make?

"Is there any other way?" Spencer asked.

The woman's smile broadened. "There's always another way to do things, but there's only one right one." She indicated the seat next to Spencer. "Do you mind if I join you?"

Spencer took a peek over her shoulder. The bar was only half-full, so the woman had her choice of seats. But she was wearing an Indie necklace, too, so she was probably feeling just as alone as Spencer was. "Feel free."

The woman took a seat and ordered a martini of her own. "Extra dirty. Kind of like me," she added with a wink. She held out her hand to Spencer and introduced herself. "I'm Hannah Rogers. And you are?"

"Spencer Collins."

"Pleased to meet you. I'm a real estate agent." Hannah's handshake was so firm Spencer had been expecting to hear her say she crushed bricks for a living. "What do you do?"

"I'm in IT."

"So if I'm having issues with my computer, you're the person I should call to tell me to reboot and try again?"

Spencer couldn't count how many times she had heard that line. Sometimes, though, a simple restart was all that was needed to fix a problem that seemed unsolvable. Perhaps this trip would be the reboot she needed to get her systems working again. "More like I'm the person who prevents you from having the issue in the first place."

"So you're a computer technician?"

"Not quite, but you're getting warmer. My teammates and I write the scripts for the antivirus software that prevents end users from having unwanted intrusions."

"Is that a nice way of saying it's your job to protect me from myself?"

"No one can prevent people from succumbing to the urge to click on suspect links or attachments in malicious email—that's why hackers keep sending it out in droves—but I try to limit the damage."

"Cheers to that." Hannah took a sip of her drink and looked Spencer up and down. The examination was naked in its appraisal, leaving Spencer feeling exposed even though she was fully clothed. It had been a long time since she'd been subjected to a look like that. It made her feel slightly uncomfortable, but it excited her a little, too. Hannah's attention made her feel desirable, something she had started to wonder if she would ever feel again. "With that accent, I'm guessing you're from someplace south of the Mason-Dixon Line."

"Guilty as charged. I'm from a small town in southwest Georgia, but the company I work for is headquartered in Seattle."

"Really?" Hannah arched a well-manicured eyebrow. "That's where I'm from. My office is in Seattle, but I live in Kirkland, which is about twenty minutes away from the city center. How often are you in the area?"

"I work remotely so I only have to put in face time a few times a year. When I'm there, I don't see much more than the designated meeting space and my hotel room."

"I used to think nothing could be better than working from home—it's a hell of a lot cheaper than renting office space—but I've gotten used to the routine of getting up, getting dressed, and heading to work."

"So have I, but my commute is a lot shorter than yours."

"*Touché.*" Hannah raised her glass in a toast. "You should give me a call the next time you're out my way. If you haven't paid a visit to some of our local attractions, you're missing out. There's more to Seattle than overpriced souvenirs in the Space Needle and smelly guys tossing raw fish in Pike Place Market. I'd love to show you the things publishers don't print in the guidebooks. You haven't lived until you've visited the Gum Wall in Post Alley in the heart of summer or snacked on steamed oysters next to a roaring fire on a crisp fall night."

"That does sound pretty good. I've been living off junk food for so long I can't remember what a real meal tastes like."

"It's about time you changed that."

It was about time she changed a lot of things.

"Are you here for the mixer, or are you meeting someone?" she asked.

"Both, actually." Hannah slid an olive off her swizzle stick with her teeth. "I'm traveling with a friend, but she prefers to be fashionably late for everything. I keep telling her she'll probably be late to her own funeral."

"Why rush when you're the guest of honor? It's not like they can start without you."

"That's what Bonnie says. I wish she were here. You two would probably get on swimmingly. She's always had a weakness for Southern belles. She gets positively weak in the knees every time *Gone with the Wind* airs on TV."

Spencer laughed. "I don't think anyone would ever mistake me for Scarlett O'Hara."

"No, I can't picture you ever wearing a set of curtains as a ball gown, but I bet you'd look smashing in one of Rhett Butler's suits."

Spencer felt her cheeks warm at the compliment. "Are you and Bonnie together?"

"As in are we a couple? God, no. Neither of us is cut out for traditional relationships. In my mind, two's company, but three's a good start." Hannah trailed a finger across the back of Spencer's hand. "In case you're wondering, real estate isn't my only area of expertise."

"I'll keep that in mind."

"I hope you do." Hannah pulled a business card from the pocket of her Capri pants and wrote something on the back. "In my business, it pays not to beat around the bush so I'm not going to do that now. If you're in the market for a new place to stay," she said, tapping the front of the card, "here's my contact information." She spun the card around. "If you're looking for a bit of adventure this week and don't feel like going ashore, you can find me here."

Spencer recognized the cabin number scrawled on the back of the card as one of the high-end suites she had passed as she tried to find her way to her own stateroom. Hannah wasn't lacking for either money or assertiveness. That much was obvious. "Thanks for the card. If I ever decide to relocate to Seattle, I know who to call."

The sound of relieved laughter drew Spencer's attention across the room. She turned to find Amy and a woman with long black hair and tawny skin that hinted at Hawaiian or Polynesian roots standing in the doorway.

Hannah followed Spencer's line of sight. "Don't even think about it. I can't blame you on either score, but believe me when I say they're both lost causes."

"Why? Are they an item?"

"I don't know if they're sleeping with each other, but what I do know is they're not allowed to sleep with clients. Company policy. It's not in the brochure, but someone needs to add it to the fine print to keep people from getting their hopes up."

"People like me, you mean?"

"People like any lesbian with a pulse. I think we both fit that description, don't you?"

Hannah gave Spencer a pat on the back. Spencer liked hanging out with her. She hoped their chance meeting wouldn't prove to be a one-time thing. Even though Hannah wasn't what she was looking for romantically, Spencer could tell she was exactly what she needed in a friend. Someone who wasn't afraid to laugh at herself and who knew how to have a good time. Maybe she would take her up on her offer. For dinner, that was. At the moment, sleeping with one woman was a stretch. If she tried to sleep with two at the same time, she might pull a muscle. Not to mention the kind of effect it would have on her heart.

"You two look happy about something," Hannah said after Amy and the woman with her joined them at the bar.

The woman's name tag read, "Breanna." Spencer realized she must be the woman Amy had mentioned earlier. The person who was in charge of keeping the Indies entertained this week.

Breanna jerked a thumb in Amy's direction. "False alarms tend to have that effect when you're as high-strung as this one is."

"What happened?" Spencer asked.

Amy and Breanna exchanged a look. "You might as well tell them," Breanna said with a shrug. "It's a relatively small ship. The rest of the passengers are bound to hear about it sooner or later anyway."

As she apparently debated whether to take Breanna's advice, Amy opened one of the two bottles of mineral water she and Breanna had ordered and took a sip. "The security team received several reports of gunfire," she eventually said, "but the culprit turned out to be a guest who has never been on a cruise before and brought her collection of video games with her to help her stay calm. She started playing one after we weighed anchor, but she had the sound turned up too loud on her console and spooked some of the people in the rooms near hers. They thought someone was trying to take over the ship."

Spencer nodded. "She must have been playing *Grand Theft Auto*, *Battlefield*, or *Mortal Combat*. Their violence quotient is pretty high and the game content is so realistic, people often mistake it for the real thing. What kind of system was she using? Xbox? Nintendo? Android? PS4?" She had thought about bringing one of her portable systems along, but she hadn't wanted to seem like an even bigger nerd than she already was. If she had followed her instincts, she could have found one of those kindred spirits she was looking for. Talk about a missed opportunity.

"Are you a gamer?" Amy asked.

"Yes, why do you ask?"

"Because this is the most excited I've seen you get since you've been on board." Amy grinned. "Concerts by Grammy-winning artists don't do much for you, but video games do, huh?"

"Since I work on computers all day, you'd think I'd want to stay far away from them at night, but gaming helps me relax. When I pick up the controls and put on my headset, the hours fly by." Sometimes, the voices of the people she was playing against constituted the only human contact she had all day. She'd once thought that would be enough. Now she wasn't so sure. Being here stirred a sense of community. A sense of belonging. She wanted more of both. And she wanted more of Amy Donovan.

"Do you field calls like that often?"

"Like that particular one, no, but I am constantly on the go. It's part of the job."

"Better you than me," Breanna said. "I'd rather help a roomful of strangers break the ice than run around putting out fires."

"To each her own," Hannah said. "Do you need some help getting set up?"

"Sure," Breanna said. "I thought we could play a few games of bingo, SOS Tours-style, to help the participants get to know each other better. You can help me round up players and pass out the game cards."

"I know bingo isn't as action-packed as the games you're used to," Amy said, "but would you like to play, Spencer?"

"Maybe. How does it work?"

"It's not too far removed from traditional bingo." Amy handed her one of the game cards. Words instead of numbers were printed in each of the twenty-five squares. "The object of the game is to find someone who is or has done each of the items listed. The first person to write a name in all twenty-five squares wins."

Spencer read some of the entries. *"Plays on a softball team. Has at least one cat. Loves to cook. Has a caffeine addiction.* I can write my own name in most of these boxes."

"That's the catch. You're not allowed to use your own name, and you can't write down anyone else's name more than once. Here. I'll help you get started." Amy pointed to the square in the center of the game card. *"Hates chocolate.* That would be me."

Spencer looked at her hard. "You're kidding, right? Who in her right mind doesn't like chocolate?"

"I have a weakness for strawberry cheesecake, but on the whole, I prefer my treats to be salty rather than sweet."

"Do you like your women the same way?" Spencer asked before she could stop herself.

"Unfortunately, yes," Amy said with a laugh. "That probably explains why I'm single."

"And it probably explains why I have so many fillings in my teeth. I keep a bowl of candy next to my computer monitor and snack on the contents while I work. More often than not, a handful of miniature chocolate bars serves as breakfast, lunch, and dinner." She glanced at the game card Amy had given her. "What's the prize if I win?"

"Besides a chance to meet twenty-five new people?"

"Twenty-four." Spencer pointed to the mark she had made in the center square. "Thanks to you, I already got a head start, remember?"

Amy lowered her voice to a conspiratorial whisper. "Don't say that too loud or you might get disqualified for cheating. I don't know what the prize is, but I'm sure Breanna has picked out something good from the company stash. You wouldn't want to miss out on winning some sweet swag, would you?"

She wouldn't want to miss out on a chance to spend some quality time with Amy, either. "Are you going to play?"

Amy shook her head. "I know most of the people here so I'd have an unfair advantage."

"Then you sound like you could be the perfect wingman."

"If I didn't have a meeting I need to get to in a few minutes, I might take you up on that." Amy turned to leave, then seemed to think better of the idea. "If you save me a seat at dinner, I'd love to hear all about how the game went. Breanna has a tendency to embellish from time to time. I'd prefer to hear the details from someone with a more reliable point of view."

SOS Tours had set aside reserved seating for the Indies at each meal, meaning Spencer wouldn't have to eat alone. With no reasonable excuse for staying in and ordering room service, how could she turn down Amy's offer? But before she said yes, there was one thing she had to know.

"Why are you being so nice to me?"

"What do you mean?"

"We're on a ship filled with thousands of passengers, yet I've run into you twice in a matter of only a few hours. Are you paying me extra attention because you want to or because it's part of your job description?"

Amy seemed taken aback by the question, even though Spencer suspected it was one she had probably fielded dozens of times before. "I'm being nice to you because I like to get to know the women who travel with us. Because you allow us to share your vacations with you, you're much more than clients. You're like family. Does that answer your question?"

Amy flashed a disarming smile, but Spencer didn't let her guard down. She thought about the conversation she'd had with Hannah a few minutes before. "I heard SOS Tours employees aren't allowed to get involved with clients. If that's true, I wouldn't want you to get in trouble for fraternizing with me."

"My fellow employees and I aren't permitted to become intimate with clients during trips, no," Amy said carefully, "but we're allowed to 'fraternize' with whoever we choose. Because we want to, not because we're told to. I'm not trying to pressure you into doing something you don't feel comfortable with, Spencer. If you'd prefer to have dinner with someone else—"

"Someone who doesn't have an aversion to chocolate, you mean?"

Amy laughed and Spencer felt the growing tension dissipate. She also felt a heavy weight fall off her shoulders. Knowing Amy was off-limits made it easier to spend time with her. She could relax and be herself, not worry about making an impression favorable enough to win her over. Like that could ever happen.

"This is going to be a continuing issue between us, isn't it?" Amy asked.

"Yep. I don't know if I'll be able to share a table with someone who turns up her nose at the greatest confection ever created, but I'm willing to give it a try if you are."

"In that case, I'll see you tonight."

Even though she knew nothing could come of it, Spencer couldn't remember the last time she had looked forward to something more.

❖

Jessica began to address the list of questions Amy handed her. Queries that SOS Tours personnel had received from guests since the ship had sailed but were unable to answer. Most questions were as simple as the hours the gym were open. Others were more complex. Leanna Lafaele, the head of the Wahines on Water program, for example, had received a question from a passenger whose partially paralyzed partner was interested in taking part in a spin class but only if she wouldn't end up feeling like the center of attention while she did so.

"I make sure all of my classes are inclusive," Jessica said. "I don't believe in separating participants by skill level. I find it's much more enjoyable when everyone's together having fun. I have several recumbent bikes available. I'm sure the passenger would be able to use one of them during a class. I can adjust the routine to account for her physical challenges, but I hope she doesn't expect me to go easy on her."

"No, I think she wants you to push her as hard as you do everyone else. Harder even since she's a former Marine."

"Awesome." Jessica loved helping people test their limits. From the sound of it, she wouldn't have to push her new client too hard to reach for hers. "I'm looking forward to it."

Jessica scrolled down the rest of the list. She answered each question as thoroughly as she could, but it quickly became apparent that Amy wasn't paying attention to anything she was saying. In fact, Amy had seemed distracted throughout their meeting, which Jessica found disappointing. When Breanna Lafaele, Leanna's sister, had called a few days ago to talk about this week's trip, she had mentioned that Amy would be acting as cruise director for the first time. Jessica had been skeptical of Amy's ability to do a good job her first time out, but Breanna had praised Amy's professionalism.

Jessica hadn't worked with Amy before so all she had to go on was Breanna's word. She had always thought Breanna was a pretty good judge of character—and she wasn't saying that simply because she and Breanna had started hooking up during a trip to the Mexican Riviera two years ago. Okay, perhaps she was. Her thinking process got a little muddled whenever she remembered some of the sexy things Breanna could do with her tongue. Amy's behavior today, however, made Jessica wonder if Breanna's assessment of her was clouded by the blinders of friendship. Or were Breanna and Amy hooking up, too? Jessica and Breanna had never made any claims on each other, but Jessica felt a definite pang of jealousy when she thought about Breanna and Amy hitting the sheets.

"Is there anything else you need to know?" she asked as a passenger walked in and headed to the treadmill.

"Hmm?" Amy jerked as if waking up from a nap. "Oh, no, that's all for now. I'll let you get back to work. Thanks for meeting with me." She gathered her things but didn't rise from her seat. "I apologize if I seemed out of sorts today."

So Jessica hadn't been imagining things. Even though Amy had confirmed her suspicions that she had been spaced out for most of their meeting, Jessica decided not to hold it against her. "No problem. Being in charge of a group this size has to be challenging."

"That's one way of putting it. Do you have any idea when the boutiques close?"

Jessica was thrown for a loop by the unexpected question. Had Amy been thinking about shopping the whole time? "Not for a couple of hours. Why?"

"I need to find an outfit for dinner."

"What's the matter?" Jessica didn't try to disguise the sarcasm in her voice. "Did you burn through a week's worth of clothes in only a few hours?"

"No. Aside from one dressy outfit I brought to wear to the formal farewell dinner on the last night of the trip, I packed mostly casual clothes because I planned to hit the buffet all week instead of the main dining room."

"What changed?"

Amy looked somewhat embarrassed. "There's a passenger on board who seems a bit out of her element, and I was hoping I could help her find her sea legs."

"I see."

Now Amy's behavior today was starting to make sense. Jessica knew from experience how easy it was to lose focus on the task at hand whenever there was a woman involved. Even though Amy was trying to downplay her dinner plans with the passenger she had mentioned, Jessica could see a spark of interest in her eyes. She could also see why Amy had inspired such loyalty in Breanna. Amy didn't buckle under the yoke of responsibility, and she wasn't afraid to own up to her own shortcomings. Jessica felt like kicking herself for rushing to judgment. And she felt terrible for potentially having a hand in placing the trip's success at risk.

SOS Tours had a lot riding on this cruise. After the debacle that had taken place in Cancún six months ago, the company couldn't afford another misstep. Not if they wanted to retain the customers that had remained loyal instead of deciding to do business with someone else. If Brandon tried to sell drugs to the wrong passenger or someone overestimated how much their body could handle, the consequences could be catastrophic for everyone.

"Good luck," she said.

Because they just might need it.

NIGHT ONE

Jessica wasn't easily impressed, but she looked on slack-jawed as the passenger who had entered the gym during her meeting with Amy continued her workout. The passenger, a tall African-American woman with muscles for days, possessed a rare combination of power, agility, and endurance. She put in a brisk thirty minutes on the treadmill and stepped off without even breathing hard. Then she picked up a jump rope and went through one of the intricate workouts boxers put themselves through while they were in training for an upcoming fight. She whipped the rope through the air so fast it was little more than a blur as it skipped under her feet and over her head. Jessica wouldn't have lasted five seconds at that rate, let alone the fifteen minutes to which the woman subjected herself. After she finally managed to break a sweat, the woman ran a towel over her face, arms, and close-cropped hair.

"Can I have a spot?" she asked as she settled onto one of the weight benches.

"Sure." Jessica pulled a back brace from her duffel bag and wrapped it around her waist. The woman's expression was wary, her body language guarded. She seemed as if it took a great deal of effort to earn her trust. Jessica felt honored the woman had chosen to trust her, however briefly. "How much weight would you like?"

The woman lifted her broad shoulders in a shrug. "One fifty's a good place to start."

Jessica whistled in admiration. The woman appeared to be in her late twenties. At her age, she should have been able to bench press around sixty-five percent of her body weight. Based on Jessica's estimate, the amount of weight the woman had requested was closer to ninety percent.

"You're probably only a buck twenty soaking wet," the woman said with a sly grin. "Do you think you're up to the job?"

"I'm stronger than I look." Jessica cinched her back brace a little bit tighter. If she had to step in, thankfully she wouldn't have to lift her burden too far. Otherwise, they'd both be in trouble. As the woman lifted the weighted barbell off the rack, Jessica positioned her hands under the bar, ready to intercede if the woman had overestimated her own strength. "What's your name?"

The woman took a deep breath as she lowered the weight to her chest and exhaled as she slowly straightened her arms. "Raquel," she said between lifts, "but my homies call me Raq. You're Jessica, right?"

"Have we met before?" Jessica had worked with so many passengers over the years that she had forgotten most of their names. Raq's striking looks, however, made her hard to forget.

"Nah, I heard the blonde who just booked it out of here call you that while you two were talking. Are you kicking it with her?"

"No, we just work together. I can get her number for you if you'd like me to."

Raq chuckled. "Thanks for the offer, but I think my girl would have something to say about that. Since she's a cop, I try not to get on her bad side. I don't want her to slap me in handcuffs unless it's in the bedroom, you know what I'm saying?"

"I hear you. Are you in law enforcement, too?"

"In a way. I'm what you might call a consultant. Kind of like Sherlock Holmes on *Elementary*. I help crack cases, but I don't get to carry a badge."

"I've always been fascinated by how people decide what they want to do for a living. How did you get started?"

"I used to provide security for one of the biggest drug dealers in Baltimore."

Jessica didn't know what she had been expecting Raq to say, but it definitely wasn't that. "Were you one of his bodyguards or something?"

"No, he had a squad of guys a lot bigger than I am to make sure he stayed out of harm's way. My job wasn't nearly as glamorous. I used to keep the corner boys safe while they did their thing. I let them know when the five-oh was about to roll up, and I kept rival dealers from encroaching on our territory."

The description sounded like some of the services Jessica performed for Brandon. She didn't have to worry about keeping the competition at bay since they had the market to themselves, but that didn't prevent her from looking out for him in other ways. It wasn't part of her job description, but she was willing to do whatever it took to keep their operation running smoothly—and to keep everyone involved in it from winding up in prison. They had successfully rolled the dice dozens of times without crapping out, but she was tired of pushing her luck. The time had come for her to cash in her chips.

"I never carried a gun, though," Raq said. "I still don't. That's one of my rules. I've always fought my battles with these." She held up her fists. "Sometimes, I was paid to do it. Sometimes, I wasn't. A friend back home who owns a boxing gym keeps trying to convince me I should try out for the Olympics or take a shot at going pro, but there's no money in women's boxing and I can't eat a gold medal."

"There's good money to be had in product endorsements. Some athletes make more money off the field than they do on it."

"Maybe, but there's no way a company with a ton of loot would take a chance on putting someone with my background on a cereal box. The side of a milk carton, maybe."

Jessica was curious about Raq's about-face. "But you said you don't live that life anymore. How did you go from working for drug dealers to helping to catch them?" When she got out, she intended to walk away without looking back. She wasn't interested in seeking justice, righting wrongs, or making amends. She just wanted to be free.

"The guy I used to work for was Ice Taylor."

Jessica recognized the name. At his peak, Isaac "Ice" Taylor was the biggest drug dealer on the East Coast. He built a vast multimillion-dollar empire, using his legal businesses to launder the money he earned from his illegal ones. Almost as swiftly as he had risen to power, he had been knocked off his perch. And Raq was partially responsible for both his meteoric rise and his spectacular downfall.

"I threw in with Ice because I didn't think I had a choice. I grew up in the 'hood, and the money he offered seemed like my only way out. I took his money, but I never let him take my principles. I met Bathsheba, my lady, when she went undercover and took Ice down. I fell for her before I knew who she was. When I found out she was a cop, I felt trapped between the only life I'd ever known and one I never dreamed I could have. Being with her made me realize I was selling myself short. I had choices. I just had to decide to go the hard way instead of taking the easy route. Staying on the straight and narrow doesn't pay as much as running the streets, but Bathsheba makes it worth the sacrifice. Taking her on this trip is kind of my way of thanking her for helping me turn my life around."

"Is this your first time traveling with SOS?"

"Yeah. Bathsheba's, too." Raq finished a set of ten reps and lowered the weight onto the bar to give the muscles in her arms and shoulders time to rest. "I love her, but she's like a Boy Scout sometimes. She's always gotta be prepared. I found our room, the dining room, the gym, and the bars. I'm good. While she's sitting through orientation, learning everything there is to know about what to expect this week, I'm hanging out here trying to take my mind off the fact that I'm surrounded by all this water. I can swim, but I ain't no Michael Phelps, you know what I mean?"

"There's no need to be nervous. I've been on dozens of cruises and the worst that's ever happened is a day or two of choppy seas." Jessica thought it best not to mention the norovirus outbreak that had plagued her last trip. Raq was on edge enough as it was.

"There's always a first time. I brought plenty of video games to keep me distracted on the days we can't see land, but that didn't work out too well today."

"Why not?"

Raq took a sip of water from the bottle between her feet. "Bathsheba and I went back to our room after the Reagan Carter concert, and I started playing one of my games to take my mind off the fact that the ship was moving. I didn't think I had the volume turned up that loud, but when she heard me waste one of the characters in the game, the federale in the room across the hall came busting into the room like she was leading a raid on a drug den."

Jessica felt a knot form in the pit of her stomach. "We have a federale on board?"

"Yeah, her name's Luisa Moreno, and she's based in Mexico City. She's not on duty this week, though. She and her girlfriend, a writer for some travel magazine, were part of that whole mess that took place in Cancún a few months ago. They got vouchers for a free vacation and decided to cash them in on this trip. Once we got over the shock of her practically kicking our door down, she and Bathsheba hit it off right away. Cops are cops, no matter what color their uniform."

"I suppose." The news that Luisa Moreno wasn't traveling in an official capacity made Jessica feel marginally better, but she wasn't completely comfortable with the idea that a Mexican federal police officer was roaming around the ship. And hadn't Raq said her girlfriend was a police officer, too? One who specialized in arresting drug dealers?

Bathsheba's and Luisa's presence on the same ship was probably nothing more than a coincidence, but what if they— and Raq—were working together to take on a new target? If that was the case, Jessica could wind up being collateral damage. She swallowed hard as she wondered if the life she was trying to leave behind was about to become her downfall.

She needed to find Brandon ASAP. She wasn't in the habit of telling him how to do his job, but this was an emergency. Her ass was on the line, too, not just his. She had to convince him how important it was for him to maintain a low profile this week. If he drew too much attention to himself as he tried to sell the product she had helped smuggle on board, the wrong person might take notice. If he went down, he'd more than likely try to do everything he possibly could to break his fall. Once he started naming names, it wouldn't take him long to get to hers.

"Ready for the next set?" Raq asked.

"Yeah, I got your back."

As she spotted her during her next set of repetitions, Jessica looked down into Raq's cautious brown eyes. Raq's story had made it seem like the love of a good woman was the only thing that had helped her change her life, but Jessica suspected the effort had taken all of Raq's obvious physical strength as well as copious amounts of mental fortitude. When the time came, she hoped she had it in her to follow Raq's example.

"How long have you been doing this?"

For a heart-stopping moment, Jessica thought Raq was referring to something other than working as a fitness professional. "Since high school," she said after she took a second or two to regain her composure. "My first job was as a locker room attendant in a local gym. I swept floors and washed towels for a few months before I got the itch to lead the classes instead of cleaning up after them. The owners hired me as a trainer after I got certified, but they could only afford to take me on part-time. I applied for a job at one of the twenty-four-hour places across town. The manager called me in for an interview, but it didn't take me long to realize I didn't want to deal with the corporate environment. When I heard Centennial Cruises was hiring, I decided to sign on with them instead. The schedule's flexible, so I was able to accept Centennial's offer without giving up my gig at the gym. The pay isn't that great, but the perks are incredible. I get to see the world, practice running my own gym, and meet a ton of interesting people along the way."

"If you say so."

"You sound skeptical."

Raq blew out a breath as she completed another repetition. "I'm not trying to offend you. If this is what you want, go for it. All I'm saying is I'd much rather keep my feet on solid ground."

"Give it a day or two. The views on the open water are amazing. The first time you see the sun rise while we're at sea, you'll be just like Leonardo DiCaprio in *Titanic*. Standing in the bow of the ship with your arms spread wide, shouting you're king of the world."

"Not gonna happen. You remember how that movie ended, don't you? Dude went from calling himself king of the world to bobbing like an ice cube. It doesn't pay to fuck with Mother Nature. No matter how powerful you might think you are, she wins every time." Raq set the barbell down and retrieved her water bottle. "You're cool people," she said after she took a sip. "Where are you from?"

"Coral Springs. It's a few miles north of Fort Lauderdale. My parents still live there, but I have an apartment in the city." Jessica mentally scolded herself for sharing too much personal information. Raq was a bit too inquisitive for her comfort. When she answered Raq's questions, she needed to provide the bare minimum, not tell her life story. Otherwise, her openness could come back to haunt her.

Raq tossed her empty water bottle in a nearby recycling bin. "I'm about to take a shower and find my girl so we can catch some dinner. Are you going to be here all week?"

"During the day, yes. After hours, you're more likely to find me hanging out in a bar or the disco."

"Cool. If I don't spot you macking on some honey on the dance floor tonight, I'll see you tomorrow. We're going to be sailing all day and I'm going to need a distraction. I'll probably be here a while, so you'd better get used to seeing my face."

Raq was easy on the eyes, but Jessica couldn't afford to have her shadowing her all day long. "There's plenty to do on board besides work out. Tomorrow, Sinjin Smythe and Laure Fortescue are doing a question-and-answer session. Since they own a vineyard in France, maybe they'll offer free samples."

"I'm not much of a wine drinker, but Bathsheba's been going on and on about the session since she found out Sinjin and Laure were going to be on board. She had the hots for both of them before they retired, so she's planning to be front and center tomorrow. Now that I think about it, it might be a good idea if I tagged along with her. I need to make sure she doesn't throw her underwear at the stage like a groupie at an Usher concert. I'll drop by after—unless she gets too worked up and needs my help burning off the extra energy. If that's the case, I won't be able to move for a couple of days, let alone work out."

"Then I guess I'll see you when I see you."

Jessica always tried to keep her dealings with Brandon on the down low, but with Raq spending a significant amount of time in the gym every day, she would have to be more discreet than ever. Raq seemed nice, but Jessica wasn't comfortable with the idea of a police consultant becoming her new BFF. Was Raq being straight with her, or was she simply plying her for information?

She tried to rationalize her way out of a full-blown panic attack.

"You can do this," she told herself. "All you've got to do is keep your nose clean for eight days. Then, when you get home, you can start over fresh. Just don't do or say anything stupid in the meantime. And when she isn't watching you, make sure you've got eyes on her. In the grand scheme of things, you're just a minnow. If she is on the hunt, she has her sights set on someone a whole lot bigger than you are."

Her outlook began to improve until she remembered a very important fact: the best way to catch a big fish was to start with a small one.

The dress code for dinner was supposed to be smart casual, so Spencer felt pretty good about her chosen outfit—khaki pants, a red polo shirt, and her favorite pair of Doc Martens. But that was before she left her room. Her opinion changed as soon as she headed downstairs and caught a glimpse of the crowd of nattily attired women filing into the main dining room. Then she went from feeling like a million bucks to feeling more like a country bumpkin venturing out on the town for the first time. Considering the population of the small town she called home, she didn't think the analogy strayed too far from the truth. In Pipkinville, no one got too dressed up unless they were going to a wedding or a funeral. And sometimes not even then.

She searched for the nearest exit, wondering if she should use her cruise card to buy a more upscale outfit from one of the many boutiques on board.

"Stop," she told herself as she tried to keep from psyching herself out. "Just relax and be yourself. You can't get anywhere by pretending to be someone else."

She hadn't gotten anywhere by being herself either, but she had to make a stand at some point.

"There's no time like the present."

She took a deep breath and slowly released it before she headed inside. Because she had been given an early seating assignment, she had expected the crowd to be sparse. She couldn't have been more wrong. Even though it was only a little after six p.m., most of the seats surrounding the elaborately decorated tables were already filled. Servers carrying trays piled high with steak, seafood, and an assortment of luxurious desserts hustled to and fro. Bartenders worked double-time trying to keep up with dozens of orders for beer, wine, champagne, and mixed drinks. So many corks were being popped it sounded like someone was throwing an indoor fireworks show minus the colorful pyrotechnics. And it was only the first night.

Spencer's stomach growled when she saw a selection of mouthwatering appetizers being delivered to a nearby table. Lobster-avocado cocktail, toasted ravioli, bacon-wrapped asparagus, and roasted grapes, to name a few.

"No wonder Mom insists on losing ten pounds before she goes on a cruise. By the time this week is over, I'll probably be wishing I'd done the same thing. Oh, yeah," she said when she saw a fountain spewing geysers of melted chocolate, "I think it's time I renewed my gym membership."

Spencer was grateful that assigned seating would prevent her from wandering around as aimlessly as a high school outcast desperate to be invited to eat with the cool kids.

"Been there, done that," she said, tamping down unwanted memories.

She scanned the room as she tried to locate her designated table. She hoped she had been given a spot in a quiet corner so she could discreetly take in all the sights and sounds as her fellow travelers greeted old friends or introduced themselves to new ones. No such luck. Her table was located in the center of the room. Perfect if she wanted to see and be seen. Terrible if she wanted to maintain her usual low profile.

"I hope you weren't planning on being a wallflower tonight. If so, you're not blending into the background very well."

Spencer relaxed when she heard a familiar voice. She turned to find Hannah standing behind her. Hannah was wearing a long-sleeved white silk shirt, black tuxedo pants with a line of silver sequins trailing down the outside of each leg, and a pair of sexy black stilettos. "Wow. You look amazing."

"Do you want to trade outfits? Given a choice, I'd rather wear your shoes than mine. My feet are already killing me, and I haven't even hit the dance floor yet."

"I wouldn't be able to make it two steps in those heels, let alone attempt to look semi-coordinated on the dance floor. My mother tried to teach me how to walk in heels before my first school dance, but the lesson didn't last long. My dad said I looked about as graceful as a cow trying to walk on ice."

"Your father doesn't pull any punches, does he?"

"He definitely operates without a filter, that's for sure. He'd never be mistaken for Archie Bunker, though. His comments are always funny rather than mean-spirited. Even so, I'm sure my mother wishes he would keep some of them to himself." Her father's boyish charm kept him from putting his foot in his mouth, but as she had demonstrated that afternoon when she'd revealed to Amy that her mother had purchased the ticket to her cruise on a resale site, Spencer's skills in that particular area weren't as highly developed. Unlike her father, she could take a conversation from comfortable to awkward in sixty seconds flat. Surprisingly, her slip of the tongue with Amy was her only conversational faux pas today. Then again, the night was still young. She took a peek over her shoulder, but Hannah appeared to be alone. "Is Bonnie running late again?"

"Of course she is. Her personal slogan should be 'I'm so far behind, I thought I was first.'"

Bonnie had been a no-show at the mixer that afternoon. Spencer was hoping to meet her tonight before they headed off to their respective tables. "Tomorrow, you should tell her dinner's at five. Maybe she'll show up on time."

"I like the way you think." Hannah tucked her clutch bag under her arm. "Are you getting the lay of the land before you break bread, or are you waiting for someone?"

"Before the mixer started, Amy asked me to save her a seat tonight. She's not an Indie, but I doubt anyone at the table will mind her bending the rules a bit."

"You're dining with our lovely cruise director this evening? Color me green with envy."

"It's not a date or anything like that," Spencer said before Hannah could start barreling down the wrong track. She had spent all afternoon drumming the idea into her head that Amy was more interested in her opinions than she was in her. She didn't want to undo all the hard work she had put in. Otherwise, she wouldn't be able to string two sentences together, let alone carry on an entire conversation. "She just wants to pick my brain about how the trip's going so far."

She hated surveys. In her mind, they were little more than massive wastes of time since the majority of respondents were so eager to put the tedious task behind them, they didn't take the time to share their true feelings. Yet she had eagerly volunteered to answer Amy's list of questions. Did she have the guts to tell Amy how she really felt, or would she cave and tell her what she wanted to hear?

"I have a few things she could pick," Hannah said. "Rest assured my brain isn't one of them."

Spencer couldn't help but laugh at the stark contrast between Hannah's polished exterior and her constant stream of off-color jokes. "You're terrible, you know that?"

"As my friends say, you can take me anywhere but out." Hannah made eye contact with a woman in a colorful sari across the room. The woman flashed a flirtatious smile before she returned her attention to the group of Indies sharing the table with her. Hannah's nose twitched like she was a hound dog on the hunt. "Have fun talking shop. I see someone who needs to hear about some exciting real estate opportunities. Starting with my stateroom."

Spencer watched as Hannah made her way through the crowd, shook hands with the woman in the sari, and slid into the chair next to her. The number on the table didn't match the one on Hannah's cruise card, but it didn't seem to matter. Hannah had the woman hanging on her every word in no time at all. Spencer could feel the heat between them all the way across the room. "I'll be surprised if they remain upright until dessert."

When she saw Amy walk in looking even more luscious than the Belgian chocolate streaming down the sides of the three-tier fountain, she wished the same sentiment could be applied to them.

❖

Amy's impromptu shopping spree had set her back several hundred dollars, but the appreciative look she saw on Spencer's face made the unexpected expense worth every penny.

"You look nice," Spencer said.

"This old thing?"

Amy looked down at the outfit she had chosen to wear that night: a flowing sundress and a pair of strappy, low-wedge sandals she had bought from the boutique across from the bustling casino on the opposite end of the deck on which they now stood. She thought the items, elegant but not too fancy, fit her personality. Spencer's outfit seemed to suit her to a T as well. Her polo shirt and chinos perfectly matched the buttoned-up computer programmer she was by day; the scuffed Doc Martens on her feet hinted at the adventurous video game enthusiast Amy had recently discovered her to be.

Amy suspected there were many more surprises lurking beneath Spencer's inscrutable surface, and she was eager to unwrap them all. She wished she had the freedom to do so, but if she wanted to keep the job she had worked so hard to earn, she needed to keep her hands to herself for the next week or so. After that, all bets were off.

Exploring her body might be more fun, she thought as Spencer's penetrating gaze wandered over her, but exploring her mind could prove to be more rewarding.

Spencer was mysterious. Intriguing. Awkward in some social situations, but thoroughly at ease in others. She was the kind of woman you could share a memorable one-night stand with and never see again, or spend a lifetime getting to know. When Spencer flashed a lazy smile that made her stomach turn somersaults, Amy knew she could get into a boatload of trouble no matter which route she chose. One path could result in her losing her job, the other might cost her something even more dear—her heart.

"Old? Are you sure about that?"

Spencer jerked her chin toward Amy's left shoulder. Following Spencer's line of sight, Amy spotted a price tag dangling from one of the spaghetti straps on her dress. How had she missed that? She hurriedly reached to remove the tag, but Spencer held her at bay.

"Here. Let me."

Spencer lifted the strap and slid two fingers underneath to trap one end of the plastic string holding the price tag in place. Amy's breath caught when Spencer's fingers brushed against her skin. Spencer's touch was strong and sure, but tender at the same time. Like someone who was used to working with both her hands and her brain.

Spencer gave a quick tug, and Amy heard a snap. The sound was the plastic string breaking, not her control. Somehow, that remained intact. For the moment, anyway, though she had no idea how long that might last. For as long as she could remember, temptation had always proven to be something she would rather give in to than resist.

"Thank you," she said after Spencer tossed the price tag and broken string in the trash. "If I need help getting dressed, I know who to call."

"In that case, I'd better update my résumé."

"You never know when a skill like that might come in handy." Amy hadn't meant to flirt with Spencer. It just came so easily. She wiped images of Spencer dressing and undressing her from her mind, then switched to a more neutral subject after they took their seats at the table. "Why did you decide to go into computer programming?"

"When I was in elementary school, my favorite subjects were always math and science. After I took a computer math class in middle school, I realized I had found my niche. We wrote a few programs in class, and I was fascinated by what could result from a few simple commands. I started writing more and more of them, both for class and for fun. Even before I got to high school, I knew what I wanted my college major and future profession to be."

"Doesn't it get old after a while?" Amy asked as they examined their respective menus. "In my job, there's always a new resort, cruise ship, or excursion to explore. There's only so much you can do with a bunch of zeroes and ones."

Spencer set her menu down. "Gender isn't binary, and neither is coding." Her eyes burned with an intensity that belied the gentle tone of her voice. "Computer programs are more than a bunch of random letters, numbers, and symbols. For me, reading a complex program is just as enjoyable as reading a classic piece of literature. When a program's written well, it can be like poetry."

"I believe you." Amy thought Maya Angelou, Emily Dickinson, or Robert Frost might beg to differ, but she found it hard to refute Spencer's argument when she could see how passionate Spencer was about the subject.

A member of the wait staff ventured to the table to take their drink orders. Spencer ordered a glass of white wine, while Amy settled for a glass of sparkling water. She would kill for a glass of champagne, but she couldn't drink anything alcoholic for a few more hours. Her workday wouldn't end until after the second of tonight's two scheduled shows. When that finally happened, she might eschew the glass and drink straight from the bottle. Today was the first of many long days to come. She could only hope the days that followed would be as relatively uneventful as this one. Aside from this afternoon's false alarm, the rest of the day had been drama-free. Just the way she liked it.

"Would you like to go ahead and order dinner, or do you need a few more minutes?" the waiter asked.

Amy forced herself to turn her attention from Spencer to the eight women sharing the table with them. "I can't stay long. I have to head back to work soon."

"At this time of night?" Spencer asked.

"There are two shows scheduled for tonight. I have to make sure both go off without a hitch before I'll be able to call it a day. In the meantime, why don't we start with a round of appetizers for the table?"

"Sounds good," someone said. "Why don't you do the honors?"

Amy ordered a mix of light and heavy appetizers from the vast menu. The small snacks probably wouldn't fill her up, but they should provide enough fuel to get her through the next few hours. Then she could grab something from the buffet before she crawled into bed and fell into an exhausted sleep or hit the disco to dance off what remained of her nervous energy. First days were always a challenge, and today certainly hadn't disappointed. At least the guests seemed to be having fun. In the end, that was all that mattered.

"When was the last time you had a real sit-down dinner?" Spencer asked after the waiter left.

"A meal that involved more than a few pieces of shrimp and didn't arrive in a cardboard or Styrofoam box? Longer than I care to remember."

"Then it sounds like we have something in common. I'm used to putting in long hours, especially when a project's due." Spencer spread her arms. "I have to say, though, that the view from my office isn't usually this nice."

"It's addictive, right?" one of the women at the table said. Her name was Sheila Ford, and she was a tax attorney from Cincinnati. Amy recognized her and her wife from past trips. "That's why Mavis and I wouldn't dream of traveling any other way. We spend all of our vacations—and most of our disposable income—with SOS."

"As a matter of fact," Mavis said, "we've already signed up for our next trip. We weren't planning on going on another one so soon, but the deep discount for booking onsite is pretty hard to pass up."

"Awesome." Amy loved repeat customers. They not only kept the company afloat, they helped cement its reputation. At the moment, SOS could use as much positive publicity and good word of mouth as it could get. "Which trip did you book?"

"The luxury cruise to Tahiti. I've dreamed of going there since the first time I saw the series of paintings Paul Gauguin created while he lived on the island."

"She wants to frolic naked on the beach," Sheila said. "I just want to sit around drinking something deceptively strong from a pineapple shell."

Amy took a sip of her mineral water. "I'm glad we could help you make one of your dreams come true."

"Are you going to be in charge of that trip, too?" Spencer asked.

"I don't know yet. It's a long way off. We'll see when the time comes." The resort was incredible the first time she had visited it. She would love to make a return trip, but she would be equally grateful if the company was still in business by then. Her bosses kept telling her this trip wasn't make-or-break, but she couldn't stop feeling like the company's future was riding on her shoulders. "How did the mixer go this afternoon?"

Spencer's face lit up. "It was awesome. I didn't expect to enjoy myself, but I had a really good time."

Icebreaking events were usually hit or miss. They were either rousing successes or colossal failures. They didn't often fall somewhere in between. Amy was glad to hear that the event Breanna planned had gone well. Surely that boded well for the rest of the week.

"Did you win?" she asked as the waiter set three platters of steaming appetizers in the center of the table.

Spencer began to fill her plate with some of the delectable dishes. "Hannah won the first round so fast we wouldn't let her play again. I came close in the second game, but I lost by one square. I couldn't find anyone who's been to Coachella."

"I didn't have as much fun there as I did at Burning Man," Amy said, "but I'd still recommend it."

"See? I knew you should have stayed."

"Maybe next time. What do you have planned for tomorrow?"

Spencer took a bite of her grilled shrimp. "Why? Do you want to pick my brain about that, too?"

"If you don't mind."

"That's not really a fair tradeoff, is it? You asking all the questions while I get to have all the fun."

Amy shrugged. She and Breanna had scouted the trip well over a year in advance. She had already taken part in most of the excursions Spencer had yet to experience. She and Breanna had already formed their own opinions about the outings. She was eager to hear someone else's. "I have to stay close to the ship this week to make sure nothing goes wrong. I have to live vicariously through someone. Why shouldn't it be you?"

"Because you might be bored to tears, that's why. Have you considered that possibility?"

Amy had considered many possibilities since she'd met Spencer Collins that afternoon, but being bored definitely wasn't one of them. "Why don't you let me be the judge of that?"

"Because I can't trust the judgment of someone who hates chocolate."

Amy couldn't help but laugh as Spencer returned to what was becoming a familiar refrain. "I'll tell you what. If you have dinner with me every night this week, I will spend the last night of the trip eating every chocolate-themed confection you place in front of me."

"That sounds like a challenge."

"Are you up for it?"

Spencer leaned toward her. "I'm game. Are you?"

Amy was more than ready to play, but would she be willing—or able—to stick to the rules?

"Count me in."

DAY TWO

Located on the promenade deck, the Illusion Lounge was the *Majestic Dream*'s main showroom. Instead of a concert or comedy show, the expansive space was currently serving as the venue for an informal question-and-answer session featuring retired tennis stars Laure Fortescue and Sinjin Smythe. Even though Spencer had made it a point to arrive early, space was hard to come by. All of the seats closest to the stage were already filled, as were many in the soaring balcony overhead.

"There are a few seats left in the back of the room, if you don't mind craning your neck to see over some of the heads in your way," the SOS Tours staffer at the door said. "If you'd prefer to have an unobstructed view, you'd be better off heading up to the balcony."

Spencer took a quick peek upstairs. A long line of women was steadily streaming down the aisles, guaranteeing that the seats that hadn't yet been claimed wouldn't remain that way for long.

"A bird in the hand beats two in the bush," she said to herself. "Down here's fine."

"Cool," the staffer said with a bright smile. The name tag pinned to her yellow polo shirt said her name was Sunny, an apt name given her cheerful disposition. She tore a small rectangular ticket off the large roll in her hand and handed it to Spencer.

"Make sure you keep this in a safe place. At some point during the session, Amy's going to give away a BOGO."

"What's a BOGO?"

"A buy one, get one free. My favorite shoe store has them all the time."

"So does my favorite grocery store, but I can't imagine SOS doing something similar. Wouldn't it cut into your profit margin?"

"I'm no economics expert by any means, but I'd be willing to bet a booked room beats an empty one every time."

Spencer couldn't argue with Sunny's logic. "How many BOGOs do you do on average?"

"Not many. They're only a fraction of our overall business. We'll probably give away four of five of them this week, and we send emails to chosen customers throughout the year as spaces become available. Before you ask me what the catch is, there isn't one. Instead of being able to get two pairs of killer shoes or, to use your example, two bags of potato chips, for the price of one, whoever wins is able to book two passengers on a trip and pay for only one fare." Sunny lowered her voice to a conspiratorial whisper. "You didn't hear it from me, but the trip Amy's giving away today is a riverboat cruise from Montpellier to Monaco. The trip's been listed on our website for only a few days, and the reservations are filling up fast. At this rate, most of the cabins are going be sold out. Not surprising, given the riverboat holds less than a hundred passengers."

"That sounds intimate. How long is the trip?"

"Eight days and seven nights with a two-night stay in Marseille featuring dinner in an honest-to-God chateau. If you book the vacation stretcher, you can zip over to Barcelona and spend some time walking up and down Las Ramblas. It's kind of touristy, but that just makes for better people-watching."

Spencer memorized the number on the front of her ticket before she slipped it into one of the many pockets on her cargo shorts. The trip sounded amazing. And expensive. But, hopefully, she wouldn't have to pay full-price.

She had never won a raffle in her life, but she desperately wanted to win today's giveaway. Not for herself. A trip as romantic as this one sounded should be taken with someone you love, not by yourself. Or, even worse, with a friend who was gracious enough to tag along to keep you company. Woefully short of friends and lovers, Spencer longed for a chance to repay her parents' generosity. Her mother loved French food, and her father adored James Bond. Her mother would be over the moon at the prospect of being able to have a multi-course meal in an historic chateau. Her father, meanwhile, had always longed to don a tux and play a few rounds of blackjack at the Casino Royale, the ritzy establishment that served as the primary locale for Ian Fleming's first book featuring a certain globetrotting and bed-hopping spy. If she were able to give both of her parents what they wanted, she'd earn brownie points for life, freeing her up to look for love on her own schedule instead of someone else's.

"Good luck," Sunny said.

"Thanks."

Spencer took a seat in the back of the room. The stage was so far away it seemed like she and it were located on opposite ends of the ship. Not that she was complaining. Far from it. She felt giddy, and she hadn't had even a single drop of wine from any of the dozen or so bottles lining the display table that had been placed behind the three director's chairs in the center of the stage. She was excited about several things. The upcoming program and the chance to win a luxury vacation, naturally, but she was even more geeked at having a chance to see Amy again so soon after their laughter-filled evening the night before.

Amy hadn't mentioned she would be facilitating this morning's Q and A session before they parted ways last night, so her presence today was an unexpected surprise. They had plans to meet for dinner tonight, but that was hours away. And even though the meal was work-related, it wasn't the same as seeing Amy in action.

Spencer liked watching people do their jobs, especially when they enjoyed their work as much as Amy seemed to. She liked her job, too, but the long hours she often put in occasionally made her feel like she was on the verge of burning out. The money was nice, but the stress level was often off the charts. She envied people like Amy who could work practically around the clock without losing their desire to show up and do it all over again the next day.

Amy had many other attributes that were worthy of admiration as well, but Spencer was trying to ignore those. Trying and failing. She could still see Amy wearing that sexy little sundress she had been sporting last night. She could still feel Amy's smooth skin beneath her fingers as she removed the price tag Amy had forgotten to discard. She wondered what kind of outfit Amy would wear tonight. Something casual but professional, or something even more alluring than that sundress?

"Is this seat taken?"

Spencer stopped daydreaming about fashion choices and looked up to find a gorgeous brunette pointing at the empty seat next to hers. The brunette, who appeared to be in her mid to late twenties, had soft brown eyes, a dazzling smile, and tawny skin that hinted at Latin American roots. "Not yet."

"Do you mind if I join you?"

"No, please do."

"Thanks." The brunette claimed the seat next to Spencer and stuck out her hand. Her wrist was adorned with a series of plastic, metal, and fabric bracelets that made her liberal political affiliations clear. One bracelet read *Resist*. Another sported the slogan *Nevertheless, she persisted*. A third read *#notmypresident*. A fourth said *We the people means everyone*. The rest of the bracelets were overlapped, preventing Spencer from seeing what they said, but she was pretty sure the wording on them was in the same vein. "I'm Jordan Gonzalez."

"Spencer Collins."

"Did you go to UGA?"

Spencer glanced at the Georgia Bulldogs T-shirt she was wearing. The agenda said today was Spirit Day. Passengers were encouraged to wear clothes or accessories that indicated what town or state they called home. Spencer had opted to advertise her college roots instead of her hometown ones. UGA had much better name recognition than Pipkinville, allowing her to spend far less time explaining where she was from.

She'd had a blast during her four years in Athens. She often wished she could go back. Not to the town but the time. She wanted to relive the sense of wonder, the sense of freedom she had experienced while she was on campus. Pipkinville was so small that everyone knew everyone else's business. In Athens, where the population was exponentially larger, she had been able to be herself, not worry about living up or down to anyone's expectations of her.

She could have set down roots anywhere after graduation. Instead, she had chosen to return home. She was starting to wonder if she had made the right choice. She adored her family and she loved her job, but her personal life often felt like it was a weak-hulled ship on a collision course with an outcropping of especially nasty rocks. So far, the trip had done nothing to dispel that feeling. The women she had met the past couple of days had made her realize she had been going through the paces in her life, not truly living it. Would she be able to resume that sad existence when the ship returned to shore next week, or would she finally be able to accept the fact that it was time for her to make a change?

"Yes, I did," she said, answering Jordan's question. "Did you go to—" Jordan's shirt seemed to have been cobbled from three other ones. Spencer slowly sounded out the seemingly nonsensical word that had been created as a result. "Wi-kle-ga? Sorry, but I'm going to need a little help with that one."

"No worries." Jordan pointed to each panel of her shirt as she explained the meaning behind it. "I grew up in Wisconsin, I graduated from UC Berkeley, and I live in Georgia."

"Really? Where?"

"Jekyll Island. My girlfriend and I run the Remember When Inn, a hotel on the beach. Technically, she runs it since she's the manager. I'm the marketing wiz behind the scenes."

"Wait. Are you talking about the place where the rooms are patterned after classic TV shows, and the employees dress up like the characters?"

Jordan beamed. "The costumes were my idea."

"Talk about a small world. My parents stayed in your hotel for their thirtieth anniversary last year. My father wanted the *M*A*S*H* room, but my mother booked the *I Dream of Jeannie* one instead."

"That's our most popular room. Circular beds tend to have a certain effect on people, if you catch my drift."

Spencer didn't want to think about the acts her parents might have performed in that circular bed. As far as she was concerned, she was a product of Immaculate Conception and no one would be able to convince her otherwise. "Should we save a seat for your girlfriend?" she asked as she looked around the crowded room.

"No, she signed up for a spin class, so she's busy working up a sweat in the gym with a hot fitness pro who looks like Shane from *The L Word*."

Spencer noticed the frown lines furrowing Jordan's brow. "Are you worried about your girlfriend or the hot fitness pro who looks like Katherine Moennig?"

"I know I shouldn't worry about Tatum, but I can't help it."

"How long have you been together?"

"Almost four years. My grandmother and I used to go on vacation together every summer. I met Tatum the year Grandma Meredith and I drove from Racine to Jekyll Island. Tatum and I fell for each other while Grandma Meredith was busy reconnecting with the love of her life, a former Army nurse she served with in Vietnam. Grandma Meredith and I must have similar taste in women because Tatum is the niece of the woman she fell for all those years ago."

"Was that the reason you chose Jekyll Island for that year's trip? So your grandmother and the woman who stole her heart could relive old times?"

"No, it was more like a happy accident, but in retrospect, I guess you could call it fate. Grandma Meredith and I always chose our destinations at random. She'd pull out a map, and I would close my eyes and point. Whatever city my finger landed on was the one we ended up traveling to. That year, our destination turned out to be Jekyll Island, Grandma Natalie's hometown."

"Did you and Tatum hit it off right away?"

"Not even close. Lincoln, her German shepherd, took to me right away, but Tatum and I butted heads from the start. We had differing opinions on pretty much everything. I'm an anti-war activist and she's a former Marine who was injured in Afghanistan."

"What happened?"

"She was shot three times when the convoy she was riding in drove into an ambush. She was confined to a wheelchair for several years, and is finally starting to walk again. She can't do it without support of some kind, but she's getting closer every day. She was an avid cyclist before she was injured, so she jumped at the chance when the fitness pro on board said she'd be able to take part in spin class. I know how badly she wants to get back to being the physically active person she once was, but I don't want her to push herself too hard and have a setback. It took her so long to get to this point. She'd be devastated if she had to start all over again. So would I."

Jordan seemed in need of comfort, so Spencer reached over and patted her hand. "The way you describe Tatum, she sounds pretty indestructible. If she survived getting shot three times, I think she can handle a measly spin class, don't you?"

Jordan grinned. "My concerns sound pretty silly when you put it that way."

"It's not silly to be concerned about someone you love." And Spencer could practically see Jordan's love for Tatum oozing from her pores. "But we're on a ship filled with lesbians, which means there's probably an inordinate number of doctors, nurses, police officers, and paramedics on board. If something does happen to go wrong during the session, I'm sure Tatum will be in good hands.

"That's what she said." The smile in Jordan's eyes matched the one on her face. "The next time your parents are thinking of traveling to Jekyll, shoot me an email and I'll make sure their preferred room is available."

"I'll be sure to let them know, but I'm hoping I'll be able to give them a trip to France instead."

"If you're talking about the BOGO, you don't have a chance because I've got the winning ticket right here." Jordan patted the front pocket of her bright orange board shorts. "Do you want to trade?"

"No, thanks. I think I'll take my chances with the one I already have."

"If you do win, have you figured out a way to sneak your father onto a women-only cruise?"

"I haven't worked out that tiny little detail yet. Maybe I can persuade someone to bend the rules."

"Good luck with that. Some of the passengers take the women-only thing seriously. That's why they chose to book this cruise instead of the family and friends trip in November that follows the same itinerary." The house lights dropped, letting everyone know the program was about to begin. Jordan squeezed Spencer's hand as the audience began to buzz with excitement. "Thanks for talking me off the ledge. If you don't have any plans this afternoon, I'd love to introduce you to Tatum and buy both of you a drink. I can afford to be magnanimous when the drinks are all-inclusive."

"In that case, make mine a double."

❖

As she waited to go onstage to host the Q and A, Amy referred to the notes she had written on the index cards in her hands. She had jotted down several talking points she wanted to address during today's session. She gave them one last once-over to make sure she had an equal number of questions about both Laure's and Sinjin's tennis careers.

Laure had been the more accomplished singles player—she had won three Grand Slam titles, compared to Sinjin's one—but they had been a formidable doubles team and were now partners in life as well as in business. Amy had been fans of both when they were on tour, and she didn't want to appear to favor one over the other now.

"You don't need those." Sinjin, the more gregarious of the two, plucked the index cards from Amy's hands and held them out of reach. Six foot one and still within five pounds of her playing weight, even though she had been off the tour for almost six years, she was easily able to fend off Amy's attempts to retrieve the cards. "If you start off by asking Laure a question about wine, she'll talk for at least an hour uninterrupted, and neither of us will have to say anything except *Hello* and *Thanks for coming.*"

Laure, who had always been reserved during her matches and the press conferences that followed, pursed her lips to keep from smiling. "Obviously," she said in the sexy French accent that had earned her nearly as many admirers as her gorgeous backhand, "you're planning on sleeping alone tonight."

"In that case, forget I said anything." Sinjin returned the cards, swept Laure into her arms, twirled her around, and gave her a lingering kiss.

Amy loved the rapport Laure and Sinjin shared. Even though she hadn't met them prior to the trip, she was well aware of their love story. They had been friendly rivals for years before they began to fall for each during the last tournament either would ever play. Laure had lost in the semifinals of Wimbledon that year. Sinjin had taken the trophy home. She had also captured Laure's heart along the way.

Even if she hadn't been privy to the details of Laure and Sinjin's relationship, Amy could tell they had been friends before they became lovers. Each made jokes at the other's expense, as most athletes were wont to do, but their jibes were tempered by their obvious affection for each other. Amy wanted a love like that. Someone who didn't allow her to get too full of herself, but looked at her like she was the only woman in the world. One day, when she could finally slow down long enough to start looking, maybe she'd be able to find it.

"Okay, you've convinced me." Amy tossed the index cards aside. "Let's just go out there and have an organic conversation. We'll banter back and forth for a while, open it up to the audience for questions, hold the raffle for the riverboat cruise, then segue into the wine tasting."

"Or we could start with the wine tasting, then spend the next hour getting hammered," Sinjin said. "If we go with that approach, I won't have to work quite so hard at pretending to be charming. An English accent helps, but it can take me only so far."

"All jokes aside," Laure said after she finished laughing at Sinjin's latest. "Would you like us to set aside some time for autographs after the session?"

Laure was always generous with her time when she was on tour. Willing to sign every souvenir and shake any hand that was thrust in her direction. Amy was pleasantly surprised to see she hadn't changed. "An autograph session would be a wonderful addition to the program, but I don't want to impose on your time.

I'm sure most of the guests in attendance would probably be satisfied simply having an opportunity to interact with you."

"It isn't an imposition," Sinjin said. "We're retired, remember? We've got nothing but time."

Amy was used to dealing with artists who wanted to cut their performances short, not extend them. That way, they could do less work for the same amount of money. Laure and Sinjin were offering to do more work for free. Their request was practically unheard of, but Amy was more than willing to fulfill it.

"I'll make the announcement before we conduct the drawing for the giveaway. Thanks for making my job so easy."

The rotating team of comedians and musicians who provided entertainment for SOS Tours were easy to deal with because they were practically part of the team. The special guests who dropped in from time to time, however, were often more problematic to deal with. Amy was glad she didn't have to worry about fulfilling any exotic contract riders or keeping anyone's fragile ego in check. Then again, the week wasn't over yet. She still had a celebrity chef to deal with. Now that everyone and her sister was a foodie, some celebrity chefs could be even bigger prima donnas than most A-list actors.

"I'll go out first, welcome the audience, and read both your bios," Amy said. "Then I'll introduce you, and you can walk onstage together."

"I would make a comment about age before beauty," Sinjin said, "but considering I've already been put on notice, I think it's best if I refrain."

"Good idea." Amy watched as Wendy Crane, SOS Tours' resident lighting and sound expert, fitted Laure and Sinjin with wireless headset microphones. She preferred a cordless microphone because she liked having something to hold on to. That way, she didn't have to worry about what to do with her hands when she got nervous. "I'll see you out there. Thanks again for agreeing to do this."

"It's our pleasure," Laure said.

"How are your accommodations?"

"Spectacular."

Laure and Sinjin were staying in one of the VIP suites on the navigation deck. The suite featured a king-sized bed, a hot tub, a living room, a dining room, a dressing room, a pantry, a full-sized refrigerator, floor-to-ceiling windows, and a private veranda. Amy, in contrast, was residing in the crew quarters deep within the recesses of the ship. The rooms were cramped and the views were terrible, but the parties the members of the crew and SOS Tours employees threw after hours made everyone forget about their surroundings. Depending on how much alcohol they had downed, they sometimes forgot the commitments they had made to the people waiting for them at home, too. Amy had never been in their shoes. She couldn't decide if that was a blessing or a curse. She liked being able to have fun guilt-free, but she often wondered how it would feel to have someone greet her at the airport at the end of a trip. To have something to go home to other than an empty apartment.

Sinjin draped her arm across Laure's shoulder. "This is the best working vacation we've ever had. I'm tempted to remain on board rather than disembarking in Puerto Rico like we planned."

Amy hoped Sinjin was kidding. If not, she would have to scramble to find accommodations for Griffin Sutton, the celebrity chef who would be performing a cooking demonstration during the leg from St. Maarten to Nassau. "The ship's full and your room has already been allotted to the next VIP," she said tactfully, "but I'd be happy to send you some information about future trips."

"Please do."

Amy was overjoyed to see SOS had made a favorable impression on the three VIPs she had spoken to at this point. After her concert yesterday, Reagan Carter had said she planned to make a return trip. Now Sinjin and Laure were echoing her sentiments. If the paying guests felt the same way, the debacle in

Cancún might become nothing more than a distant memory. She and the rest of SOS Tours' employees were eager to put that dark day behind them for good. Today represented another step on the path, and she was eager to continue the journey.

❖

Spencer didn't have a clear view of the stage from her vantage point. Thankfully, she didn't need one. Oversized images of Amy and her guests were splashed across the large projection screens located on either side of the stage. Spencer watched as Amy interviewed Laure Fortescue and Sinjin Smythe. No, interview wasn't the right word. Amy seemed to be conversing with them, not interrogating them. They chatted like they were old friends. Amy asked Laure and Sinjin a series of questions about their lives before, during, and after their tennis careers. No matter if their responses were funny or touching, they seemed thought out rather than rehearsed.

"She's a natural," Jordan said.

"She's like Ellen DeGeneres without the jokes."

"I was thinking more along the lines of Rachel Maddow without the professional lesbian haircut, but I'll go along with that."

"If anyone has any questions," Amy said, "raise your hand and Sunny will bring you the microphone so everyone can hear what you have to say."

An African-American woman in the front row raised her hand. She had the bearing of either a soldier or a law enforcement officer. Her posture was so perfect it prompted Spencer to improve her own. "I have a question," the woman said as Spencer sat straighter in her seat.

"What's your name, and where are you from?" Amy asked.

"My name is Bathsheba Morris, and I'm from Washington, DC," the woman said after Sunny handed her a cordless microphone.

"Thanks for coming today, Bathsheba," Laure said. "What's your question?"

"I would ask you to say my name again, but I think my partner might take issue with that."

"You're damn right I would," the woman next to Bathsheba said. Her voice projected so well she didn't need a microphone to make herself heard throughout the room.

"I might have a problem with that, too." Sinjin jogged to the edge of the stage to give Bathsheba's partner a fist bump as the butches in attendance roared in approval.

"Now that Raq's day has been made and my dreams have been dashed," Bathsheba said, "let me say it was a privilege to watch you and Sinjin play. I've always dreamed of having a backhand like yours, Laure, or a serve like yours, Sinjin. Since I was blessed with neither, I'm much better at watching tennis than I am at playing it. Both of you walked away relatively early. Laure, you were twenty-seven. And, Sinjin, you were just twenty-five."

"I think you know our bios better than we do," Sinjin said, prompting a round of laughter.

"My question is," Bathsheba said after the laughter died down, "do you still watch the game, or did you completely leave it behind when you retired?"

"That's a great question," Laure said as Bathsheba returned the microphone to Sunny and resumed her seat. "Even though people speculate we left the game too soon, I think I speak for both of us when I say we left because we both knew we had nothing left to prove. For me, winning the French Open fulfilled a lifelong dream. Winning Wimbledon did the same for Sinjin. Once we accomplished those goals, we were ready to get on with our lives. We don't regret our respective decisions, but we do miss the game. To answer your question, there are far too many tournaments for us to keep track of every single result, but we do pay close attention to each of the Grand Slams because they're the pinnacle of our sport, and it's always awe-inspiring to watch someone make history. Thank you for your question, Bathsheba. And for having such a beautiful name."

"So no chance of a comeback?" someone shouted without waiting for Sunny to hand her the microphone.

"I wouldn't rule it out," Sinjin said, "but I wouldn't count on it, either. I wanted to be a tennis player from the moment I held a racquet in my hands. Walking away from a sport I loved was simultaneously the easiest and the hardest thing I've ever done. Hardest because I was walking away from the only life I had ever known. Easiest because I knew I was heading toward a life I always wanted."

Spencer couldn't help but tear up when Sinjin clasped Laure's hand. Jordan's reaction was slightly different.

"I could eat her up with a spoon, couldn't you?"

"I think that's the perfect segue into the next part of our program," Amy said. "In case you weren't aware, Laure and Sinjin own a vineyard in Saint-Tropez. They have generously brought a few bottles along with them today. Would you like to try some?"

The women in the audience whooped so loud Spencer's ears rang.

"Before we pop the corks," Amy said, "let me point out that Laure and Sinjin's vineyard is a popular location for picnics, weddings, and tours. It is also the site of an optional excursion during SOS Tours' upcoming riverboat cruise from Montpellier to Monaco. All food and drinks are included. Each dinner will feature a French entrée, and local cheeses will be included in the dessert course. The centerpiece of the trip, aside from the excursion to the vineyard, of course, is a three-course meal served in a chateau overlooking the Mediterranean Sea. We'll have two of your favorite SOS Tours entertainers on board as well."

"She makes the trip sound even better than Sunny did," Spencer said.

Jordan clutched her ticket. "I'll tell you all about it when Tatum and I get back."

"I can skip directly to the wine tasting if you like," Amy said, "or I could give away a buy-one-get-one for the riverboat cruise. What do you say?"

"BOGO, BOGO, BOGO," the crowd chanted in unison.

"I thought you might say that. Sunny, may I have the numbers, please?"

As Sunny handed Amy a black drawstring bag, Spencer pulled her ticket out of her pocket and stared at the numbers she had already committed to memory.

"Good luck," Jordan said.

"You, too."

"The tickets in this bag correspond to the ticket each of you were given when you walked in earlier," Amy said. "I hope you held on to your half because Sunny will have to take a look at it in order to verify the winner. Winners have to be present to win, and if you think you won't be able to take part in the trip, please let everyone know so someone who can attend will have a chance to win." She gave the bag a good shake and pulled it open. "Sinjin, would you do the honors?"

"I'd be happy to."

Spencer's palms began to sweat when Sinjin stuck her hand in the bag, pulled out a ticket, and handed the ticket to Laure. She felt like someone who had used her last dollar to buy a lottery ticket and the winning numbers were about to be drawn. Life would go on if she didn't win, but it sure would be a hell of a lot better if she did.

"Please say five-seven-nine-six-two," she whispered. "Please say five-seven-nine-six-two."

"The winning number is five, seven…" Laure paused as several groans of disappointment echoed around the room. "Nine."

Jordan took part in the next round of groans. "I'm out. How about you?"

Spencer held up her ticket. "I'm still in it. For the moment, anyway."

Jordan crossed her fingers in solidarity.

"Six." Seeming to enjoy drawing out the suspense, Laure paused again. "And the final number is two."

Spencer felt like she was having an out-of-body experience. There was some kind of disconnect between what she was seeing and what she had heard. There had to be. Because if there weren't, that meant—

"Hey, those are your numbers," Jordan said. "You won!"

"Do we have a winner?" Amy shielded her eyes with her hand as she scanned the crowd.

Spencer wasn't quite sure what she was supposed to do. Jump up and down like someone who had won the Final Showcase on *The Price is Right* or exhibit a modicum of restraint like someone who had just triumphed on *Jeopardy!*

Jordan dug an elbow into Spencer's ribs to get her attention. "If you don't say something, they're going to draw another number and give the trip to someone else."

The reminder that she might lose the trip she had barely won spurred Spencer into action. She raised her ticket over her head and leaped to her feet. "Here! Over here!" She squinted when the blinding beam of a spotlight played across the crowd and came to rest on her face.

"May I see that?" Sunny reached for Spencer's ticket and checked the numbers. She nodded after she confirmed that the numbers on Spencer's ticket matched the numbers Laure had announced. "What's your name, and where are you from?"

"Spencer Collins from Pipkinville, Georgia." She pumped her fist when the other Georgians in the room made their presence known. *I'm starting to think I should have brought more business cards.*

"Congratulations, Spencer," Amy said from the stage. "Can you go on the trip?"

Dozens of people turned to face Spencer, waiting to see if she would say yes or no. Deep down, she knew she probably wouldn't be able to give the trip to her parents as she had originally planned. Did she want to keep the prize for herself, or give someone else—someone in a relationship—a chance to win?

"Yes," she said, deciding to take a chance on herself for once, "I can go."

"Awesome. Come see me at the conclusion of today's presentation to claim your prize."

"Change of plans," Jordan said after Spencer reclaimed her seat. "I'm not buying this afternoon. After this turn of events, drinks are on you."

Spencer couldn't help but laugh at Jordan's joke—and at her own good fortune. "Cool. Because I think I see a bottle of chardonnay with my name on it."

Jessica's adrenaline was pumping too hard for her to pay attention to the burning in her legs. She typically averaged between fifteen and twenty miles for a beginner spin class, thirty for an advanced one. Since attendees of all levels had taken part in today's session, her mileage total had fallen somewhere in between. Some women had dropped out shortly after the class started. Some had bailed after forty-five minutes. Only a few had kept pedaling for the full hour. She was pleased to see that Tatum, the former Marine who was recovering from a spinal injury, was one of them. After the timer on her watch hit the sixty-minute mark, she raised her arms over her head to indicate the class had come to an end.

"Good job, everyone. Give yourselves a hand." She climbed off her bike and led the weary warriors who remained in a round of applause. "Thanks for spending part of your afternoon with me. I hope to see you tomorrow. Enjoy the rest of your day."

She chugged a bottle of water while the women made plans to meet up later for drinks, lunch, or dinner. She wished she could work SOS Tours cruises on every trip. The energy that developed was always supportive, not cutthroat like it could be on some of the straight cruises. If given a choice, she would prefer to see women lifting each other up, not tearing each other down.

"How was it?" She resisted the urge to offer a helping hand as Tatum climbed off the recumbent bike and used her crutches to drag herself to her feet. She knew from experience not to offer assistance to people with a physical challenge unless they asked for it beforehand.

"Incredible." Tatum's face glowed from a rush of endorphins. She, like Jessica, obviously didn't need to take drugs to get high. Exercise had the same intoxicating effects. "Aside from meeting my girlfriend, I haven't felt this happy in years. Do you do this every day?"

"I have to do something to burn off all the free alcohol."

"I hear you. I seriously doubt my liver will be on speaking terms with me by the end of the week."

"Make sure to drink plenty of water. That's my secret. I'm teaching a Zumba class tomorrow. Are you planning to attend that, too?"

"I wish I could, but my girlfriend has made plans to go parasailing in Grand Turk tomorrow, and I'll be lounging in a cabana on the beach cheering her on."

"Such a hard life you lead."

"I know, right? Seriously, though, thanks for going out on a limb to make this possible for me."

"No big deal."

Tears welled in Tatum's eyes. "Yes, it was." She reached into her backpack to retrieve her buzzing cell phone. "That's probably my girlfriend, Jordan, texting to check up on me. She was afraid I might overexert myself today." She looked at the phone's display. "Okay, I was only half-right. The text is from

Jordan. She wants to know how much longer I'm going to be. There's someone she wants me to meet."

"You sound like that happens often."

"Are you familiar with the phrase 'never met a stranger'? That's Jordan in a nutshell. She introduces herself to everyone she comes across. Five minutes later, they're BFFs. Unless the subject of politics comes up. Then all bets are off."

"Are you the same way?"

"Not even close. It takes a long time for me to warm up to people. For me, trust is earned, not implicit."

"Did you trust Jordan when you met her?"

"Oh, God, no. I live on Jekyll Island, so I have a love/hate relationship with the summer people who flock into town every year. When I met her, I thought she was a flighty, insufferable tourist more concerned about working on her tan than anything else. I made the mistake of judging her by her friends instead of trying to get to know her. When I spent more time with her, I realized what a big heart she has. I might not understand her need to march in every protest within a five-hundred-mile radius or lend her support to so many causes, but I know she does it because she cares. I didn't mean to talk your ear off, but you got me started on one of my favorite subjects."

"Sounds like you have a full day planned. I'll have to work all that frivolity out of you when you come back for another spin class."

"I'm looking forward to it. Thanks again."

"You're welcome." When Jessica turned to watch Tatum leave, she spotted Breanna standing near one of the treadmill machines. She had been so focused on her conversation with Tatum she hadn't heard or seen Breanna enter the room. "Hey, beautiful lady. When did you get here?"

"Somewhere between your benediction and your coronation. I wouldn't have pegged you for sainthood."

"Good. Because I'm certainly not aiming for it."

Breanna sauntered across the room. Breanna was Hawaiian, so she rarely if ever did anything in a hurry. She always got the job done on time, but she never seemed to be rushed. Jessica loved that about her. Especially in bed. The time they spent together on a cruise didn't feel like a few days. It felt like a lifetime.

"That's welcome news. I was starting to wonder since I hadn't seen much of you this trip. Where were you last night? You missed out on a killer party below decks."

Her conversation with Raq had prompted Jessica to lay low after she finished her shift. She had fixed a to-go plate from the buffet and sought out Brandon so she could warn him that there was a Mexican federal police officer on board, but he'd been too busy trying to get into the pants of a cashier from one of the clothing boutiques to listen to what she had to say. God, she hoped he knew what he was doing. Because like it or not, her future was tied to his.

"I didn't want to overdo it on the first night. I'm trying to pace myself."

Breanna poked out her lower lip in a sexy pout. "What's the matter? Did you find someone else to play with? I know we never tried to define what we mean to each other, but I thought we were having fun."

"We were."

"Past tense?"

"Stop trying to read between the lines. I've always been an open book. You know that."

"Prove it."

Jessica kissed her to erase Breanna's fears and assuage her own guilt. "You're the sexiest woman I've ever met in my life. I want you just as much as I ever did."

"Then I'm counting on seeing you tonight. It's seventies night in the disco. I hope you packed platform shoes and plenty of polyester."

Breanna turned to leave, but Jessica called her back.

"Yes?" Breanna said.

Jessica wanted to tell her everything. She wanted to confess all of her sins so there would be no secrets between them. She wanted to tell Breanna she had done something incredibly stupid. Something that might put everything and everyone they knew at risk. But something held her back.

She and Breanna were occasional bedmates, not lovers. They were friends with benefits, not soul mates. They were, in Breanna's words, just having fun. Their relationship, such as it was, was too delicate to survive such a weighty admission. She chose to keep quiet rather than risk ruining a good thing.

"Save the last dance for me."

Amy treated herself to a small glass of wine from the display table. She was still on the clock, but she couldn't pass up a chance to sample some of the wares from Laure and Sinjin's vineyard. She let the wine fill her mouth before she swallowed, allowing the flavors of apple, pear, and oak to coat her palate. "That's definitely worth fifty dollars a bottle."

"You're not drinking on the job, are you?"

Amy turned to find Spencer standing behind her. "The last time I saw you, you were surrounded by a horde of well-wishers. I started to join you, but I didn't want to interrupt the party."

"They're really interesting people." Spencer pointed out the four couples with whom she had been conversing. "Luisa and Finn met on the Cancún trip. Luisa's the Mexican federal police officer who offered to trade herself for one of the hostages. Finn's a travel writer who was assigned to write an article about the trip but ended up having an entirely different story to tell."

"I've met them."

Amy had been given strict instructions by her bosses to do everything in her power to make sure Finn and Luisa had an uneventful vacation. All the clients from the Cancún trip had been given vouchers for free vacations to make up for the trip that had been ruined when members of a drug cartel invaded the resort in which they were staying. Finn had used her voucher to book this cruise. A voyage that had gotten off to a rough start when Luisa had mistaken the sound effects in her neighbor's video game for gunshots. Amy couldn't blame Luisa and Finn for being skittish after everything they had experienced a few short months ago. She just hoped yesterday's mix-up would turn out to be nothing more than an amusing footnote instead of a portent of things to come.

"I'm sure you've met Bathsheba and Raq, too," Spencer said, "since Raq told me she was the reason for your false alarm yesterday."

"Did you tell her you're a gamer, too?"

"I did. Raq and I gave each other our online handles so we can play a few games against each other when we get home. I'm looking forward to testing my skills against someone new. I've been playing the same set of online friends so long I've learned all their patterns. Then again, I'm sure they can probably say the same about me. In any case, it'll be good to switch things up."

"Who are the other couples?" Amy had assigned herself the daunting task of introducing herself to each passenger during the trip. She thought she was off to a pretty good start, but she hadn't been able to get around to everyone yet. When she and the rest of her teammates lined up to bid farewell to the departing passengers next Saturday, she hoped she would be able to connect the right name to the right face. Otherwise, all her efforts would be for naught.

"Jordan and Tatum are fellow Georgians. Jordan sat next to me during the presentation. Tatum joined us afterward. They manage a hotel in Jekyll Island. I met Hannah at the mixer yesterday. She and Maneet had dinner together last night. Hannah says she doesn't do relationships, but she and Maneet seem mighty cozy."

"You learned all that from one brief conversation?"

"More like a series of conversations."

Amy remembered how shy and withdrawn Spencer had seemed when she met her the day before. "You came out of your shell in a hurry."

"Alcohol might be bad for you, but it certainly helps to loosen the tongue." Spencer took a sip of her wine. The merlot, from the looks of it. "I had forgotten how much fun it was to be around people. This cruise is a far cry from the last one I went on, that's for sure."

"In what way?"

Spencer held up her hands as if she were warding off an invisible attacker. "The less said about that first trip, the better."

Spencer's reaction to such a seemingly innocuous question piqued Amy's curiosity. Now she really wanted to know what had happened during Spencer's previous voyage. Since Spencer looked like she was uncomfortable with the conversation, Amy decided not to test her boundaries. If Spencer wanted to share her story, she would when she was ready to do so. Until that day came, Amy's imagination would be working overtime trying to fill in the missing pieces.

"I don't want to keep you from your friends," Amy said. "The envelope containing your voucher for the Montpellier trip is in the cruise director's office. I'm using the space since the ship's cruise director has the week off. I'm headed there now. You can follow me if you'd like to pick it up, or I can give it to you later. It's your choice."

Amy had experienced mixed feelings when she realized Spencer had won the drawing for the riverboat cruise. She was thrilled she would have a chance to see Spencer again, but she was bummed that the opportunity would be in a professional rather than a personal capacity. She liked the idea that Spencer might become a repeat client, but she hated the fact that it meant Spencer could never become more than that.

Spencer pointed to the cluster of women behind her. "We're about to grab some lunch in the grill. Would you like to join us? There's no need for you to pick my brain at dinner since you participated in the most exciting part of my day."

"The day's not over yet."

"I know, but I doubt anything can top this."

Amy was tempted to say yes, but she needed to establish some distance before she allowed Spencer to get too close. "Thanks for the invitation, but I have some things I need to take care of before the disco ball tonight. When you're ready to pick up your voucher, you know where to find me."

At arm's length, not by her side.

NIGHT TWO

Spencer's cheeks hurt from smiling. She couldn't remember the last time she had laughed so much. She could have spent all day listening to everyone's stories. She very nearly had. What was supposed to be a quick lunch had ended up lasting most of the afternoon.

First, Bathsheba and Luisa had taken turns trying to one-up each other with tales of their often hair-raising adventures in law enforcement. Then Raq and Tatum had traded war stories, Tatum's based in the battlefields of Afghanistan and Raq's on the mean streets of Baltimore. When Tatum and Raq were done, Finn had regaled everyone with anecdotes culled from her many trips to exotic destinations around the world. Maneet was a former aid worker, not a travel writer, but she had visited nearly as many countries as Finn and had just as many memories to share.

As they dined on a wide variety of burgers and grilled sandwiches, each of the women around the table had had a story to tell—even Spencer—but Hannah's had turned out to be the most memorable.

As she headed to her room to shower and change for the evening's festivities, Spencer laughed to herself as she visualized Hannah taking a couple of clients on a tour of what was supposed to be an empty condo, only to walk in on the owners having sex in the master bedroom.

"The owners might not have closed the deal, so to speak," Hannah had said as everyone devolved into fits of laughter, "but I still made the sale."

Spencer hadn't been surprised to hear Hannah had been able to convince her clients to buy the condo despite the X-rated floorshow. The woman was such a smooth talker she could probably sell ice to an Eskimo.

Spencer slowed to check out the decorations on her neighbors' stateroom doors. A few of the designs were relatively simple, but some were as elaborate as a float in a holiday parade. Spencer had never been especially crafty, but she was tempted to get in on the fun. But what theme should she use? Her room was her home away from home this week. It deserved to be more memorable than the real one.

Spencer felt a pang of melancholy as she wondered how she could feel such a deep connection with a group of women she had known for only a few days while her bonds with some of the people she had known most of her life were irreparably frayed. Would she ever be able to outrun her past, or was she doomed to keep paying for the stupid mistake she had made on her ill-fated senior trip?

She let herself into her room, grabbed a bottle of water from the minibar, and headed out to the balcony to enjoy the view as the ship continued to make its way toward Turks and Caicos. She took a deep breath, drawing the crisp salt air into her lungs.

"What would Summer and Madison say if they could see me now? Easy," she said, answering her own question. "The same thing they said in high school."

Back then, she had been the nerd everyone wanted to cheat off of in class but no one wanted to hang around with after the bell rang. In their eyes, not much had changed.

"I'm still the freak who has plenty of book smarts but no common sense."

Why else would she allow herself to entertain the fantasy that someone like Amy could be interested in someone like her?

She had been down that road before, and the journey had brought her nothing but heartache. She wasn't ready—or willing—to make the same mistake.

She did wish she had been more forthcoming when Amy had asked her why she hadn't enjoyed her last cruise, however, but she hadn't known how to broach the subject. How was she supposed to tell someone who thought she had her act together that most of the people she grew up with thought she was a total loser?

Spencer could still hear the derisive laughter and the chants of "Kamikaze Collins" that provided the soundtrack for the worst night of her life. The night she had mistaken Summer's concern for something else. The night she had tried to—

A knock on her stateroom door drew Spencer out of the past and back to the present. "Housekeeping."

She opened the door to find a uniformed maid standing in the hallway.

"Would you like turndown service?"

"Sure. Why not? It's all part of the experience, right?"

She stepped aside and allowed the maid to enter the room. She wasn't in the mood for whimsical towel animals or mood lighting when she didn't have anyone to help her appreciate either, but she didn't want to prevent anyone from doing her job.

The maid went about her business with a practiced ease. Spencer watched from the other side of the room as the maid turned down the covers, placed candy and candles on the nightstand, and, with a few flicks of her wrist, folded a plain white towel into an elephant.

"Are you Spencer Collins?" the maid asked as she placed a flower in the elephant's upraised snout.

"Yes. Why do you ask?"

"I was asked to give these to you." The maid retrieved an envelope and a note from her cart. "Enjoy your evening."

"You, too."

After the maid softly closed the door behind her, Spencer examined the items she had left behind. The envelope bore the SOS Tour logo on the upper left corner. Someone had typed *Riverboat Giveaway* in the section usually reserved for the recipient's address. Spencer flipped the envelope over and slid her finger under the flap. Inside, she found a voucher entitling the bearer to two discounted tickets for the Montpellier to Monaco cruise as well as a copy of the planned itinerary for the trip. The voyage wouldn't cover much distance—less than four hundred nautical miles—but it seemed like the trip of a lifetime.

Spencer knew her parents would be over the moon when she gave them the prize she had won. She imagined slowly cruising along the Mediterranean Sea, dining in a chateau, walking the rows in a vineyard, or dressing up to spend an evening gambling in a glamorous casino. Instead of her parents, the images in her head were of her and Amy.

"Yeah. Like that would ever happen."

Spencer stopped herself before her fantasy could go too far. What was it about cruise ships that made her start seeing things as she wanted them to be instead of how they really were? Amy was interested in her as a client. Nothing more. If Spencer had harbored any doubts about that, the note accompanying the voucher made it clear Amy was more interested in her business than she was in her.

Congratulations on winning the giveaway, the note read. *I'm looking forward to seeing you and your guest on next year's cruise. Spending eight days and seven nights in the south of France sounds incredibly exciting. If you would like to spend even more time in paradise, please be sure to stop by the reservations desk to book one (or both) of the vacation stretchers. Fancy a trip to Toulouse or Genoa? We can make your dreams come true.*

Disappointed by Amy's transparent efforts to convince her to spend extra money upgrading her trip, Spencer locked the voucher in the in-room safe and tossed the note aside. Some dreams, obviously, were meant to be just that.

Even though Amy was born almost a decade after the 1970s came to an end, she had always had an affinity for the time period. She wasn't a fan of the often gaudy fashions, but she loved the music, the movies, and the live-and-let-live attitude that defined the Me Decade. She was living in what was commonly referred to as the Golden Age of TV, but most of the memory in her DVR was taken up by reruns of *Maude, Fantasy Island, The Mary Tyler Moore Show,* and *The Love Boat.* Some of the shows were groundbreaking classics, and some were cheesy relics, but she loved each one of them, dated references and all.

After she squeezed herself into a pair of bell-bottom jeans and a light blue halter top, she feathered her hair into a close approximation of the style Farrah Fawcett had made famous while she was chasing bad guys on *Charlie's Angels.* She didn't plan on arresting anyone tonight. She just wanted to lose herself in the music, forget about all her responsibilities, and have a good time while she danced her cares away. She doubted it would happen, but it was worth a shot.

Her growing attraction to Spencer was proving to be even more problematic than she had feared. Instead of focusing on fulfilling all her clients' needs, she wanted to cater to only one. That was acceptable behavior for a personal assistant, not a cruise director.

Her priorities were shifting, her thoughts were jumbled, and her emotions were all over the place. She was filled with anticipation one moment, dread the next. She couldn't wait to spend time with Spencer and hear about the exciting new things she had experienced that day, but she couldn't stop wishing she could experience them with her.

"That's not how it works," she reminded herself. "SOS Tours employees aren't allowed to sleep with clients. Like it or not, Spencer is a client, so you need to keep your hands—and everything else—to yourself."

Her desire to establish some distance between herself and Spencer was the main reason she had asked one of the maids to deliver the voucher for the riverboat cruise instead of waiting for Spencer to stop by the office and pick it up herself. The note she had included with the voucher had been intentionally impersonal. She had cribbed a few lines from a marketing brochure and signed her name at the bottom of the page. She felt like a coward for doing so, and for deciding to have dinner in the buffet tonight instead of the main dining room, but she needed time to clear her head. She needed time away from Spencer.

The best way for her to resist temptation was to avoid it completely. There were only so many places she could hide on a ship, even one that held two thousand people, so she knew she would run into Spencer sooner or later. Given a choice, she'd go with later.

"I hope you got some beauty sleep," Leanna said when Amy joined her and Breanna backstage for the first of two shows featuring four of the biggest divas from disco's heyday. "I have a feeling tonight's going to be a long one."

"That's exactly what I was hoping for."

The more time she spent doing her job, the less time she'd spend thinking about the woman who could cause her to lose it.

Spencer didn't know what to make of Amy's no-show at dinner. Had work gotten in the way, or had she found something better to do?

"So much for our deal."

She would hate missing out on the opportunity to spend the last night of the trip plying Amy with as much chocolate as she could find, but she hated the thought of missing out on a chance to spend some quality time with her even more. Even though several other women had shared the table with them last night, Amy had made her feel like she was the only one in the room. She wanted to feel that way again. Not just for a night or a week. She wanted to feel that way every day for the rest of her life.

One of her father's favorite sayings was, "You're old enough to know your wants won't hurt you." She wished he was here now so she could tell him how wrong he was. Because there was nothing more painful than wanting something and knowing you weren't able to have it. Wanting a relationship was one thing. Entering into one was another. How was she supposed to make someone else happy when she hadn't been able to perform the same trick on herself?

She ate dinner mechanically. More out of necessity than hunger. The contrast between tonight's desultory meal and the almost celebratory lunch she'd had that afternoon couldn't have been starker. When she was done, she was tempted to call it an early night so she could wipe the slate clean and get a fresh start tomorrow, but she had promised Raq she would meet her and Bathsheba in the disco so Raq could teach her some of the line dances she had no idea how to perform. She knew all about the Bus Stop, the Texas Two-step, and the Boot Scootin' Boogie. The Wobble, the Cupid Shuffle, and the Cha-Cha Slide? Not so much.

She hoped she wouldn't make a fool out of herself when Raq tried to teach her the steps. But if she did, what else was new? Just because she was used to being the butt of someone else's joke didn't mean she had to like it.

"Are you having a good time?" a guy in plaid pants, a wide-collared shirt, and a puka shell necklace asked as she headed to the Illusion Lounge for the early performance. Even though he was out of uniform, Spencer recognized him as one of the porters she had seen helping passengers with their bags before and after they had boarded the ship on check-in day.

"Yes, I am. How about you?"

"I'd be better if I didn't have to wear this getup."

"I can imagine."

He was wearing so much polyester he was a walking fire hazard. Spencer's clothes—a pair of white jeans and a yellow T-shirt with a picture of a seagull on the front—fit the night's theme, even if they weren't accurate to the time period they were supposed to represent. She'd bought the jeans a couple of years ago, and she'd purchased the T-shirt from an online retailer last week because the sun-washed colors reminded her of the tropical countries she would soon be visiting.

"You look like the kind of woman who likes to party. If I'm right about you, I can hook you up."

Spencer couldn't tell if the line was meant to be a clumsy come-on or an overture for something else. Before she could ask him to clarify, a woman with shaggy brown hair, pouty lips, and toned arms joined the conversation.

"Some guys just can't take a hint, can they?" the woman asked as she hiked up her low-slung patchwork jeans. "Two thousand lesbians on board and he still thinks he's got a chance. Piss off, Brandon. Maybe you'll have better luck on the next trip."

Brandon stared at the woman, his eyes glinting with what looked like malice. Spencer thought he was about to lash out and say something juvenile, then his lips curled into a smile. "You never know until you try. See you around, Jess."

Jessica watched Brandon walk away. She could tell his feathers were ruffled, but he'd be sure to change his tune when she told him he almost tried to make a deal with someone she had seen having lunch with a large group of people that included Raq and her cop girlfriend. Jessica didn't know if the woman was a police officer, too, but she hadn't been willing to take the chance.

"Thanks for riding to my rescue."

"No problem." After they introduced themselves, Jessica tried to satisfy her curiosity. "I'm one of the fitness pros on board. What do you do?"

"I write computer software."

"Cool." Jessica had been half-expecting to hear her say she was a DEA agent on assignment, not a tech geek. "Are you headed to the early show?"

"No, I might check out the second one. I told some friends I'd meet them in the disco. Well, they're not really friends. I just met them this afternoon."

The admission made Jessica feel marginally less paranoid. "From what I've seen, it doesn't take long to make friends around here. Enjoy your night."

"You, too. I'll be sure to call you the next time I need someone to run interference."

"I'm here all week."

And then what? After she stopped working as a mule, she'd have to stop working for the cruise line, too. She didn't want to give up such a sweet gig, but she'd have to if she wanted to put as much distance between herself and her past as she possibly could. She'd miss the perks, she'd miss the passengers—some of them, anyway—and she'd definitely miss hooking up with Breanna whenever their paths crossed, but she was excited to see what the future had in store for her. She might not be able to fulfill all her dreams, but she'd be able to live her life without worrying if today would be the day she'd finally get caught.

She took a deep breath, giddy at the thought of being able to choose her own destiny instead of subjecting it to the fickleness of fate.

Brandon cornered her outside the entrance to the showroom. "What the fuck was that about?" he asked in a fierce whisper. "Were you trying to bust my balls to help you pick up chicks or what?"

Jessica eyed the women streaming in for the upcoming concert. A few glanced her and Brandon's way, but none, thankfully, seemed to have overheard their conversation. "I was saving you from a very long prison stint," she said after she pulled him out of earshot. "The woman you were trying to sell to just now is friends with the cop and the police consultant I warned you about. If she tells them or the federale that you tried to sell her drugs, how long do you think it would take for you to end up in handcuffs?"

Brandon's face paled beneath his tan, but he tried to play off his obvious unease. "You said the cop's from DC and the federale's from Mexico. Take a look around. We're nowhere near either of those places. The most they can do is say something to the ship's security team. Do you think I'm scared of those guys? They're nothing more than well-dressed rent-a-cops. They'd shit themselves if they had to deal with anything more serious than breaking up a bar fight between a couple of overserved passengers."

"You're a lot more certain about that than I am."

"That's because I've been doing this a lot longer than you have. You're new to the game, but I've been slinging since I was a kid, and I've never been caught."

"There's always a first time."

"Not for me. Do you know why? Because I know what I'm doing. I know how to sell and who to sell to. I can also smell a cop from a mile away. Relax, Jess. Don't get your panties in a bunch. You did your job. Let me do mine. You've been trying to tell me how to handle my business for days. You don't see me trying to tell you how to handle yours, do you? I'm no better at teaching an aerobics class than you'd be trying to move a key of coke. Thanks for giving me the heads-up about the fuzz on board, but I can take it from here. Why are you so worried anyway? I thought you wanted out."

"I do."

"And give up all that easy money?"

"Your definition of easy must be a lot different than mine because I don't see anything easy about the risks I've been taking."

"The risk is what makes this shit so much fun," Brandon said with a grin that was even cockier than his attitude. "If we're done here, I'm going to try to find someone to keep me company tonight."

"Happy hunting, but you'd probably be better off trying to find a needle in a haystack."

"Like I said before, you never know until you try."

Brandon wasn't known for giving good advice. In fact, Jessica had often found she was better served doing the opposite of anything he suggested. This time, she hoped he was right. About everything.

❖

The concert served as the perfect warm-up for the disco ball. The energy was electric when the final performance ended and even more so when the party began. The disco ball was already underway when Amy, Leanna, Breanna, and Jessica arrived. They carved out some space for themselves on the crowded dance floor and joined the party.

Amy waved a glow stick in the air as she took in all the wild outfits and the even wilder gyrations. Nights like this reminded her why she loved her job. But she had forgotten that most of the songs from the '70s were exponentially longer than modern releases. And DJ AZ was playing all of her favorites. Breanna and Jessica disappeared after four songs. Leanna stuck around for two more before she announced she was heading to the bar to grab a drink.

"Are you coming?" Leanna asked.

Amy was winded, she was sweaty, and her feet were starting to hurt, but she didn't want to stop dancing. Because the moment she did, she would have to start examining her feelings instead of ignoring them. Tonight, she didn't want to process. She didn't want to ponder what she might be missing out on. She just wanted to have fun.

"Not yet."

"Suit yourself."

The mood on the dance floor changed from sexy to downright sultry when DJ AZ switched from one of the Bee Gees' greatest hits to a Donna Summer classic that had often been described as a seventeen-minute orgasm set to music.

Amy was left without a dance partner when Leanna bailed, but she didn't remain unaccompanied for long. Spencer and the group of friends she had made at the wine tasting that afternoon were dancing nearby. Spencer was the only one without an official partner so she and Amy ended up getting paired with each other.

If she'd known Spencer was in such close proximity, Amy would have accepted Leanna's invitation to get a drink instead of turning it down. You couldn't avoid someone if she was right in front of you. As the music swirled and pulsed around them, Amy wondered how Spencer managed to make a simple ensemble like jeans and a T-shirt look impossibly sexy. Or was it more accurate to say she was more attracted to the woman inside the clothes than the outfit itself?

Spencer looked at her expectantly. Was she waiting for Amy to explain her absence at dinner, or was she waiting for her to move closer? Most of the other couples on the dance floor were practically joined at the hip. Amy longed to follow their lead, but her job prevented her from doing so.

"Did you get my note?" she asked, trying to keep things light.

Spencer nodded. "I wasn't expecting courier service. You really know how to make a girl feel special."

Spencer was smiling, but her body language said she was far from relaxed. Amy suspected she was partly to blame for Spencer's tension, but she didn't know how to relieve it since she wasn't allowed to implement her preferred solution—taking Spencer in her arms and kissing her breathless.

"Are you looking forward to the trip?"

"Not really," Spencer said. "I'm still trying to enjoy this one."

"With my job, I always have to plan ahead."

"If you're always looking toward the future, do you ever take time to enjoy the present?"

"Not often," Amy was forced to admit. "I'm either looking ahead to the next trip, or looking back to review the most recent one."

Client satisfaction was one of the company's top priorities. Amy and her fellow employees were always looking for ways to improve the customer experience, whether by selecting more luxuriously appointed ships, more exotic destinations, more quality entertainment, or more engaging activities. Customer feedback was helpful in determining what worked and what didn't, but travel trends were notoriously hard to predict. Certain cities remained popular year after year, but which previously anonymous locale would become the next go-to destination? It was her job to find it before everyone else did, and to make sure SOS Tours' clients enjoyed themselves when they arrived.

"I feel like I'm constantly on the go," she said. "And for good reason."

"Do yourself a favor." Spencer leaned forward and placed her lips close to Amy's ear. Close enough that Amy could feel Spencer's breath on her skin. "Stop working long enough to enjoy some of the things you've worked so hard to earn. You go on vacation for a living, but when was the last time you took one yourself?"

It had been several years since Amy had visited a city for fun instead of work. Hell, it had been years since she had done anything that wasn't work-related. But that didn't mean she hadn't had fun. Or did it? Was she mistaking complacency for happiness or was she, in the immortal words of Oprah Winfrey, living her best life?

"I have a job to do," she said, resorting to her usual mantra.

"Let someone else do it for a while."

"And what am I supposed to do in the meantime?"

"Everything. Nothing. Whatever the hell you want."

Spencer made playing hooky sound incredibly tempting, but Amy felt guilty at the thought of shifting the burden of her job onto someone else's shoulders. Breanna had a zip-lining excursion planned with her Indies tomorrow, and Leanna would be taking her Wahines on a snorkeling trip near Governor's Beach. Someone had to keep an eye on things on the ship. Maybe she could do both. If something happened to one of the passengers on the *Majestic Dream* while the rest were onshore, she was just a radio call away. As long as she didn't venture too far, she could be where she was needed in a matter of minutes.

"It would be cool to rent a bike or a golf cart and take a tour of the island," she said.

"I've heard the views from the lighthouse are out of this world," Spencer said enthusiastically. I've already got one ticket. I don't mind paying for another if you care to join me."

"It's a deal."

Amy barely managed to convince herself not to say *date*. In time, perhaps she would be able to convince herself that it wasn't one.

Day Three

Spencer got out of bed and threw open the curtains, treating herself to the welcome sight of land. The *Majestic Dream* was scheduled to arrive on Grand Turk Island, the capital of Turks and Caicos, at eight. That was a little more than an hour away, but she could see the port looming in the distance. The logical side of her said the ship's navigation systems were top-notch, but being surrounded by water all day made the skeptic in her wonder if the captain truly knew where they were headed. She had the same fear each time she traveled on a flight with poor visibility. If she looked out the window and saw nothing but clouds, how could she be certain the flight crew had a better view than she did? Visibility wouldn't be an issue today, though. Both the sky overhead and the water beneath the ship were crystal clear, gleaming a bright turquoise that could only be found in nature.

Dozens of cruise ships lined the harbor as the *Majestic Dream* made its way into port. Spencer took a quick shower, then pulled on a loose-fitting T-shirt and a pair of comfortable shorts. After she brushed her teeth and laced up her tennis shoes, she stuffed some essentials into her backpack and headed to the buffet to meet Amy for breakfast before they headed onshore.

She normally settled for little more than a cup of coffee and a muffin for breakfast, but she piled scrambled eggs, bacon, French toast, and fresh strawberries on her plate today. Amy's plate was almost as loaded when she joined Spencer at their table, both seeming to realize they would need plenty of fuel to prepare themselves for a full day of exploring the island.

"What time did you get to bed last night?" Amy asked after she washed down a bite of sourdough toast with a sip of fresh-squeezed orange juice.

"I think I finally fell asleep around three."

"Me, too. The party might have officially ended at two, but I think the after-party's still going on."

"Is that why it's so empty in here?"

Amy looked around the sparsely populated room. "I think a lot of people will be getting off to late starts today."

"That's one way of putting it." Spencer hadn't had much to drink the night before. She hadn't needed alcohol to cloud her senses. Not when she had Amy around. When she had asked Amy to put work aside for a while and spend the day sightseeing with her, she hadn't expected Amy to accept either her challenge or her invitation. She had been pleasantly surprised to hear Amy consent to both. "It's going to be a hot one today. Do you want to rent bikes or a golf cart?"

"I don't know about you, but I got more than enough exercise last night. A golf cart works for me."

"I was hoping you'd say that. I wasn't looking forward to embarrassing myself when I crashed and burned trying to crest one of the hills we're bound to come across. Now all I'll have to do is figure out which side of the road I'm supposed to drive on."

"The left. And unless you want a speeding ticket, make sure you don't go faster than forty miles per hour."

"Now you're taking all the fun out of it."

"I hope not. I've been looking forward to this for hours. I don't think I've thought about anything else since I left you last night."

"This morning, you mean?" Spencer felt remarkably refreshed for having had only four hours' sleep. She attributed her good spirits to the good food warming her belly and the good company warming her heart. What else could it be? "I haven't danced like that since college. When we weren't cramming for exams, my friends and I used to head to the clubs downtown every chance we got so we could hear the local bands play."

"What kind of music do you like?" Amy asked as they headed to the purser's office to retrieve their passports.

"A little of everything, but I have a special affinity for R.E.M. and the B-52's because they were both formed in Athens, the city where I went to college. What about you?"

"My playlists are pretty schizophrenic, too. If you scroll through the music app on my phone, you'll see everything from ABBA to ZZ Top."

Spencer could picture Amy rocking out to the Swedish quartet whose tight harmonies and even tighter spandex costumes had ruled the music charts for the better part of a decade. A trio of hairy blues rockers from Houston, Texas? Not so much. She couldn't wait to discover what other surprises Amy had in store.

After they left the ship and passed through passport control, they headed to one of the many rental stands lining the beach. They split the price of a golf cart rental, listened to a quick tutorial from the stand's owner, and joined the hordes of tourists treating themselves to self-directed or guided tours.

After she slid behind the wheel and buckled herself in, Spencer was so distracted by the beautiful sights and sounds of the small island that she had a hard time keeping her eyes on the road.

"It's gorgeous, isn't it?" Amy asked after they drove past yet another picturesque beach.

"I don't know how anyone who lives here can get any work done. I'd be too busy staring out the window to focus on my computer screen."

"Granted, I haven't known you very long, but I think it's safe to say you don't have a problem staying focused, no matter what your surroundings."

"Then you obviously didn't see me almost run off the road while I was checking out those parasailers over there."

Amy stuck her head out the side of the golf cart to check out the parasailers floating overhead. Spencer wondered if Jordan was one of them. Luisa had volunteered to accompany Jordan while Finn and Tatum lounged in a cabana on the beach. Bathsheba and Raq had signed up for a zip-lining excursion, while Hannah and Maneet planned to do some shopping in the dozens of merchant stalls lining the port. All those activities sounded like worthy endeavors, but none of them had really appealed to Spencer. Some sounded a little too exciting, others a little too sedate. Today's trip seemed to offer the best chance for her to enjoy herself without putting her life on the line in the process.

When they reached the Grand Turk Lighthouse, Spencer handed her ticket to the attendant out front and paid to purchase a ticket for Amy. The three-dollar admission fee could be used toward the purchase of any item in the gift shop or snack bar. Since a bottle of water cost exactly three dollars, Spencer opted to pick up two of them so she and Amy could keep cool and stay hydrated while they wandered the grounds.

"Hungry already?" Spencer asked after Amy set a handful of apples on the counter.

"They're not for me," Amy said with a mysterious smile.

"Then who are they for?"

"You'll see."

They lingered in front of the display panels detailing the history of the island, then headed over to the main reef that extended nearly three miles into the ocean. Spencer wished she could climb to the top of the lighthouse so she could take a look at the reef from a higher vantage point, but visitors weren't allowed to enter the sixty-foot tall structure. The views she could see, however, were breathtaking.

The lighthouse and the lighthouse keeper's house were located on a small limestone hill overlooking North Creek. The lighthouse, made of whitewashed cast iron, had been built to warn sailors about the shallow reef that extended from the northern end of the island. Mangrove trees dotted the coast. A ropes course with several zip lines had been set up on the grounds, and dozens of people were lining up to take their turns.

"Do you want to have a go?" Spencer asked. "It's only a hundred bucks a person."

"Save your money." Amy put her hand on Spencer's arm to prevent her from reaching for her wallet. "I have something even better in mind. Follow me."

Spencer followed Amy to one of several trails leading from the lighthouse to the beach. They had gone only a few steps when Spencer realized why Amy had made her mysterious purchase in the snack bar.

A pair of wild burros snacking on tufts of grass lifted their fuzzy gray heads when they heard Spencer and Amy approach. They appeared to be mother and child. Spencer stopped walking, afraid she might spook the animals. Instead of shying away, the burros began to walk toward them, the mother in front and her foal following closely behind. The mother nudged the bag in Amy's hand with her nose.

"Would you like some breakfast?" Amy reached into the bag and pulled out one of the apples. She balanced the apple on her palm and extended her hand. The burro greedily downed the treat while her foal brayed, begging for his own handout. "A little help?"

Amy tossed the bag in Spencer's direction. Spencer caught it and fed one of the apples to the baby burro. Spencer laughed when the mother nudged the bag again.

"Do you still want to go zip-lining?" Amy asked as she fed the mother a second apple.

Spencer ran a hand over the baby burro's coarse fur after he plucked another apple from her hand. As she watched the animals make quick work of their treats, she couldn't think of anywhere she'd rather be. Or anyone else she'd rather be with.

"No, I'm good right here."

As she and Spencer debated whether they should go horseback riding on the beach or pop into a local bar to down a couple of drinks and a basket of conch fritters, Amy resisted the urge to pull her walkie-talkie out of her bag and check in with the ship's crew. Before she disembarked, she had turned the sound on the walkie-talkie down low so she could keep track of everyone's transmissions while she was onshore. A few problems had arisen over the course of the day. One passenger had sprained an ankle after slipping on a loose cobblestone, another had cut her foot after stepping on a broken shell on Pillory Beach, and a few had returned to their cabins early after receiving a bit too much sun. But none of the incidents had been serious enough to warrant her personal attention.

Amy was relieved nothing had gone wrong so far, though she was a bit disappointed not to be needed. The success or failure of this trip depended on how well she and her team performed. How would she know if she truly had what it took to handle a crisis if she wasn't confronted with one? She was grateful that there had been only a few minor hiccups since they left Fort Lauderdale, but how much longer could their luck hold out? Hopefully, at least five more days.

"Horseback riding sounds like fun," she said, "but the ship is scheduled to leave at three. That's less than two hours from now. Since we didn't make reservations, the walk-up lines at all the horseback riding venues are bound to be a mile long. Chances are we wouldn't have time to reach the front of the line before we'd have to report back to the ship."

"You're probably right."

"If you'd rather take a breather and enjoy some great views of the ocean, I know a place we can go. The exterior's a little iffy and the service can be slow at times, but the locals swear by it. It's supposed to have the best food and some of the best views on the island. It's also one of the few bars and restaurants in this part of town that stays open after most of the cruise ships leave port."

"Sounds good to me. I'd rather spend time in a local hangout than a tourist trap any day." Spencer tossed her the keys to the golf cart. "Since you know the way, why don't you drive?"

Amy knew several couples whose roles were so defined that only one partner was allowed to drive and the other was designated to navigate. Even though she and Spencer weren't a couple, she couldn't resist making a joke at their expense. "I'm glad to see this isn't the kind of relationship where only one person is allowed to take the wheel."

"I'm nothing if not flexible."

"Good to know."

As she navigated the golf cart through the clogged city streets, Amy forced herself to stop thinking about work and return to the task at hand. Spencer had asked her to come onshore today so she could enjoy herself for a few hours. The memories she had made so far were bound to last much longer than that. Had that been part of Spencer's plan? If so, the plan was working like a dream.

Amy couldn't help but smile as she thought back to the time she and Spencer had spent feeding apples to the wild burros that roamed freely on the grounds of the lighthouse. The look on Spencer's face—part shock, part awe, and completely endearing—was one Amy wouldn't soon forget.

"How did you find out about the burros?" Spencer asked as Amy turned onto Front Street.

"Breanna and I read about them on the internet before we visited the island to scout it as a potential destination. One post said the burros are so used to receiving handouts, they'll even eat the snacks in your cart if you leave the cart unattended."

"Is today the first time you ran across them?"

"No, but it was by far the most memorable."

Not just memorable. Unforgettable. Because she had been able to share the moment with Spencer.

Amy had been afraid this would happen. She had tried to establish distance between herself and Spencer so she could control her growing feelings. Today, she felt even more connected to Spencer instead of less. Should she keep fighting the bond that was forming between them, or should she just give in? She knew what the answer should be, but for one of the few times in her life, what she should do was in direct opposition to what she wanted to do. Her job was important to her, but was it more important than allowing herself a chance to fall in love?

"Those burros were cute, weren't they?" Spencer asked after Amy parked in front of a building whose nondescript façade belied both the incredible food and spectacular views that could be enjoyed from the open-air patio on the other side of the exterior doors. "Especially the foal. His pointy ears reminded me of Donkey from the *Shrek* movies. Every time he looked at me, I kept expecting to hear Eddie Murphy's voice come out of his mouth. I can't believe they're so tame."

"They're not," Amy said after they took their seats at one of the picnic tables out back and ordered drinks, a diet soda for her and a local beer for Spencer. "They're just used to people."

"Is there a difference?"

"Of course."

"Then I'm all ears. Please explain."

Spencer put her elbow on the table and propped her chin on the heel of her hand. Amy didn't know which sight was more breathtaking—the ocean a few yards away or the woman sitting across the table from her. Spencer's eyes glinted with curiosity as she waited to hear what Amy would say next.

Despite her assertions to the contrary, Spencer was a wonderful conversationalist. True, she didn't always say much, but she was able to pack a great deal of meaning into just a few words. And she was an incredibly attentive listener. She had a way of looking at you like there was no one else in the world. No one else who mattered, anyway. Not at that moment. That was exactly the way she was looking at Amy now. And Amy didn't want the moment to end.

"You can do everything possible to turn a wild animal into a pet," Amy said. "Feed it. Love it. Be kind to it. But no matter what you do, you'll never be able to make it forget its true nature. You'll never be able to turn it into something it's not."

"You sound as if you're speaking from experience."

"I've never tried to turn a wolf into a lap dog, if that's what you're implying."

"But has someone tried to do something similar to you? Asked you to change who you are into someone they preferred you to be?"

"No."

"Probably because they knew better."

Now it was Amy's turn to ask for an explanation. "What do you mean?"

"There's a popular expression that says you are what you eat. Where you're concerned, I think it's more apt to say you are what you do." The waitress brought out two chilled mugs dripping with condensation. Spencer took a sip of her beer and carefully set the mug on the table. "You obviously love your job. Your face lights up every time you talk about the places you've been or the people you've met along the way. I can't imagine you doing anything else."

"Neither can I, but my job isn't nearly as glamorous as it seems. It's a lot of hard work. If I met someone with more money than God and she offered me a chance to put my feet up, sip champagne all day, and never work another day in my life—"

"You'd head for the hills."

"How can you be so sure?"

"Because I'm the same way. I may complain about the long hours and the tight deadlines I'm often subjected to, but when it comes down to it, I love what I do. So do you."

Amy couldn't deny the truth. She didn't know how long the company would remain in business, but she had devoted way too much time to building her career to walk away from it now. "What do you say to those people who say you should spend less time making a living and more time living a life?"

Spencer grinned. "People who say silly things like you go on vacation for a living but never take one yourself?" she asked, paraphrasing the question she had posed the night before.

Amy returned Spencer's smile. "Yeah, what do you say to people like that?"

"Nothing. I avoid those people like the plague."

"Perhaps I should start taking your advice."

"Only if you want to be led astray."

Amy reached into the basket of conch fritters the waitress placed on the table. She broke one of the streaming fritters in half and gave it time to cool before she popped it into her mouth. "I've never been much of a fan of sticking to the beaten path."

"I gathered that. But if we play our cards right, we might be able to find our way off the beaten path and stumble onto the right one. We'll be arriving in San Juan tomorrow at noon. Would you like to do this again in a slightly different locale?"

Amy's head told her to politely decline, but her heart directed her to do something else. "I'd love to."

Night Three

Even though she had been on the move most of the day, Spencer decided to go for a long walk after dinner. Her mission was twofold. She wanted to burn off some of the many calories she had taken in since she boarded the ship three days ago, and she needed some downtime so she could have a chance to clear her head. One task proved far easier to accomplish than the other.

By the time she completed her second lap of the promenade deck, her heart rate was up and she had broken a sweat, but her thoughts were just as jumbled as they had been when she'd left her cabin.

Today had been everything she had hoped for and more. Spending time with Amy had been like something out of a dream. Better even, because most of her dreams didn't have happy endings. She didn't have any reason to believe the outcome of this dream would be any different, but she couldn't stop wondering if this was the rare occasion when reality surpassed fantasy. Even though she kept reminding herself of the many reasons why she and Amy couldn't possibly make a go of it, she kept coming up with reasons to explain why they should give themselves the opportunity to find out.

When she was with Amy, she didn't feel like the awkward misfit who was accustomed to being the butt of jokes instead of the person telling them. She felt confident. Comfortable. Capable of anything. Even outrunning her own past. She couldn't tell if she was losing sight of who she was, or discovering who she had never given herself a chance to be.

She headed up to the lido deck and took a look around. The deck was even more deserted than the buffet had been that morning. A woman in a black bathing suit and a matching swim cap was doing a brisk backstroke in the pool, but most of the lounge chairs surrounding the pool were empty. That was fine by Spencer. She wanted to stare at the stars twinkling overhead, not make conversation.

"It's a beautiful view, isn't it?"

Spencer turned her gaze away from the Big Dipper and focused on the woman who had spoken to her. Finn Chamberlain, the travel writer she had met after the wine tasting the day before, was stretched out on a lounge chair on the other side of the pool with an electronic reader propped on her lap. The e-reader's touch screen cast a faint glow just bright enough for Spencer to read the words on Finn's T-shirt: *If I Die, Please Delete My Browser History*. Finn seemed to possess nearly as many humorous T-shirts as she did stories about her many travels around the world. Before she met Luisa, her only companion on her voyages was the Porky Pig figurine she tucked into her backpack before each trip. Spencer could see herself doing many things on her own, but flying solo to a country where she didn't know anyone and couldn't speak the language wasn't one of them. She admired Finn's sense of adventure.

"I didn't expect to see you here," Spencer said. "Where's your other half?" She searched the deck but didn't see Luisa anywhere.

"She's getting a massage in the spa. I signed up for one, too, but I rescheduled mine for tomorrow so I'll be able to enjoy it. If I climbed on the table now, I'd probably fall asleep after five minutes. For the price I'm paying for the service, I want to enjoy every second."

"Why are you so wiped out? Did you have a long day onshore?"

"Word to the wise: don't ever take an excursion with a group of adrenaline junkies. After Luisa and Jordan finished parasailing, they convinced me and Tatum to accompany them to an aerial adventure park. I thought I was in decent shape, but I was exhausted by the time we were done. My arms and legs still feel like rubber."

"Did Tatum take part?"

"Take part? Before long, she was leading the charge."

"But she told me she wasn't comfortable with heights."

"If she wasn't before, she is now. All it took were two mojitos and a dare from Jordan to convince her to push her boundaries."

"It takes more than a couple of stiff drinks and a double dog dare to convince me to risk life and limb. I learned that rather painful lesson years ago."

Finn shut off her e-reader but didn't make a move to join Spencer on her side of the pool. "You remind me of me, you know that?"

"How?" Spencer asked with a laugh. "You've been everywhere, and this is only my second trip out of the country."

So far, the trip had proven to be much better than her first, but she didn't want to celebrate too soon. The week wasn't over yet. She had plenty of time to screw things up. To revert to form instead of adhering to the new standard she had established. She was starting to feel like Cinderella: enjoying her time at the ball while dreading what would happen when the clock struck midnight.

"That's not what I meant," Finn said. "We're part of the same secret society. Introverts always recognize one another when they cross paths."

"Yes, we do, though I never would have pegged you for one."

Finn tossed her hair over her shoulder like a supermodel playing up to the camera during a photo shoot. "Don't let the designer eyeglasses, fashionably messy hair, and globetrotting lifestyle fool you. I grew up in a small town, and no matter what part of the world I find myself in, I'm still a small-town girl at heart."

Spencer felt like she was listening to her own story instead of hearing Finn's. Fascinated, she bridged the gap between them. "But you seem so confident," she said after she took a seat in the chair next to Finn's.

"Confidence covers a variety of sins. I used bravado to fake my way through a lot of situations. I let people in, but I pushed them away before they could get too close."

"Why?"

"I wanted everyone to see the carefully crafted image instead of the person I was underneath. I wanted them to see me as a sophisticated journalist instead of a former stutterer with social anxiety. I wanted to seem fiercely independent instead of admitting I was lonely."

Spencer knew exactly what Finn meant. Her job paid her well, but it kept her isolated. Initially, the great paycheck had seemed like a fair tradeoff for the loneliness. Now her perspective was starting to change. *She* was starting to change. "Did you play those games with Luisa, too?"

"I tried, but she's a federal police officer. She's been trained to recognize bullshit when she sees it. She saw right through me, but she liked me anyway. That's the dream, isn't it? To find someone who gets you and decides to move closer instead of running the other way?"

It was a dream Spencer couldn't allow herself to have. Not if she didn't want to wake up disappointed.

"Before I met Luisa, I was content to live my life alone," Finn said. "I wanted to be able to do things on my own terms without having to answer to or explain myself to anyone. To not have someone mistake my acts of self-preservation for a lack of desire to be with her. I still have moments, like now, when I need some time to myself, but those don't happen as frequently as they once did. Luisa says I've morphed into something of a social butterfly, but I wouldn't go that far."

"She sounds like a total badass, both in and out of uniform. How did you know she was the one you were meant to be with?"

"I didn't. Not at first. I met her in a bar in Dallas/Fort Worth International Airport while we were waiting for our respective flights to be called. We flirted for a bit and got to know each other better in a nearby hotel before we had to head back. When we left DFW, I never expected to see her again. But when we left the hotel room, I knew I'd be willing to move heaven and earth to make sure I did."

"Then she ended up risking her life in order to save yours."

"I told her that was overkill. To paraphrase Renée Zellweger in *Jerry Maguire*, she had me at hello. Or, in our case, *Is this seat taken?*"

Spencer marveled at the thought of a one-night stand turning into happily ever after. How many times had that happened? With her luck, she'd most likely end up as the subject of a cautionary tale instead of the costar of a fairy tale.

"We might not have figured out whether we want to put down roots in Mexico or the States," Finn said, "but it doesn't matter where we end up as long as we're together. It's funny. When we met, neither of us was looking for a relationship. I told myself I didn't have time because I was always rushing to catch a flight, and she had convinced herself that it was easier for her to do her job without having someone worrying she might not make it home in one piece."

"What changed your minds?"

"Some very bad men with some very big guns made us realize there are many things to be afraid of in life," Luisa said, joining the conversation, "but love isn't one of them." She sat on the end of Finn's chair and placed a hand on Finn's knee. "Did you enjoy your you time?"

The intimacy in Luisa's touch as well as her voice made Spencer feel like she was intruding. She tried to make herself invisible while Finn and Luisa continued their whispered conversation.

"Yes, I did." Finn's eyes and face glowed as she gazed at the woman she loved, making Spencer feel even more like a fifth wheel. "How about you, super cop?" Finn pushed a lock of Luisa's dark hair behind her ear. "You look relaxed. Did your masseuse give you a happy ending?"

Luisa flashed a dimpled grin. "She didn't offer, and I didn't ask. I was kind of hoping you would volunteer to take care of that part."

"I think that can be arranged." Finn leaned forward and gave Luisa a teasing kiss. "Does now work for you?"

"I'll have to check my schedule, but I might be able to squeeze you in."

Spencer felt envious as she watched them interact and listened to their playful but sexy banter.

"Then we'd better get started before any potential scheduling conflicts arise." Finn took Luisa's hand and pulled her to her feet. "Good night, Spencer."

"Have fun," Spencer said.

Luisa wrapped her arm around Finn's waist. "I'm sure we will."

Spencer watched Finn and Luisa walk away. Finn had managed to overcome her doubts about embarking on a relationship and had ended up meeting the love of her life in the process.

"I hope we're as much alike as she seems to think we are."

❖

Amy tried to keep her announcements brief so the second show could begin. Tonight's featured entertainer was Rusty Connors, one of the most popular comics on SOS Tours' roster. Rusty's hour-long set during the early show had been standing room only. The crowd for the second show was just as large. Thanks to either the lateness of the hour or the copious amount of free alcohol that had flowed at dinner, the crowd was also considerably rowdier. Since Rusty loved to interact with her audiences, she was bound to have a field day. Amy didn't want to delay the fun any longer than she had to.

She had seen Rusty perform dozens of times in various locales, but Rusty updated her routine so often that each time was like the first time. During the first show, for example, she had foregone her usual jokes about her tumultuous life with her parole officer wife and their four teenaged kids so she could recount the drawn-out but hilarious tale of her run-in with a persistent vendor in the market that afternoon.

Rusty had been on the bill for the Cancún trip, too. She was one of the nearly five hundred women who had been held hostage when a drug cartel had overrun the ritzy Mariposa Resort and Spa. She hadn't worked any of the material from that experience into her act yet, but Amy had heard her laugh about it from time to time. Usually to lighten the mood during a staff meeting that was proving to be more boring than productive. The jokes hadn't been received well the first time Rusty told them. At the time, everyone was still too on edge to even talk about what had happened, let alone make light of it. Lately, though, the laughs seemed to be coming more easily. Comedy, after all, was simply tragedy plus time.

Amy felt like a school principal as she reminded everyone they should smoke only in designated areas and should refrain from getting up bright and early to claim lounge chairs around the pool even though they had no intention of occupying said chairs until they had enjoyed a leisurely breakfast and, perhaps, a midmorning nap.

"Now that we've gotten that out of the way," she said after she completed her tongue-lashing, "is everyone having a good time?" She waited for the cheers to die down before she continued. "We've almost reached the halfway point of our trip. Three days down and five more to go. Even though it sounds like you're having the time of your lives, I'm sure you're probably missing all the fur babies you left behind. If you'd like to take a moment to say hello to them, shout out their names now."

With everyone yelling at once, Amy couldn't understand all the names being said. She could, however, feel the emotion behind the greetings. She didn't own a pet. Thanks to her long hours and frequent travel schedule, the poor thing would spend way too much time alone in her apartment or boarded in a kennel. She avoided relationships for the same reasons. She couldn't, in good conscience, invite someone to become part of her life until she was ready to devote as much time and energy into a relationship as she did her job. So far, the urge to keep planning new adventures overwhelmed the desire to find someone to share those adventures with. Someone who challenged her one moment and comforted her the next. Someone who was excited by the prospect of discovering new things but also had a fondness for the past. Someone who was thoroughly modern, yet surprisingly traditional. Someone like Spencer.

Unfortunately, she would have to find someone *like* Spencer because Spencer was off-limits. The question she was almost afraid to ask herself was what would she do if, as she suspected, Spencer turned out to be one of a kind? Would she eventually meet someone who intrigued her just as much, or would she always feel like she'd missed out on an opportunity that might never come her way again?

"That's definitely a question for another day," she said as she headed backstage.

"What do you have planned for tomorrow?" Breanna asked as Rusty began telling jokes in her familiar Oklahoma drawl.

Amy took a few more steps away from the stage so her conversation with Breanna wouldn't distract Rusty while she performed. "Spencer and I made plans to take a walking tour of Old San Juan, then check out Castillo San Felipe del Morro. If we have time, maybe we'll drop by a few of the art galleries and gift shops before we head back." She paused. "By the look on your face, I'm assuming your question was meant to be rhetorical."

"It was, but thanks for dishing all the dirt. You've been spending a lot of time with Spencer this week. She even managed to talk you into shirking your duties, which is something I've never been able to do, no matter how attractive a carrot I dangled in front of you."

"That's not what today was about," Amy said defensively. "That's not what this week has been about. I'm just trying to see things from the passengers' point of view without grilling them while they're here or asking them to complete an online survey when they get back home. I want to experience it firsthand."

"That's a good idea, but you know the rules even better than I do. Because, unlike me, you've actually managed to stick to them. We're supposed to make sure our clients have a good time, not show them one. You're not sleeping with Spencer, are you, Ames?"

"No, she and I are just hanging out."

"The same way Jessica and I are hanging out?"

"I can assure you that between the two of us, the only person who's having sex on this cruise is you."

"Spencer isn't the first passenger you've treated like a pet project, but this situation doesn't feel like the others. The others were like orphaned baby birds you took in, nursed back to health, and eventually set free. Are you going to be able to do the same with Spencer after you inject her with self-confidence and teach her how to fly, or will you be making a side trip to Georgia when the trip ends?"

Amy would love to spend some time in the town Spencer called home so she could see some of the people and places that had influenced Spencer while she was growing up, but what was the point? Because Spencer was a client, she and Amy could never be anything more than friends. Either during the cruise or after. But Amy had enough friends. Being around Spencer made her want more. Made her want something she couldn't have.

"I wasn't planning on it, no."

"You know what they say. Plans are meant to be changed."

"Speaking of plans," Amy said, trying to steer the conversation onto safer territory, "why are you so interested in mine?"

"Angel was supposed to help me chaperone a shopping excursion to Plaza las Americas tomorrow, but she's been blowing chunks since four a.m. and won't be able to do it."

"I noticed she looked a little green around the gills during the staff meeting this morning. When I asked her if she needed to make a trip to the infirmary, she waved me off and said she'd be fine. She told me she was just dealing with a case of Montezuma's revenge."

"Close, but no cigar. I wouldn't say she was flat-out lying to you, but she was definitely covering her ass."

"Why?"

"So you won't be able to rat her out to the members of the executive team when we get back to LA."

"I'm not a snitch, Bree."

"No, but you're definitely a stickler for the rules."

"Says who?"

"Says anyone who's ever met you. Be honest. You were the kid the instructor left in charge of the class when she stepped out of the room to grab a smoke in the teachers' lounge or have a quickie in the supply closet, weren't you? That's what makes this whole Spencer situation so incredibly ironic."

"Please stop making me painfully aware of all my personal shortcomings and tell me what's the deal with Angel."

"Fine."

Breanna rolled her eyes as if the answer she was about to give was patently obvious to everyone except Amy. Perhaps it would be if Amy had been paying less attention to Spencer and more to everything else. If she had been doing her job today instead of slacking off.

"Angel's not sick," Breanna said. "She's hungover. I'm sure you probably already know, but in case you weren't aware, rum and late-night skinny-dipping don't mix."

"Thanks for the warning. I think I'll stay away from tequila for the foreseeable future, too. It's the only thing that prompts me to get naked in front of a crowd."

"I've seen you strip for considerably less than a shot of Jose Cuervo. Oh, wait, that was me."

"All jokes aside, if you need my help tomorrow, I'd be more than happy to pitch in."

"Don't give it a second thought. I'll ask Jessica if she thinks she'll have enough energy after she teaches her morning spin class. See? You're not the only person who can problem-solve on the fly. Given a choice, I'd rather spend the afternoon with someone I'm sleeping with instead of my boss anyway. And I wouldn't want to keep you from spending more quality time with your favorite client."

"I don't play favorites. Every one of our clients is equally important to me, whether she's a first-time traveler or someone who's been relying on our services for years."

"It seems to me one client might be more equal to you than others."

Realizing Breanna might not be the only person who had noticed her giving Spencer special attention, Amy felt a sinking feeling in the pit of her stomach. "Is this just you talking, or do the other staffers onsite feel that way, too?"

"Relax, Ames. Everyone's too busy doing their own thing to worry about what you might or might not be doing with your Southern gentlewoman. The only person on the ship who seems to be concerned about appearances is you. That goes for the passengers as well as the crew. If you like this woman, don't follow the rules. Break them."

If Amy hadn't been chosen to take the lead on this trip, she might do exactly that. But what kind of example would she be setting for the rest of her teammates if she brazenly broke the rules they had all sworn to uphold?

"You can always find another job," Breanna said, "but you might not be able to find someone who matters to you as much as Spencer seems to."

"You asked me to be honest, so I'm going to do exactly that. I'm good at my job, but I suck at relationships. Why should I turn my life—and someone else's—upside down in pursuit of something that, based on my track record, is bound to fail? I'm in the business of making dreams come true, not breaking hearts."

"Even if the cost is your own happiness?"

"Life is a series of compromises, Bree. We can't have everything we want. Some things just aren't meant to be."

Day Four

Jessica hated shopping. If she couldn't find what she was looking for online, she drove to the store, located what she wanted, paid for her purchases, and headed home. She didn't waste five hours looking through the racks, only to end up buying the first item that had caught her attention.

"Tell me again why I agreed to do this," she said as she nursed a spicy watermelon mint agua fresca in the food court of Plaza las Americas, a three-story shopping center in downtown San Juan. "Babysitting a bunch of bargain-hunting tourists while they explore every inch of the largest mall in the Caribbean isn't my idea of fun."

She and Breanna had designated the table at which they were sitting as the rendezvous point for the fifty women who had signed up for today's excursion. When the passengers finally tired of wandering in and out of the dozens of stores in the sprawling complex, they were supposed to return to the food court so Breanna could perform a head count before they returned to the ship. Based on the sound of cash registers ringing left and right, no one would be heading back to the *Majestic Dream* any time soon.

"Because I promised you could have your way with me tonight."

Jessica felt her temperature rise—and only partially because of the extra jalapeños she had asked the server at the juice bar to place in her drink. "Speaking of which, can we trim a few hours off this wonderful outing so you can give me a preview of what I can expect tonight?"

"I wish," Breanna said with a sigh, "but that's not my call. Everyone signed up for four hours, so that's what we're obliged to give them. Settle in, sweet cheeks. We're here for the duration."

Jessica checked her watch. "Great. Only three hours to go. But who's counting?"

"Remind me not to ask you to tag along the next time I want to go shopping."

Jessica rested her chin on the heel of her hand as she took a long appreciative look at Breanna's beautiful face and curvy body. With her laid-back demeanor, Breanna was the definition of languid. Jessica thought she could learn a thing or two from her example. She wanted to take her time exploring every inch of Breanna. Right here and right now. Excursion be damned. "I'm partial to your birthday suit. Why don't you model it for me more often?"

"Because we live three thousand miles apart and see each other only on the rare occasions when our schedules converge." Breanna adjusted the flower in her hair. She, like her sister, wore a fresh flower each day. Leanna's flower was worn behind her left ear to symbolize she was taken. In contrast, Breanna wore her flower behind her right ear to signal she was available. "We should do something about that one day," she said when she was done fiddling with the hibiscus blossom she was sporting today.

"Meaning?"

Breanna pointed to the flower behind her ear. "I'd like to switch this from one side to the other one day."

"One day or today?"

"Like the old saying goes, there's no time like the present."

Jessica wasn't sure she liked the direction the conversation was heading. She and Breanna had never attempted to place labels on their relationship. In her opinion, that was one of the reasons it worked so well. Why *they* worked so well. She didn't want to ruin a good thing by trying to turn it into something it wasn't. "What are you getting at, Bree? I thought we were just enjoying ourselves."

Breanna took a sip of Jessica's drink and frowned when the jalapeños kicked in. "We are."

"Then why do you sound like you're about to pull out your class ring and ask me to go steady with you?"

Breanna cocked her head as if considering the idea. "Would that be so bad? We're good together."

"We have great sex." Jessica winced at how shallow her statement sounded, but she couldn't deny it was true.

"Yes, we do. I don't know about you, but that sounds like the foundation of a good relationship to me."

Jessica looked at her hard. Even though Breanna was smiling, she didn't seem to be joking. "You're serious, aren't you?"

Breanna nodded as she reached for Jessica's hand. "I like you, Jess. I think you like me, too. So why don't we stop pretending we don't mean anything to each other and do something about it?"

Suddenly, shopping didn't seem like such a massive waste of time after all. Jessica would much rather be searching for the perfect overpriced T-shirt than having this conversation. She didn't want to hurt Breanna's feelings, but she didn't want to offer her too much encouragement either. Her life was too complicated to draw someone else into it. Especially someone she cared about. Perhaps even loved. She didn't want Breanna to get hurt. By her or anyone else.

"I look forward to hanging out with you whenever I know we're going to be on the same ship," she said noncommittally.

"Why do I feel there's a 'but' coming?"

"But I've never considered making things permanent."

"So I'm just a random hookup? Is that all I am to you?"

"Of course not." Breanna tried to pull away, but Jessica wouldn't let go. She attempted to erase the look of disappointment on Breanna's face by explaining her point of view. "I love being with you, but would what we have still be sexy and fun if we're doing dishes and arguing over whose turn it is to take out the trash instead of dancing in a disco until three in the morning and waking up at the crack of dawn to watch the sun rise over the bow of a ship? Because that sounds like the kiss of death to me."

"You've managed to spend ninety minutes in a mall without pulling your hair out. That counts for something, doesn't it?"

"It's a start." Jessica felt herself begin to weaken as Breanna's questions exposed her responses for what they really were: excuses.

Breanna rubbed the back of Jessica's hand with her thumb. "A pretty good one, I think."

Jessica was soothed yet aroused by the sensation of Breanna's thumb sliding across her skin. It got harder and harder to say good-bye each time she and Breanna parted ways. Perhaps it was time for her to look for ways for them to be together instead of coming up with reasons to keep them apart. Because she could definitely get used to this. To seeing Breanna every day instead of a few weeks a year. Now that she had decided to stop living a life of crime, perhaps she could start living a life with Breanna.

Breanna lived in one of the most image-conscious cities in the world. If Jessica moved to LA, she could build a roster of clients and become a personal trainer. If she worked out of her clients' homes, she wouldn't have to worry about opening a gym, filling it with equipment, and forking over tons of money for all the related recurring expenses. She could take some of the funds she had stashed in the bank and use them to relocate. Then she could save the rest for the future. *Their* future. Everything she wanted was sitting right in front of her. All she had to do was reach out and grab it.

Jessica tried not to get too far ahead of herself. She had to put her old life behind her before she could start a new one. She had a feeling that extricating herself from the cartel's clutches wouldn't be nearly as easy as falling into them in the first place. Once she was free, she would be able to start over. And she would be able to do it with Breanna at her side.

"Let's table this discussion for now," she said.

"For now or for good?"

"Just for now. When we get back to the real world, why don't we spend some time together and pick up where we left off?"

"I'd like that." Breanna leaned across the table and gave her a kiss on the cheek. "If you don't mind holding down the fort for a few minutes, I see a negligee over there that's calling my name. If you play your cards right, I might let you peel it off me later."

Breanna trailed her fingers across Jessica's arm. Goose bumps formed in their wake. "Who knew shopping could be so much fun?"

"I tried to tell you."

Jessica watched Breanna walk across the food court and into a lingerie shop. When she turned back, a man she didn't know was sitting in the seat Breanna had just vacated. The man was dressed head-to-toe in designer clothes. His outfit probably cost more than Jessica's car. The cheap cologne he reeked of, however, wasn't nearly as high-end. The potent fumes wafting from his side of the table made Jessica's head hurt.

"Do you mind if I join you?" the man asked in heavily accented English.

Jessica looked around. Even though the food court was bustling, there were plenty of empty seats to be found. Why hadn't the man chosen one of them? Perhaps he was looking for company in more ways than one. "As long as you don't get too comfortable. My friend should be back soon."

"If you pay attention to what I have to say and don't ask unnecessary questions, I'll be out of your hair in no time."

"What do you want?"

"Give me time and I'll tell you." The man slurped his soft drink and set the oversized cup on the table. "Your girl's hot." He jerked his chin toward Breanna, who was holding up a nightie so sinfully sexy it was probably illegal in most Southern states. "How long have you been together?"

Jessica wasn't in the habit of sharing details of her personal life with random strangers, especially smarmy ones who overstepped their boundaries. "We're not a couple. We just work together."

"In a way, you and I do, too. Though a little birdie tells me you're looking to get out of the business."

The man's icy tone made Jessica's blood run cold. She knew she was in trouble. She just didn't know how much. Remembering his admonishment not to ask unnecessary questions, she kept her mouth shut and waited for him to get to the point.

When he crossed his arms and placed them on the table, his sleeves slid up, revealing part of a tattoo on his left forearm that was similar to the one Brandon sported on the same limb. The subject was the same—a jaguar caught in mid-leap like the hood ornament on a luxury car—but the design was different. Coincidence or connection? Jessica didn't believe in one but was reluctant to establish the other.

The cartel that had overrun the Mariposa Resort six months ago was named the Jaguars. Their hit men identified themselves by tattooing an image of a jaguar on their left forearms. Was that who the man worked for? Was that who Brandon worked for? Was that who *she* worked for? The Jaguars were one of the most infamous cartels in Mexico. At least they were before Luisa Moreno had helped take out their leaders.

Ines Villalobos was the unchallenged head of the Jaguars. Before Luisa Moreno put a bullet in his head, Ines's grandson Javier was her top enforcer. The press hadn't mentioned he was romantically involved with anyone. Was he the oft-mentioned boyfriend who was always too busy working to accompany Pilar Obregon on her frequent trips? If Pilar had been involved with him, she could have easily stepped into the void created by Ines's and Javier's deaths, or used her feminine wiles to cozy up to the person who did.

Either way, Jessica was in even more trouble than she had initially thought. In their heyday, the Jaguars let hundreds of people into their organization, but no one made it out alive. What made her think she could be the first?

Not caring about her own well-being, she looked over her shoulder to make sure Breanna was still a safe distance away.

"Don't worry about your lady friend," the man said sharply. "Focus on me." Jessica dutifully turned to face him. "That's better."

"How do you know who I am?" she asked in a panicked whisper. "How did you know where to find me?" She flinched when the man unfolded his arms, certain he was about to reach for a gun.

"Our mutual employer has eyes and ears everywhere. You'd be wise to remember that." He took another slurp of his soda. "I'm not here to waste your time or mine, so I'll make this quick. If you want to cancel your arrangement, get rid of Luisa Moreno."

"Who's she?"

The man pursed his lips like a disapproving schoolmarm. "Don't play dumb. You and I both know you've been warned about the federale responsible for taking out the boss man. *La jefa* wants revenge."

"Pilar Obregon, you mean?"

"Pilar who? Never heard of her." The man's expression said otherwise, which made Jessica realize she had stumbled upon the truth. Pilar Obregon, the beauty queen turned gangster's moll, was much more than met the eye. "Get rid of Moreno and you're free to make all the plans you want with your lady friend. When you get back to your room, you'll find everything you need to complete the job under your pillow. Consider it a gift from the tooth fairy."

Jessica couldn't believe what she was being asked to do. "I'm a fitness trainer, not a killer."

"Then this could be the perfect opportunity for you to branch out. To broaden your skill set, so to speak."

"If Pilar wants Luisa Moreno gone so badly, why doesn't she hire a professional to do the job?"

"Why should *la jefa* waste money on hiring someone when she can have you do it for free? If you botch the job, it's on you, not her. I suppose you could ask Brandon to help you out, but he's got problems of his own. Lately, he's been using more product than he's been selling. If he doesn't come up with the money to pay us back, I'll be paying him a visit, too. Just like you, he'll never see me coming."

Jessica wondered what kind of Faustian bargain the man would offer Brandon. Would he try to strong-arm Brandon into doing away with her the same way he was attempting to use her to get rid of Luisa Moreno, or would he give Brandon an even more odious assignment to carry out?

"Your options are simple," the man said. "If you take care of Luisa Moreno, your courier services will no longer be required. Don't forget to send proof that the job is done. Photographic evidence and a finger or two will do nicely. Make sure you select the trigger finger. I'm sure *la jefa* would appreciate that."

Jessica nearly gagged as bile rose in her throat. "And if I don't…take care of Officer Moreno?"

The man rose to his feet. "I'm here to present the facts, not make threats."

"You could have fooled me," she said as he towered over her.

The man reached for his cup. "Do the job you've been tasked with and you can have the freedom you so desperately desire. If you refuse, you'll be expected to move product on the ships you're assigned to as well as on land."

"Wait. That's never been part of the deal before."

"It is now. Are you in or out? The choice is yours."

He walked away before she could give him an answer, which was a good thing because she had no idea what her answer was.

She felt trapped between the proverbial rock and a hard place. She couldn't keep doing what she was doing, but she couldn't possibly pay the price that had been placed on her freedom. She couldn't take someone else's life in order to fix the shambles she had made out of her own.

She held her head in her hands. A few minutes ago, she had been planning her future. Now it was becoming increasingly obvious she wouldn't be able to have a future until she paid for the sins she had committed in her past.

"Who was the guy you were talking to?" Breanna asked when she returned to the table.

"No one I know."

"He seemed to know you. Or maybe he just wanted to get to know you better. He made a beeline for you as soon as I left." Breanna blew on her fingernails and rubbed them against her chest. "I always knew I had great taste in women."

Jessica looked away as her eyes flooded with tears. The bad decisions she had made had earned her a tidy sum, but now they were costing her dearly. Would those decisions exact a toll on her loved ones, too?

Unfortunately, she knew the answer to that question, and it was a resounding yes.

❖

Even though Amy had made sure to don comfortable shoes when the ship dropped anchor in San Juan at noon, her feet were killing her. The walking tour of Old San Juan had taken a little over three hours, then she and Spencer had spent a little over forty-five minutes exploring Castillo San Felipe del Morro, a sixteenth-century fort overlooking the entrance to San Juan Bay. They would be in Puerto Rico for less than half a day, and Spencer seemed determined to take full advantage of every minute. She was currently trying to figure out if they had enough time to take the tunnel tour of nearby Castillo de San Cristobal before they had to return to the ship.

The *Majestic Dream* wouldn't raise anchor for another few hours, but Amy didn't want to spend every minute of that time on her feet. Unless, of course, she was dancing the salsa, samba, or merengue in one of the many clubs in town. One establishment even had a waterfall built into the elevator that ferried guests to an incredible rooftop bar. Amy wasn't dressed to impress, but she wouldn't mind spending an hour or two lounging on one of the leather beds while she and Spencer munched on empanadas and sipped fruit-infused cocktails. But this was Spencer's vacation, not hers, so she let her take the lead.

After several minutes of intense study, Spencer finally put her guidebook away. "You look like you could use a break from all the exploring we've been doing today. Do you want to sit and talk for a while?"

"That sounds wonderful." Grateful for the respite, Amy took a seat next to one of the cannons pointed toward the crystal clear water. "Are you having a good trip so far?"

"I'm having a blast. I'm glad I didn't follow my instincts and try to talk myself out of coming. I've made several new friends this week and experienced some things I never thought I would."

"You seem surprised."

"I am, to be honest."

"Why?"

"The last cruise I was on wasn't nearly as enjoyable as this one has proven to be."

Instead of pressuring Spencer to open up, Amy waited for her to do it on her own. Spencer looked out at the water with a contemplative expression on her face as if she were waiting for the same thing.

"When I was in high school," Spencer said at length, "my classmates and I took a cruise to Mexico for our senior trip. Five days from Miami to Cozumel."

Amy started to comment on how beautiful the sights were in Cozumel and the surrounding areas, but she stayed mum. Spencer had skirted around the subject of her previous cruise for days now. Now that she was finally ready to tell the story, Amy didn't want to impede her progress.

"We took a charter bus from Pipkinville to Miami. I talked everyone's ears off the whole way down about all the things I was going to do once we boarded the ship. I was going to participate in every activity, sign up for every excursion, and do all the touristy things and then some."

"That sounds familiar," Amy said before she could convince herself not to.

Spencer flashed a self-deprecating smile before she continued her story. "I changed my tune once we set sail. I spent so much time throwing up in my room I didn't have any time to do anything else. I'd brought all kinds of remedies for seasickness with me—pills, patches, even a wristband my local pharmacist recommended—but none of them seemed to help. Summer Colton was my roommate. Not by choice, mind you. The room assignments were given alphabetically and our last names were next to each other's on the list. If she had her way, she would have preferred to room with Madison Davis or Debbie Wells, her BFFs from the cheerleading squad. Instead, she was stuck with the geek no one wanted anything to do with outside of school, but everyone wanted to sit next to during midterm or final exams."

Amy knew firsthand that wounds inflicted in high school often ran deep. No matter how much scar tissue developed over the years, the pain still flared up from time to time. Even so, she wished Spencer would stop selling herself short. Couldn't she see that she was so much more than she was giving herself credit for?

"I was in such a sad state Summer must have felt sorry for me," Spencer said. "She was like Florence Nightingale. She held my hair while I threw up, rubbed my back when I stopped, then fed me ice chips and plied me with ginger ale until I was able to keep food down. When I finally started to feel better, she dragged me out of our room and into the sunshine. I wasn't strong enough to do much besides work on my tan, but as she put it, at least I'd be able to go home looking like I had fun instead of puking my guts out for three days. If the story ended there, it would be bad enough, but I had to go and make it infinitely worse."

"What happened?" Amy asked when Spencer seemed reluctant to continue.

"Even though we were too young to drink, a lot of people had raided their parents' liquor cabinets and smuggled several bottles of alcohol on board. Security wasn't as tight then as it is now, and teenagers will always find a way to do something when you tell them they can't. After our chaperones fell asleep, out came the booze. The parties were held in a different person's room each night so none of the crew would get suspicious. I missed the first few nights, but I made up for lost time as soon as I could. Louis Hill, the tight end on the football team, couldn't run a decent pass route to save his life, but he was an awesome bartender. His specialties were Long Island iced teas and kamikazes."

Amy thought she knew where the story was headed, but she waited for Spencer to confirm her suspicions.

"I opted for the kamikaze because it seemed like the lesser of two evils. A drink you can see through couldn't be that bad, could it?"

Interesting theory, but the hangovers Amy had experienced from downing too much tequila blanco wouldn't allow her to espouse it.

"The first drink made me feel like I fit in. The second made me feel like I was Supergirl. By the time I was halfway through the third, I was the life of the party." Spencer smiled at the memory, but her smile soon faded. "The music was blasting and everyone was having a good time so I asked Summer to dance with me. I still don't know why she said yes. To prove to her friends how cool she was, I suppose. At the time, I thought it was because she liked me. She'd been so kind to me while I was sick that I developed a bit of a crush on her. The things she'd said and done while we were alone made me think she felt the same way about me. Otherwise, I never would have tried to kiss her. Especially with everyone watching. But I did try and, of course, she freaked out. I don't remember the exact words she said. I just remember the look on her face, the sound of her laughter, and the chants of 'Kamikaze Collins' that chased me out of the room."

Amy had also fallen for the wrong person a time or two, but at least she hadn't done it with a roomful of people bearing witness to her humiliation. She didn't have to imagine how mortified Spencer felt at that moment because she could see it written all over her face.

"I kept a low profile for the duration of the trip," Spencer said, "but I needn't have bothered. No one wanted anything to do with me anyway. By the time we got home, the news had beaten us back to shore and I was even more of an outcast than I'd been before we left. I'm sure I wasn't the only lesbian in town, but it certainly felt like it during the endless summer between high school and college. I couldn't wait to head to Athens so I could finally be myself. Then, when I graduated four years later, I couldn't wait to go back."

"Why would you willingly return to a place where people tormented you simply for being who you are?"

Spencer offered a wan smile. "Because it's home. Because even though I'm not going to change who I am or who I love, perhaps they'll eventually be able to accept both."

Spencer certainly made a persuasive argument for living in a small town, but Amy didn't know if she would be able to give up the creature comforts a large metropolitan city had to offer. Changing hearts and minds was important, but so was being able to catch a nonstop flight to anywhere she wanted to go rather than being forced to spend time in several regional airports along the way.

"Thank you for sharing your story with me." Amy took Spencer's hand in hers and laced their fingers together. She could feel the bond between them growing stronger every day. Even though she knew she should, she didn't want it to break. "Thank you for sharing *yourself* with me."

"Thank you for making it considerably less painful than I remembered."

Spencer flashed that sad smile again. Amy wanted to hold her until her sadness disappeared. Kiss her until the tears pooled in her eyes turned into laughter. She wanted to do so many things. Things she wasn't allowed to do as long as Spencer was a client.

Amy's job had brought her many things. At the moment, though, she hated what it might be preventing her from having: a chance to craft a relationship with the most amazing woman she had ever met.

Amy's phone rang. Naturally, Breanna's name was printed on the display. Work often intruded on Amy's personal life. Why should today be any different?

"Hey, Bree," she said after she excused herself to take the call. "What's up?"

"I just wanted to let you know that everyone who signed up for the shopping excursion is accounted for and safely ensconced on the ship."

"That's good to hear." Amy looked down at the waves breaking on the rocks. "Was it a successful event?"

"Everyone seemed to have fun. Based on the number of shopping bags I spotted on the shuttle bus, I think it's safe to say the Puerto Rican economy received a substantial boost today."

"That's good. After all the lost tourist dollars as a result of Hurricane Maria, the island can use the income. But why do you sound so depressed?"

"I'm fine, Ames. Everything's cool."

"If everything's as fine as you're trying to make it out to be, you would have hailed me on the radio instead of calling me on my cell." Amy lowered her voice in an attempt to keep her conversation as private as she could. Even though Spencer was maintaining a respectful distance, several other people hovered within earshot as they took selfies in front of the piles of cannon balls or crowded next to the worn stone walls to admire the view. "Talk to me, Bree. Tell me what's wrong."

"I shouldn't say anything. It's probably just my imagination."

"Tell me anyway."

"I told Jessica I wanted to take our relationship to the next level."

"Really?" Amy couldn't hide her surprise. Like her, Breanna preferred to keep her relationships casual. "What did she say?"

"She was taken aback at first, but she seemed to warm to the idea. At least I thought so. Now I'm not so sure. She's been acting weird for a couple of hours now. She says nothing's wrong, but I think there's something she's not telling me."

"Something like what?"

"Beats me. Tell me I'm not imagining things."

Amy wanted to say something to ease Breanna's mind, but she didn't have enough information to do the job. Plus she had been single for so long she was woefully out of practice at doling out relationship advice. Breanna might have been better off reaching out to her sister for help with this particular problem. Since she wasn't willing to take that route, the situation had to be much more serious than Amy had initially given it credit for. Breanna didn't shut her family out of her life unless she was dealing with something she didn't want them to worry about. Her relationship with Jessica was obviously giving her cause for concern. "Have you talked to her since you left the mall?"

"No, she said she needed to check on the gym to make sure her replacement didn't screw anything up while she was gone."

Jessica's explanation sounded plausible, but Amy could tell Breanna wasn't buying it. "Do you think there's more to the story?"

"I know there is. I just don't know what."

"What do you need, Bree?"

"Tell me I'm being silly. Tell me I'm reading way too much into this situation than what's actually there. Tell me—"

"That you're not falling for her? Sorry. No can do."

"I was afraid you'd say that. What am I supposed to do?"

"Hang up the phone, find her, and talk to her. She's the only person who can give you the answers you're looking for."

"But what if she says something I don't want to hear?"

"We'll deal with it together. That's what friends are for, right?"

"Right." Breanna laughed. "I thought I was supposed to be the one talking *you* off the ledge on this trip, not the other way around."

Amy's heart fluttered when she saw Spencer staring at her with a concerned expression on her handsome face. Spencer couldn't have looked more adorable if she'd tried. "Don't worry," Amy said, wondering how long she would be able to resist Spencer's considerable charms. "I'm sure you'll get your chance sooner or later."

Night Four

Even though both locks on her stateroom door were engaged, Jessica had never felt more vulnerable. She sat on the foot of her bed and stared at the gun resting on her pillow like a perverted after-dinner mint. She didn't know anything about guns so she had no idea what make or model this one was, but she knew one thing: it looked dangerous.

How could something so small bear so much weight? She was tempted to throw it overboard, but what was the point? If she got rid of it, another would probably appear in its place.

Everything had looked normal when she had returned to her room a few hours ago. Then she had looked under her pillow and discovered the gun the man in Plaza las Americas had promised she would find. Loathe to touch it, she had picked it up while making sure not to leave any fingerprints behind. She had been in a standoff with it ever since. She doubted she could come out on top, but she had to try. Because this was one game she couldn't afford to lose.

She hugged her knees to her chest. She had a couple of theories about how the gun had made its way into her room. Either the maid had been paid to plant it while she performed her daily turndown service or she had been asked to look the other way while someone else performed the deed. But none of that mattered now. What mattered was what happened next. Jessica needed to figure out what to do, and she needed to figure it out fast.

She could barely muster enough courage to swat a palmetto bug that wandered into her apartment. How was she supposed to find the strength she needed to do away with a person?

"There's no way I could ever commit murder," she said, thinking out loud. "I am so screwed. And not in a good way." She fisted her hands in her hair. "Fuck! What am I going to do?"

She had been relying on her own instincts since she was old enough to earn a paycheck, but it was plain to see the time had come for her to seek outside counsel.

"Yeah, but who am I supposed to turn to? The retainer alone for a good attorney would cost me every penny I have, and I can't trust an ambulance chaser to keep me out of jail."

Surely there had to be a way she could do the right thing without losing everything she had worked so hard to earn in the process. Her career. Her good name. And most importantly, her freedom.

"It's just like you tell your clients," she said with an air of resignation. "You can't have your cake and eat it, too."

Something had to give. She'd either have to bankrupt herself paying restitution for the crimes she had committed or be forced to sell her soul in order to commit more.

"Which is more important, getting rich or clearing your name?"

Breanna deserved to be with someone who was worthy of her. So far, Jessica had done little to merit the honor.

"I can't keep her in the dark. Even if she decides to walk away once she hears the truth, I've got to tell her what's going on."

She wrapped the gun in a towel and stashed it in the bottom of her underwear drawer. Trying not to imagine the look of disappointment she expected to see on Breanna's face when she revealed her misdeeds, she tried to figure out what to say. How was she supposed to even broach the subject, let alone confess to committing multiple crimes, some of them right under Breanna's nose?

"She's going to hate me. She'll probably never talk to me again."

But Breanna had a generous, compassionate soul. She could ignore even the most egregious insult in order to maintain her mental equilibrium. "It's not worth the bad karma," she would calmly say when most people would have flown into a rage. Perhaps one day she would find it in her heart to forgive Jessica as well.

Jessica nearly jumped out of her skin when someone knocked on her stateroom door. She hadn't realized her nerves were so on edge. Then again, they had reason to be.

After she took a couple of deep breaths to slow her racing heartbeat, she opened the door to find Breanna standing in the hallway. "I was just about to come find you."

"Really? Why?"

"We need to talk."

"I was thinking the same thing."

Jessica ushered Breanna inside. Like most ship employees, her quarters were small. She often joked she'd have more leg room in the overhead bin of an airplane. Today, however, the compact space felt almost claustrophobic. When Breanna took a seat in the chair next to the bed and Jessica sat opposite her, their knees practically touched.

"Do you want to go first," Breanna said, "or shall I?"

Jessica rubbed the back of her neck as she fought through a sudden bout of nerves. She had known telling Breanna all the secrets she had been keeping would be hard, but she hadn't expected it to be quite this tough. Seeing Breanna's soft brown eyes boring into her, begging her for answers to questions she didn't want to face, she lost her nerve. "Why don't you get things started?"

"Okay." Breanna rubbed her hands along the tops of her thighs. One leg bounced up and down like she was nervous, impatient, or both. Going with nervous, Jessica offered her what she hoped was a reassuring smile. "Something's been off between us since our conversation at the mall this afternoon. I know I said some things you weren't expecting to hear, but I hope I didn't do or say anything to drive you away."

"Why would you think that?"

"Because you've been acting strange ever since. Is it me who's got you off stride, or the guy you were talking to?"

"What guy?"

"The one who sat with you after I left. The one you said you didn't know but who seemed to know you."

"The one who took great pleasure in telling me how hot you are? I'm the one who should be jealous, not you. Besides, you know he's not my type."

Jessica reached to caress Breanna's cheek, but Breanna swatted her hand away. "I'm not jealous, Jess. I'm scared."

"Scared of what?" Jessica felt a knot form in the pit of her stomach. Had the man approached Breanna, too? Had he threatened her in some way? If so, he had proven that he and Pilar were willing to do whatever they had to in order to get their way.

"There's something going on with you and I can't figure out what it is. Is it because I told you I want to try for something serious instead of settling for something frivolous? Is that why you ran away?"

"I didn't run away."

"No? Then what would you call it? When we got back to the ship, you said you had to go to the gym. When I went there looking for you, Kendra said she hadn't seen you since last night when you asked her to switch schedules with you today. Have you spent all afternoon holed up in here trying to think of a way to let me down easy?"

"Of course not. I would never string you along like that. When I said I wanted to talk things through, I meant it."

"Then why have you been avoiding me?"

Jessica wanted to tell Breanna all the thoughts that were racing through her mind. She wanted to confess her sins and give Breanna the opportunity to decide if she wanted to continue pursuing a relationship with her or call it quits. She wanted to tell her all the things she couldn't find the words to say. But she couldn't. She didn't have it in her heart to break Breanna's.

"I've been avoiding you because I'm scared, too. I don't want to lose you, Bree."

As tears began to roll down Jessica's cheeks, Breanna sat next to her and wrapped her arms around her shoulders. "What makes you think that's going to happen?"

"Because I'm a screwup, that's why."

"Who isn't?" Breanna turned Jessica to face her. "No one's perfect, Jess. I love you *because* of your faults, not in spite of them."

Jessica knuckled away her tears. "You do?"

"Yes, I do." Breanna placed her hand over Jessica's heart. Jessica felt the warmth of Breanna's skin even through the thick cotton of her T-shirt. "No matter what happens, we'll always be *'ohana*. We'll always be family. In my culture, family is forever. We stick together no matter what. There's nothing you could ever do or say that would make me turn my back on you." She pressed a kiss to Jessica's forehead. "Now that I've had my say, what did you want to tell me?"

"I wanted to tell you that I love you, too."

"Are you sure that's all?"

"That's all that matters. *You're* all that matters."

Jessica kissed her slowly and tenderly, then made love to her the same way.

She didn't know what she had done to earn the unwavering faith Breanna had placed in her. From this night on, though, she was determined to do everything in her power to keep it.

❖

Spencer felt like she had exorcised a demon. The story of her ill-fated senior trip had haunted her for years. At home, she couldn't live it down. Here, it was just one more thing she had in common with so many women like her.

On the way back from Castillo San Felipe del Morro that afternoon, Amy had told her about the time she had embarrassed herself in front of her entire high school when her bra strap had snapped while she was giving a campaign speech during student body elections.

"Talk about a lack of support," Amy had said while Spencer had tried rather unsuccessfully not to laugh.

It hadn't occurred to Spencer at the time to ask Amy if she had won the seat she had sought despite the actions of her wayward undergarment. She'd have to make up for the oversight tomorrow. She smiled at the thought of what new adventures tomorrow might bring.

The ship was scheduled to be docked in Phillipsburg, St. Maarten, for seven hours. When they went onshore, Luisa and Finn planned to take a guided underwater tour while wearing pressurized helmets. Both had been leery of the water since Finn had saved Luisa from drowning while they battled a madman in Cancún, and they hoped the excursion would help alleviate their fears. Hannah and Maneet had an exciting trip planned, too. They were heading to Maho Beach to watch planes skirt the ground as they came in for a landing at nearby Princess Juliana International Airport. Tatum, Jordan, Bathsheba, and Raq were thinking of tagging along with them.

Spencer wasn't keen on the possibility of being blown into the water by jet blast from airliners passing less than a hundred feet over her head, so she had made other plans. Pic Paradis, the highest point on the island, rose nearly fifteen hundred feet into the sky. She intended to spend the day exploring the mountain and the nature sanctuary located on it. She would have to venture to the French side of the island to do it, but Amy had assured her they would be able to make it to Loterie Farm and back in plenty of time.

No matter how hard she tried, Spencer couldn't figure Amy out. Some days, it felt like Amy was only doing her job by hanging out with her. On days like today, it seemed like Amy's job was nothing more than a convenient excuse she used to continue spending time with her.

Maybe being a guinea pig isn't so bad after all, she thought as she slowly swayed in the hammock on the patio outside her room. The lights of San Juan were gradually fading in the distance and the stars were shining bright overhead. It was so peaceful she was tempted to sleep out here tonight instead of in her bed. With her luck, the ship would get hit by a rogue wave and she'd wind up getting swept overboard

"Or maybe I watch too much TV. Mom's always saying I have an active imagination. Speaking of which."

She grabbed her cell phone from the in-room safe and called home. She hadn't talked to either of her parents since Saturday, when she had phoned to let them know she had arrived at the port safely. She was surprised her mother hadn't blown up her phone every night to request details about her trip. Her mother was probably bursting at the seams to hear all the gossip. Spencer wasn't one to kiss and tell, but it felt good having fun stories to relate—and to have someone who was interested in hearing them.

"You sound relaxed," her mother said when she answered the phone.

More than relaxed. Spencer felt positively content. "Now I know why you and Dad are on the road all the time. Returning to work is going to be a shock to my system."

"It feels good to get away from home every now and then, doesn't it?"

"It does. Next year, I get to do it all over again."

"Did you take advantage of the onboard discount to book another cruise? I always say I'm not going to, but I get pulled in every time. Where will you be going?"

"I won a trip to France."

Spencer could still feel the charge that had surged through her body when she realized that the numbers on the winning raffle ticket matched the numbers in her hand. Her mother evidently felt the same excitement because she squealed so loud Spencer had to hold the phone away from her ear. The sound must have startled her father as well because she could hear him in the background asking what was wrong. "Nothing," her mother said. "Spence won a free cruise."

"Fancy that," her father said. "I ain't never won nothing but a summons to jury duty. I'm at the courthouse more often than the lawyers are. Ask her if she wants to trade seats."

"The trip's not exactly free, Mom. More like half price."

"One of those buy one, get ones? That's even better. You'll pay less money and you'll be able to share the experience with someone else. Who are you planning to take with you, one of your video game friends or someone from work?"

"Actually, I was planning to give the prize to you and Dad. I know both of you have always dreamed about going to France."

"That's sweet of you, but don't worry about us, honey. Your father and I will get there in time. And there are plenty of places for us to visit closer to home if we don't. They speak French in Montreal, too, don't they? And I hear the Eiffel Tower at Paris Las Vegas looks almost exactly like the real thing. Invite someone to tag along with you and have the time of your life."

"Are you sure?"

"Sure I'm sure. Now stop running up your bill and hang up this phone. Those international charges sneak up on you before you know it."

"It's okay, Mom. I can afford it."

"Just because you can afford it doesn't mean you have to pay for it. Go find some trouble to get into. Make sure it's the good kind so you can tell us all about it when you get back. Your father's been itching to have a good, old-fashioned cookout. I can't think of a better reason to celebrate. Would you like burgers or steaks?"

"Surprise me."

"Where are my glasses? I need to start making a list of all the things we'll need. Let's see. Burgers, buns, baked beans, coleslaw. Oh, and potato salad, too. For dessert, do you want me to whip up a sweet potato pie or buy some fresh fruit?"

"It's a party. Why can't we do both?"

"I've taught you well."

"That you have." Spencer chuckled softly. Her mother was single-minded when she was on a mission and she was certainly on one now. "I'll leave you to it. I love you, Mom."

"We love you, too, honey. Don't forget to have fun."

"I won't."

But would she still remember how to do it in a few days' time?

Day Five

Amy stuck her arm out the passenger's side window as Spencer drove their rented car along Suckergarden Road. They were headed to Loterie Farm, a luxurious hideaway that offered something for everyone. Adventurous types could explore the numerous hiking trails on foot or glide over the treetops on a zip line. Gourmands could have a delicious meal or down an exotic cocktail in the tree house bar and restaurant. And music lovers could dance their cares away during one of the themed pool parties that took place throughout the year. Amy didn't know if a pool party was planned for today, but she was wearing her swimsuit under her clothes just in case.

"How long do we have?" Spencer asked.

"The farm's only thirty minutes from here. It opens at nine and closes at three thirty. The ship leaves at three, so I suggest we start heading back no later than two in case we get stuck in line when we return the rental car."

"Five hours to explore one hundred thirty-five acres? Piece of cake." Spencer took her foot off the gas when the automated voice programmed into the navigational software on her phone suggested an alternate route. "My GPS is acting a little wonky today. If I didn't know better, I'd say it's trying to get us lost. If we have to pull over and ask a local for help, how's your French?"

"It got me through my junior year abroad, but that was years ago."

Spencer grinned as she shifted gears. "I'll take my chances."

Amy closed her eyes and lifted her face toward the sun. There were few things she liked better than riding on a beautiful stretch of road with the top down, music blasting, and a gorgeous woman by her side. It seemed almost unfair she was getting paid for this. *There are worse ways to earn a living.*

"Careful." Spencer's voice drew Amy out of her reverie. "I think your nose is starting to burn."

Amy peered at her reflection in the mirror attached to the back of the sun visor on her side of the car. "I do have a distinct Rudolph the Red-Nosed Reindeer vibe going on. It happens every time. No matter how much sunscreen I slather myself with, my nose is the first thing that burns." When she applied a fresh layer of protectant, the skin on her nose felt warm and was already becoming tender to the touch. Hopefully, she wouldn't start peeling until she got home, but she doubted she'd last that long. One, perhaps two more days at the most before she started looking like a snake shedding its skin.

"I have a baseball hat in my backpack if you'd like to borrow it."

"That would be great. Thanks." Amy reached into Spencer's backpack, pulled out a faded Tampa Bay Rays cap, and threaded her hair through the hole in the back. Then she checked her reflection again. Windswept, sunburned, and her nose covered in bright white goo. Perfect. She pointed to the insignia on the cap. "You're not a Braves fan?"

"Pipkinville's closer to Florida than it is to Atlanta, so my dad has always rooted for the Tampa-based teams. The Rays. The Buccaneers. Even the Lightning when he's in the rare mood to watch hockey. He draws the line when it comes to college sports, though. Then it's the University of Georgia all the way."

"He must have been proud of you when you decided to attend college there."

"When he read the acceptance letter, I think he jumped even higher than I did. He couldn't wait to tell all his friends I'd gotten in. With a full scholarship, to boot. The only time I've ever seen him cry is when I walked across the stage to accept my diploma. Mom says he cried when I was born, too, but I was too busy bawling myself to remember it."

When Spencer talked about her family, Amy could tell from the sound of her voice how close she was to them. No wonder she still lived near them. For her, home was truly where the heart was.

"What about you?" Spencer asked. "Are you a sports fan?"

"Not really. I always get caught up in the spectacle surrounding a major sporting event, but I'd rather participate than watch."

"I can tell."

"What gave me away?"

"As a cruise director, I would expect you to be tethered to your desk all day, but you seem happier when you're on an excursion with me than you do when you're on the ship."

Amy had noticed the same thing. She liked hearing about the passengers' experiences when she chatted with them each night, but she enjoyed sharing experiences with Spencer even more. Breanna was the only person who had commented on it, but the rest of her co-workers were probably on to her as well.

Her job used to be the only thing that mattered to her. Now it was starting to seem more like a necessary evil. It paid the bills, but it didn't satisfy her soul. Not like it used to less than a week ago. Her job had allowed her to meet Spencer, and it was also keeping them apart.

"Am I right, or am I wrong?" Spencer asked.

"You're right."

"Do you care to elaborate?"

Amy didn't want to respond to the question because she wasn't ready to deal with where the conversation might lead. But

Spencer was waiting for an answer, and she felt obliged to give her one. An honest one. "I enjoy spending time with you because being with you doesn't feel like work."

"What does it feel like?"

Amy's heart skipped a beat when Spencer took her eyes off the road long enough to turn and face her. She couldn't see Spencer's eyes through the dark lenses of her sunglasses, but she could feel them on her. Examining her face. Staring into her soul. "It feels..." Like coming home. Like where she was supposed to be. "It's better than chocolate."

Spencer frowned. "You don't like chocolate."

"It's starting to grow on me."

And so was Spencer.

Spencer ordered a virgin strawberry daiquiri from the bar and held her half-frozen drink over her head as she lowered herself into the crowded but expansive pool. The clear water felt cool against her skin, providing a sharp contrast to the warm air that had caused her to work up a serious sweat while she and Amy hiked a few of the numerous trails dotting the vast property.

Amy followed closely behind her as they waded across the elaborately decorated pool to get to the outcropping of rocks on the other side. The trees and lush foliage surrounding the area made it seem like they had immersed themselves in a lake in the middle of a jungle instead of a manmade creation. Their damp clothes were drying on the back of a lounge chair on the pool deck. Amy's oversized beach bag rested in the chair's seat, her cell phone and walkie-talkie stashed inside. Spencer hoped neither device sparked to life any time soon. She was enjoying herself way too much to stop now.

When she reached her destination, she pressed her back against the rocks and turned to survey the steadily growing crowd. The shallow end of the pool, the part closest to the DJ, was filled with so many people the resulting waves looked like whitewater rapids.

Spencer watched a scantily clad couple in color-coordinated swimsuits float by on a giant inflatable swan. The guy was wearing a neon green Speedo. Dental floss would have covered more territory than his companion's string bikini managed to. Spencer looked down at her black sports bra and matching boy shorts, which seemed demure in comparison. "I feel like I'm in the Playboy mansion without the bunnies and D-list celebrities."

"It feels more like we wandered through the Looking Glass."

"Wherever we are, I don't ever want to leave."

"Neither do I."

Spencer tried not to stare when Amy adjusted the fit of her yellow bikini bottoms, but she couldn't help admiring the view. "What dance is that they're doing?" she asked when she finally managed to drag her eyes away from Amy's gorgeous body.

Amy sipped from her bottle of mineral water as she watched the people in the shallow end perform a line dance with so many steps Spencer couldn't keep up with all of them. "Something that will probably make its way to the States in six months or so. My parents were on vacation in Acapulco the first time they saw someone do the Macarena. They had never heard of the dance or the song, even though everyone else in the restaurant they were in seemed to. A few weeks after they got home, they couldn't escape it."

"What do your parents do for a living?"

"My mom's a registered nurse, and my dad is a used car salesman."

"The kind that airs all the crazy ads on local TV?"

"You guessed it. His name's Lawrence, so he calls himself Loopy Larry and dresses up like a demented circus clown. When I was in high school, my friends teased me relentlessly each time he released a new commercial. It was so mortifying at the time.

I wanted to bury my head in the sand like an ostrich. When I got my learner's permit and was in the market for my first car, I was happy to have the inside track. I didn't need to waste my time visiting every car dealership in town. All I had to do was stop by my dad's lot. We bickered over the price for a while," Amy said with a wink, "but he ended up giving me a good deal."

"Having an ace in the hole always comes in handy, even when you're not playing cards."

"What about your parents? What do they do?"

"My mom was a history teacher and my dad was a plumber. They saved every dime they could when they were younger so they could afford to retire early and spend their golden years traveling as much as possible. Now they're on the road more often than they're home."

"You don't ever go with them?"

"I'm too busy working so I'll be able to afford to follow their example one day."

"Have you ever had a real family vacation?"

"We tried a couple of times. They usually ended up like a plot from a Chevy Chase movie. One summer, we packed up the car to drive to an amusement park in Atlanta. When we finally arrived, we discovered it was closed for repairs."

Amy grimaced. "What did you do instead?"

"My dad was so mad he wanted to turn around and drive home, but my mom talked him out of it. Her brother owns a cabin in Blue Ridge, a small town close to the Tennessee border. He wasn't using it that week so Mom asked if we could borrow it. We canceled our hotel reservations and spent the weekend in Uncle Darrell's cabin. My parents and I had more fun fishing, grilling, and hanging out in the local restaurants than we would have in the amusement park. Until this week, that was the best vacation I've ever had."

"I'm happy to hear SOS made the list. What do I have to do to push us to the top?"

Amy scooped a handful of water from the pool and let it dribble across Spencer's shoulders and chest, which were starting to turn bright pink from the reflected rays of the sun. Spencer shivered at the sensation. An incredibly sexy song by a former boy band member was playing. Spencer wished she and Amy could act out the lyrics, their hands moving nice and slow as sweat dripped off their bodies.

"Just keep doing what you're doing and I'm sure you'll get there."

Spencer took a sip of her drink to cool off. When she looked up, she noticed that the couple in the inflatable swan had floated their way again.

"Are you two exclusive, or do you like to have fun?" the guy in the Speedo asked.

Spencer wasn't interested in taking him up on his offer. Amy didn't seem too keen on the idea, either, so Spencer slipped a possessive arm around Amy's waist. "I don't like to share."

The woman in the string bikini slowly ran her tongue over her lips. "I don't blame you."

Amy draped her arm across Spencer's shoulder and nuzzled her cheek. "I should probably kiss you to make the illusion complete, don't you think?" she asked in a whisper.

"Probably," Spencer responded in kind.

Spencer's knees nearly buckled when Amy pressed her body against hers. She rested her hands on Amy's lower back. Not too low, but low enough to feel the rise of her hips. When Amy leaned toward her, Spencer had to force herself to remember to draw air into her lungs. Then Amy's lips were on hers, breathing life back into her. For a second, Spencer forgot they were only pretending.

"I think that's our cue," the guy in the Speedo said as he and his companion began to float away.

Amy broke the kiss but remained in the circle of Spencer's arms. "It was nice meeting you," she said to the couple. Then she turned back to Spencer. "Thanks for playing along."

"No problem."

"Are they still watching?"

"I have no idea." The only person Spencer could see was Amy.

Amy finally pulled away. "We've got a boat to catch. We'd better start heading back."

"Good idea." Spencer followed Amy out of the pool. After they got dressed, she downed the rest of her drink in a futile attempt to quell the growing heat between her legs.

Amy removed the Rays cap and held it out to Spencer. "Thanks for letting me borrow this."

"Keep it. It looks better on you than it ever did on me."

"I doubt that, but thanks."

Amy turned to make her way to the car, but Spencer grabbed her arm before she could leave. "I know there are all kinds of rules you have to follow about what you can and can't do with me, but I need you to do me a favor."

"What?"

"The next time you kiss me, do it because you want to, not because someone might be watching."

"Understood."

Except Spencer didn't think she did. How could she unless she was starting to feel the same way? Spencer knew that was impossible. Amy was married to her job, and no one could ever come between them.

Night Five

Jessica checked the schedule posted near the entrance to the fitness room as she debated whether she should close early. The gym's official hours were six a.m. to ten p.m. She and three other instructors led a series of classes from nine to six every day except Saturday, when passengers were either just settling in or preparing to return home.

The late morning and early afternoon classes were traditionally the most popular. Crowd participation usually took a severe nosedive once the first dinner service began. When the twice-nightly shows started, the chances of someone walking in for an impromptu workout went from slim to none. A few stragglers occasionally wandered in for some self-paced exercise, but not often.

Today was par for the course. The gym had been practically deserted since Kendra's Zumba class ended three hours before.

"I can think of much better ways to spend the next hour than watching over an empty room."

Namely, making love to Breanna. God, Breanna. Just thinking about her made Jessica smile. Being with her was always memorable, but last night was truly an experience she would never forget.

She had never opened her heart to someone the way she had with Breanna yesterday. Admitting she had feelings for her had been scary but liberating, too. Jessica couldn't wait to share even more of herself with her. But how could she when she couldn't truly let Breanna in?

She wanted to keep Breanna safe. Keeping her safe meant keeping her as far from the situation as she could.

Breanna had said she would love her no matter what. That there was nothing she could do to make Breanna turn her back on her. Breanna had sounded like she meant every word, but Jessica was hesitant to put Breanna's loyalty to the test.

She felt a pang of guilt for not telling Breanna how she had earned most of the money currently earning interest in her savings account. For not telling her she had been working as a drug mule for the past three years. Yes, she had resolved to remove herself from the situation and do things the hard way—the right way— from now on, but was it too little, too late?

She told herself she was being brave by placing the weight of her problems solely on her own shoulders, but she felt like a coward for inviting Breanna into her life under false pretenses. Breanna hadn't asked for any of this. She hadn't asked to have a target placed on her back. She had asked Jessica to make a commitment to building a future with her. A simple request, and one that Jessica had eagerly fulfilled. Now she needed to find a way to honor her commitment. She needed to find a way to keep Breanna safe while the danger around her continued to mount.

"This is my problem, not hers. She's an innocent bystander. I'm the guilty one."

But like it or not, Breanna was as deeply enmeshed in all this drama as she was. She couldn't be charged with anything, but as long as Jessica was involved with her, Breanna would be a tool Pilar and her people could use to force Jessica to do their bidding. In a way, that was even worse.

Jessica wasn't naïve enough to think she could wave a magic wand and make all her problems disappear. If that were possible, she'd be swinging that wand until her arm fell off.

"You've got less than three days to make your move. You'd better make sure it's one you can live with."

She grabbed her keys and headed for the door. Raq pushed the door open before she could set the locks.

"You're not closing up shop, are you?" Raq pointed to the woman with her. A gorgeous Latina with long black hair and piercing brown eyes. "We wanted to work off some of the carbs from dinner. Our other halves made reservations at the Italian restaurant tonight, and we kind of overdid it on the breadsticks."

"Yeah, those things can be addictive."

"There's going to be a cooking demo tomorrow," Raq's companion said. "We need to make room for the free handouts. Do you mind?"

"Of course not." Jessica backed away from the door. "Come on in."

"Thanks, dog." Raq gave Jessica a pat on the back that nearly knocked her off her feet. "I almost forgot to provide introductions," she said as she headed for the treadmill. "Jessica, this is my new homie, Luisa Moreno. Luisa, Jessica."

Luisa smiled and extended her hand. "It's nice to meet you."

"You, too."

Jessica had never come face-to-face with someone she was supposed to kill. She hoped Luisa didn't notice how much her palm was sweating when they shook hands.

Luisa climbed on the treadmill next to Raq's and set a brisk pace. Jessica watched her while she ran. This was the woman who had almost single-handedly taken down one of the most feared drug cartels in Mexico? Based on the stories she had heard, Jessica had expected Luisa to look like an Amazon with the bulging muscles to match. Luisa was in good shape, but she seemed normal, not superhuman. She had an air of nobility about her, fitting for a person who spent most of her day in uniform. Jessica didn't see her as a threat, but others obviously thought otherwise.

Catching Jessica staring, Luisa used the mirror lining the wall to lock eyes with her. "Slow night?"

Jessica shuffled the stack of comment cards in front of her in an effort to look busy. "It usually is at this time of day." She told herself to remain unobtrusive so Luisa could concentrate on her workout, but curiosity got the best of her. "Aren't you the cop who saved the day during that incident in Cancún a few months ago?" she asked, setting the cards aside.

"I wasn't *the* cop. I was one of many."

"Don't let the modesty act fool you," Raq said between exhalations. "Wonder Woman here swooped in like she was a character in *Call of Duty* and started taking suckers out left and right. Pop, pop! Then she stole a speedboat, chased the head dude down, and took him out, too. She caught a bullet in the process, but she still managed to save the day *and* get the girl. Or did your girl save you? I always get that part mixed up."

"You were shot?" Jessica asked.

"It's not as dramatic as Raq makes it sound." Luisa tapped her chest with the tips of two fingers as she continued to run. "My Kevlar vest stopped the round, but the impact knocked me into the lagoon we were in. Finn, my girlfriend, dove into the water and pulled me out."

"After she practically chewed off her own hand to free herself from the railing she was tied to," Raq said. "I didn't think she had it in her."

"Neither did she."

"Anybody can do anything when they're about to lose something they really want."

"Is that what you did, Raq?" Jessica asked. "I mean, you said you used to do things that weren't exactly on the up and up. Now you're dating a cop and helping her catch bad guys instead of hanging out on street corners keeping the bad guys safe."

"All I knew was I wanted to be with Sheba. From the second I met her, I knew she was the one. When I found out she was an undercover cop on assignment, I wanted to wring her neck for fooling me into thinking she was down for the cause. When I came to my senses, I realized I was the one in the wrong, not her. So I walked away from the so-called life I was living and took a chance on something real. She could have had any woman she wanted, but she chose to be with me. I wanted to be more than a thug from the 'hood. I wanted to be someone Sheba could be proud of, not someone she was ashamed to introduce to her friends."

Drawn in by the passion she heard in Raq's voice, Jessica moved closer. "How did you get out of that life? Did you seek immunity or what?"

"I didn't make any deals. I didn't have to. I didn't shoot anybody or move any product, so after I helped Bathsheba and her crew bring Ice down, the po-pos offered to hire me instead of trying to lock me up." Raq reached for the towel draped across her shoulder and wiped sweat off her face. "Why are you asking? Do you know someone who's jammed up?"

Jessica resisted the instinct to say no. "As a matter of fact, I do."

"Yeah? Who?"

Jessica hesitated. Even though Raq probably could have related to her dilemma, she didn't want to admit to her or Luisa that she had been stupid enough to get herself into so much trouble. "A friend of mine got caught up in something and she can't seem to find her way out. It started out small, granting a few favors here and there, now she's in over her head."

"Is she involved in a gang?" Luisa asked.

"I'm not sure. She didn't give me all the details."

"She's either mixed up with a gang or a cartel. What you described sounds like their usual MO. They draw people in, test them out, then sink their hooks into them once their victims get a taste of the good life. After that, the recruits are like puppets on a string, desperate to walk away but powerless to do so."

Raq nodded in agreement. "I know what you mean. When I was working for Ice, I did whatever I could to keep him happy because I knew how ruthless he could be when someone pissed him off." She dried her face again, then turned to Jessica. "I gave you my card, right? When your friend's ready to talk, tell her to give me a call. I'll talk it over with Bathsheba. We'll reach out to some people and do whatever we can to help."

"Thanks for the advice. I'll tell her what you said. What should she do in the meantime?"

"Watch her back to make sure no one's trying to stick a knife in it."

Amy marveled along with the rest of the crowd as tonight's featured artists went through their paces. The Fallen Angels were acrobats whose feats of aerial wizardry were made even more breathtaking by the fact that they often performed in the nude. Their only adornments were the oversized wings they removed after they took the stage and the fine sheen of sweat that coated their sculpted bodies as they performed.

Amy had watched every awe-inspiring minute of their first show and treated herself to part of the second before she headed to the cruise director's office so she could prepare for tomorrow morning's staff meeting. She looked up when she heard someone tap on the half-open door.

"Hey, Bree. What's up?"

"Wrong one. Try again."

Amy noticed the flower in her visitor's hair was positioned behind her left ear instead of her right. "Oops. Sorry about that, Leanna."

"I've had twenty-seven years of practice. Believe me, I've gotten used to it by now. May I talk to you for a second?"

Amy set her notes aside so she could give Leanna her full attention. "Is this about Bree?"

Leanna took a seat in the cushioned chair in front of the desk. "Were she and Jessica on the outs again? If so, they must have patched things up. When I talked to her this afternoon, she sounded like they were practically engaged."

Relieved she hadn't betrayed Breanna's confidence, Amy blew out a sigh. "I was starting to wonder if they would ever get their collective act together. I'm glad to hear they've worked things out. How are things going with you? We don't see each other much outside the office."

Leanna grinned. "That's because you keep me so busy while we're *in* the office. There's only so much of you I can take."

"Whatever. What did you want to talk about?"

"I have a question about tomorrow's program."

"The cooking demo? Before you ask, yes, all the samples will be gluten-free, and there won't be any peanuts involved in case anyone's allergic."

"Good to hear, but that's not what I wanted to ask. One of my Wahines wants to propose to her girlfriend, and she wants to do it during the cooking demo."

"Why then?"

"She says her girlfriend's kind of a drama queen so she wanted to come up with a suitably dramatic gesture when she pops the question. Do you think Griffin would mind if we take up part of her time? I don't want to get in the way of her doing her thing. If she doesn't want to share the spotlight, we can try to come up with something else. But if she's amenable, we can add the proposal into her performance somehow. Perhaps she could ask the drama queen to be her sous chef and hand the mike over to her during the question-and-answer session."

"The demo's scheduled to last an hour. Griffin has a no-bake dessert planned. I can't think of a reason why she'd object to devoting part of her time to something other than meal prep."

"The last celebrity chef we booked for a cruise was a bit of a diva. We weren't allowed to have any input on her presentation, and her contract rider was longer than Mariah Carey's."

"True, but Griffin's a lot more down-to-earth than that. Even though she won one of the most prestigious cooking competitions on TV and her restaurants make money hand over fist, she's not prone to making all sorts of ridiculous demands just because she can. I'll talk to her tonight, see what she says, and try to have an answer for you by tomorrow morning. That way, we'll have plenty of time to brainstorm in case we have to come up with plan B. We've had dozens of commitment ceremonies. Have we ever had an actual proposal before?"

Leanna thought for a minute. "No, I think this is our first one."

"Then let's make sure we get it right. For better or worse, we're going to be part of this couple's story for the rest of their lives."

"I'm aiming for better."

"So am I."

And one day, perhaps she would eventually be asked to say, "I do," instead of making it possible for someone else.

Day Six

S pencer made her way to the promenade deck twenty minutes before the cooking demonstration was scheduled to begin so she could reserve a section of seats for her, Finn, Luisa, Tatum, Jordan, Raq, and Bathsheba. She wouldn't have to find places for Hannah and Maneet because they, along with Bonnie, had signed up for the poker tournament currently taking place in the casino one floor above. If the poker tournament lasted as long as the ones she watched on TV from time to time, Spencer would be able to head to the upper promenade deck after the cooking demo ended. Then she could spend the rest of the afternoon watching Hannah and Maneet compete—and finally lay eyes on the elusive Bonnie. After five days of missed connections, she was looking forward to finally being able to put a face with a name.

"Let's hope she doesn't go bust in the first hour. Otherwise, I might be telling her good-bye before we've even had a chance to say hello."

She walked through the double doors and scanned the room. The culinary arts center was stocked with so much state-of-the-art equipment it could have doubled as the kitchen of a professional restaurant. A large workstation divided the food preparation area from the rest of the room, which featured enough seats to accommodate around two hundred people. Most of those seats, unfortunately, were already spoken for. A few empty ones remained here and there, but not enough to accommodate Spencer's entire group. The rest of the seats were either already occupied or marked with laminated Reserved signs.

"The next time we do this," she said when Finn, Luisa, Tatum, Jordan, Bathsheba, and Raq finally showed up, "someone's going to have to volunteer to camp out the night before. Otherwise, we'll never be able to sit together."

Jordan stepped back to remove herself from consideration. "Don't look at me. I plan on sleeping in as long and as often as I can. This week is the first time in years I haven't been forced to share a bed with an eighty-pound German shepherd. I'm enjoying not having to hug the edge of the mattress or twist myself into a pretzel every night."

"Don't worry about it," Tatum said. "I've got us covered. Give me a sec." She conferred with an SOS Tours staffer for a minute or two, then beckoned everyone to follow when the staffer began to lead them to the front row.

"How did you manage this?" Jordan asked as she settled into one of the seven reserved seats.

Tatum grinned. "The war hero angle gets them every time. It worked on you, didn't it?"

"Not right away. I had to see you in uniform before I was truly convinced." Jordan leaned over and gave Tatum a kiss. "Nice job on the seats, though."

"I do what I can."

Raq and Luisa began a whispered conversation. Spencer couldn't hear what they were saying, but they looked much too serious to be discussing dessert and cocktail pairings, the topic of today's demonstration. Bathsheba let them talk for a few minutes before she finally stepped in. "Break it up, you two. You're supposed to be on vacation, not talking shop."

"What's going on?" Finn asked.

"Nothing to worry about," Luisa said.

"That's not what I asked you."

Seeming to realize she couldn't get away with giving Finn such a pat answer, Luisa sighed and said, "Raq and I had a conversation last night with Jessica, one of the fitness trainers."

"She teaches the spin class I've been attending," Tatum said. "She's not in trouble, is she?"

"I'm not sure," Luisa said. "She said she had a friend who needs help getting out of a difficult situation, but Raq and I both think she was asking questions on her own behalf, not someone else's. I was just asking Raq if she thinks we should talk to her again to see if she changes her story."

"I think she's ready to flip on whoever's got her under their thumb," Raq said. "She just needs someone to talk to. Someone she trusts."

"Someone like you?" Bathsheba asked.

"I made a connection with her the day after we got here. She and Luisa bonded a little last night. Maybe we can use the relationships we've formed with her to—"

"Don't," Finn said forcefully. She sounded scared rather than angry. "Bathsheba's right. We're on vacation. Leave the work stuff at home." She turned to Luísa. "This trip was supposed to put what happened in Cancún behind us. I don't want to dredge up those emotions again. I don't want to risk losing you again. I know it's your job to put your life on the line every day, but you're not on the job right now." She fingered her necklace, a misshapen bullet dangling from a chain. The bullet had been dug from Luisa's Kevlar vest after Javier Villalobos fired a round at her during the fatal gun battle that had claimed his life and had nearly claimed Luisa's as well. "I call you super cop for a reason. You're willing to take risks no one else will."

"That was before I met you," Luisa said. "I'm much more careful now."

"Then let someone else take the risk this time. There's probably nothing going on, but what if there is? If you go looking for trouble, you're sure to find it."

"Sometimes, you don't have to go looking," Bathsheba said. "Sometimes, trouble finds you."

"Hey," Finn said, "I thought you were on my side."

"Even off-duty, a cop can't turn off her instincts," Bathsheba said. "At the moment, though, none of us are in position to do something about it. If you think something's up, babe, tell the ship's security team so they can look into it. Don't get mixed up in it yourself."

"I don't want Jessica to get scared and clam up," Raq said. "Then she'll be even worse off than she is now. Let me take one more run at her before I bring someone else into it. Finn's right. Luisa and I might be overreacting. But if we're not, I want to do whatever I can to help. She's good people. She got into something she didn't expect, now she's stuck."

"What do you think she's into?" Spencer asked.

"Money laundering or drug smuggling, most likely," Luisa said. "Maybe even a bit of low-level dealing. The ships she's assigned to visit dozens of international ports each year and are filled with thousands of potential customers. Cartels would pay dearly to have someone like her on the inside."

"Like that flight attendant who got caught smuggling sixty pounds of cocaine into LAX and hauled ass without the Gucci shoes and designer luggage she left behind," Raq said.

"I remember that," Bathsheba said. "She took off like she was a member of the Jamaican sprint team."

"Jessica might be doing something along the same lines," Luisa said. "Bringing the product in and handing it over to someone else to sell. She probably only deals with one or two people and doesn't even know who she's working for."

Raq picked up on Luisa's train of thought. "But if we follow the money until we reach its source, we can find out who the top dog is and take that person down."

"This is starting to sound a little too familiar," Finn said.

Bathsheba nodded in agreement. "To me, too. Do what you have to do, Raq. Just be careful. You know better than I do that when people get backed into a corner, they tend to come out fighting."

"Then it's a good thing I've got a strong chin."

Rubbing her hands together, Jordan steered the conversation in a decidedly less serious direction. "Is everyone looking forward to this as much as I am?"

"I don't think *anyone* is looking forward to this as much as you are," Tatum said with a laugh. "You're such a chocoholic, I'm surprised your blood type isn't cocoa."

"You could coat anything in a layer of chocolate and I'd eat it," Jordan said. "Strawberries, pretzels, crickets. Even liver. I don't care. "

"You had me until you mentioned crickets, but I know what you mean," Bathsheba said. "I draw the line at chocolate-flavored wine, though. Chocolate and wine are two things I enjoy together, but not in the same glass."

"I bought a bottle on a whim once," Jordan said.

"And how was it?" Bathsheba asked.

Jordan wrinkled her nose. "Thick."

"Exactly my point."

The chocolate-themed conversation reminded Spencer of Amy and her aversion to the treat Jordan seemed to love so much. Spencer still remembered the feel of Amy in her arms. The taste of her on her lips.

The kiss they had shared yesterday had been amazing but bittersweet. Amazing because it was the best kiss Spencer had ever received. Bittersweet because Amy had kissed her in order to convince a pair of total strangers that they were a couple when odds were they would never actually become one. Not as long as Amy was willing to bend the rules but not break them.

The next time you kiss me, Spencer had told her as they prepared to return to port, *do it because you want to, not because someone might be watching.*

She wondered if that time would ever come. She hadn't seen Amy except from a distance since they boarded the ship after their trip to Loterie Farm. Was Amy using the time apart to try to figure out how to respond to the edict Spencer had given her, or was her absence the only answer Spencer needed?

Spencer turned to the group rather than continuing to dwell on a problem she couldn't solve on her own. "Who knows? Chocolate might not even be on the menu today. The theme is dessert and cocktail pairings. That could be anything."

"Well," Jordan said when the house lights dimmed, "we're about to find out."

Amy felt uncharacteristically anxious. She had addressed much larger crowds than this one with no qualms. Today, though, she was a bundle of nerves. She wondered if the brides-to-be were equally on edge. One was completely clueless about what was about to happen. The other was all too aware.

Amy practiced reciting Griffin Sutton's bio one last time. She needed to get the rhythm of the words down so she wouldn't stumble over any of them when she kicked off today's demonstration. She wanted today to be perfect from beginning to end. One way or another, today was a day to be remembered.

"Let's make sure it's for the right reasons."

When she was done practicing her lines, she strode over to Griffin, the Newport Beach-based chef who would be headlining today's demonstration. Even though Griffin was conversing with her wife, Rachel, she kept a close eye on her team of assistants to make sure the desserts she had prepared earlier and planned to serve to the audience later were being kept sufficiently chilled.

Amy knew from experience that nothing ruined a good time faster than bad dairy. During a trip to the Mexican Riviera, dozens of guests had contracted food poisoning after ordering strawberry cheesecake that had been accidentally allowed to reach room temperature. Amy was glad to see Griffin was taking all the necessary precautions to ensure her food was being handled properly. SOS couldn't afford a repeat of the previous debacle.

"I don't mean to interrupt," Amy said. "I wanted to check in with you one more time to make sure you don't mind the changes we've made to today's program."

Griffin was wearing black motorcycle boots and tight jeans with frayed hems. A faded concert T-shirt with a picture of Florence Welch on the front peeked through her unbuttoned chef's coat. "Today is supposed to be about the sexy side of food. I can't think of anything sexier than love, can you?"

"Nothing immediately comes to mind."

Rachel had been scheduled to act as Griffin's sous chef today until Amy and Leanna altered the script. Thankfully, she seemed to be taking the demotion in stride.

"I'm crushed about not being able to take my turn in the spotlight," Rachel said with a smile, "but I get to go home with the chef so I think I'll survive. Knock 'em dead, babe." She gave Griffin a kiss for luck, then left to take her seat in the audience.

Griffin's flagship restaurant was in California, where she and her family lived, but she had recently opened an establishment in New York City as well. Though both restaurants were wildly successful, Griffin didn't seem to have the requisite oversized ego to show for it.

"Thank you again for agreeing to do this," Amy said.

"It's my pleasure." Griffin adjusted her headset microphone and buttoned her chef's coat, a crisply ironed maroon jacket with her name monogrammed on one side and her restaurant's logo emblazoned on the other. "Let's do this."

The crowd applauded wildly when Amy stood on her mark in front of the workstation.

"Griffin Sutton looks like a surfer, dresses like a biker, and occasionally swears like a sailor, but please don't let her mother know."

The crowd's warm welcome had caused some of Amy's nerves to dissipate. When the opening line of her introduction drew a laugh, her nerves disappeared altogether.

"She has competed in and won the most prestigious cooking competition on television, *Cream of the Crop*, and her signature restaurant, the Sutton Family Café, is one of only a handful of establishments in southern California that has been awarded three Michelin stars. Its New York counterpart, SFC East, boasts a waiting list that's longer than the run of some Broadway shows. If that's not enough incentive to taste what she has in store for us today, I don't know what is. Please welcome Griffin Sutton!"

Griffin bounded out of the backstage area with the energy of an unbridled colt. Eager to watch her work, Amy quickly exited the stage.

"Thank you for the flattering introduction, Amy. It's a pleasure to be here and an honor to meet all of you. My wife and I have only been on board since yesterday, but everyone has made us feel right at home. Are all of you having as much fun as we are?"

Amy was pleased to hear the crowd roar its approval.

"The kitchen staff was nice enough to let me horn in on their territory today. I've been down there all morning working on a dish that's near and dear to my heart. A gooey, decadent dessert that's almost as much fun to make as it is to eat."

Amy heard more than a few murmurs of anticipation.

"Some things in life just go together," Griffin said. "Peanut butter and jelly, cookies and milk, bacon and eggs. I'd like to tell you about some other natural pairings you might not have considered. Wine and chocolate, for example." She lifted the lid on a large tray filled with bottles of wine and bars of gourmet chocolate.

"I knew it!" a woman in the front row yelled before she blushed furiously and covered her mouth with her hands.

"A fellow chocolate lover, I see," Griffin said good-naturedly. "If you're a fan of milk chocolate, try pairing it with port, sherry, or a nice pinot noir. White chocolate, I find, goes best with champagne or Riesling. Make sure the Riesling isn't too sweet or it will overpower what you're eating. Dark chocolate, which can be slightly bitter, matches well with cabernet sauvignon. I like to mix my sweets with a hint of something savory. Chocolate accented with sea salt, my personal favorite, tastes even better with a glass of merlot. And if you're feeling really wild, throw a dollop of warm caramel into the mix."

"Should we be taking notes?" an audience member called out.

Amy hadn't expected the demonstration to be quite so interactive. Griffin had set aside some time for questions after the demo was done, but the audience didn't seem willing to wait. At least they were engaged instead of bored to tears. That was a good sign.

"Just sit back and relax. I'll provide you with the Cliffs Notes later." Griffin moved to the next covered dish. "If you're in the mood for a baked dessert rather than something prepackaged, lemon bars always do the trick. Pair them with a glass of prosecco and you'll be transported to Tuscany in no time."

"What goes with brownies?" someone asked.

"A fork, a glass of port, and a bib to catch the crumbs. If you don't have a fork handy, fingers work, too. Then you can use the bib for other things."

The crowd hooted at the titillating comment, and Griffin stepped out of the way as three of her assistants cleared the dishes off the workstation. The items she had displayed, Amy knew, wouldn't go to waste. Samples would be offered to the crowd. The rest would be divided among the members of the wait and kitchen staffs.

"There's no rule that says a dessert has to be decadent, but there's no rule that says it doesn't, either. The richest dessert in my repertoire is the one I want to make for you now: a cookies and cream parfait with coffee liqueur-infused whipped cream."

The resulting moans sounded like a collective orgasm.

"There's no baking required, but the dish calls for a bit of elbow grease. Who's willing to help me out?"

Hands shot up all across the room.

"You." Griffin pointed to the woman Amy had seen Spencer sitting next to during Sunday's wine tasting. "My chocolate lover in the front row. Why don't you come up here and give me a hand?"

The woman squealed like she had been given a chance to compete for the grand prize on her favorite game show.

"What's your name?" Griffin asked after Wendy fitted the woman with a headset microphone.

"Jordan."

"Thank you for volunteering, Jordan. How skilled are you in the kitchen?"

"I can order takeout with the best of them."

"That works, too. Do you think you can handle a food processor?"

"I can try."

"Perfect." Griffin handed her a plate filled with chocolate sandwich cookies minus the creamy centers. "I need you to take a handful of these, fifteen or so, and grind them into a fine powder. We're going to use some of the crumbs as one of the layers on our parfait and dust the rest over the top of the finished product."

"I think I love you."

"Careful. Don't let your girlfriend hear you say that."

"Too late. She already did," Jordan's girlfriend said.

Amy laughed along with the rest of the crowd. Griffin was a natural at this. Jordan was, too.

This might work out well after all.

"While Jordan's taking care of the cookies, I'm going to prepare the whipped cream." Griffin gathered her ingredients. "Add two cups of heavy cream, the filling from the cookies, and a third cup of your favorite coffee liqueur into a blender and whip until you achieve the desired texture. The process normally takes about four minutes. If you keep going beyond that point, you'll end up with butter instead of whipped cream. Butter can be sexy, too, but I wouldn't recommend including it in a parfait. For an extra layer of richness, melt four ounces of semisweet chocolate in half a cup of hot milk and add that to the whipped cream."

Amy looked away from the whirring equipment. The audience seemed spellbound by what they were witnessing. If only they knew what was next on the menu.

Griffin switched off the blender. "The whipped cream's done. How are you doing over there, Jordan?"

"I think the cookies are done, too."

"Perfect." Griffin turned off the food processor and removed the lid. "Now for the fun part: plating." She grabbed two glasses from the cupboard and set them on the workstation. "Interacting with food is a sensual experience. You eat with your eyes first, especially when a dish is visually appealing. If you're preparing this dish at home, though, don't stress over trying to make it look perfect. Some of the best meals I've had were also the messiest. Sometimes, clean-up can be an adventure in itself."

Wendy held up a time cue, but Griffin was so polished she didn't seem to need it. Even with the last-minute changes, the program was right on schedule.

"Okay, Jordan, you're on. I want you to take this spoon and alternate layers of the cookie crumbs and whipped cream until you reach the top of the glass."

"Which ingredient should I start with?"

"That's up to you. Parfaits are like snowflakes. No two are exactly alike. Ready? Go!"

The audience cheered as Griffin and Jordan began a frenzied race to the finish.

"I didn't know cooking was a contact sport," Griffin said after Jordan hip checked her away from the workstation.

"It is in my house."

Griffin gave Jordan a high five, then addressed the audience. "As my lovely sous chef just demonstrated, cooking doesn't have to be as serious as some of my colleagues in the food industry make it out to be. Cooking is meant to bring people together. And, most of all, it's meant to be fun. So don't freak out if you don't get the recipe right the first twenty times you try to follow it. As Maximillien Robespierre once said, you can't make an omelet without breaking a few eggs."

The audience applauded the end of the demo.

"Before we serve these gorgeous parfaits," Griffin said as the wait staff began to gather behind her, "does anyone have any questions?"

Wendy handed Amy and Leanna cordless microphones so they could work the room. Griffin fielded a wide-ranging variety of questions before the woman sitting next to Spencer raised her hand. Amy and Leanna had agreed that Leanna should wield the microphone while this passenger posed her question, so Amy hung back while Leanna sprinted toward her.

"My question is for Jordan." The crowd gasped when Tatum pulled a ring box from her pocket and leaned on one of her crutches as she gingerly lowered herself to one knee. "Jordan Gonzalez, will you marry me?"

Amy looked at Spencer to see if she might have known about Tatum's plans ahead of time, but Spencer looked just as surprised as Jordan did.

Tears pouring down her face, Jordan abandoned her position at the workstation and helped Tatum to her feet. "Of course I'll marry you."

The room erupted as Tatum slipped the ring on Jordan's finger and their mouths met in a lingering kiss.

Amy was so caught up in the moment she almost forgot to officially bring the presentation to an end. "Congratulations, Jordan and Tatum. I'll be on the lookout for my wedding invitation."

"Once we start making the list," Tatum said, "I'm sure everyone in this room will be on it."

"I'm looking forward to it. Everyone, please join me in thanking Griffin Sutton for today's demonstration."

Griffin held up her hand to acknowledge the cheers. "Thank you for having me." She cued the wait staff to begin serving the parfaits. "Enjoy."

"Do you think Jordan and Tatum would be willing to pose for a few pictures for the company website?" Leanna asked as dozens of audience members, parfaits in hand, made their way over to the happy couple to offer their congratulations. "It would be great publicity for us, and a serious boost for both our wedding and honeymoon registries."

Amy watched Jordan and Tatum celebrate with Spencer and the rest of their friends. She longed to join them, but doing so would have felt like an intrusion. She wasn't part of this moment. She had simply been hired to help make it happen. Now that it had, she knew it would make good business sense to piggyback on the publicity. But she hadn't thought about business once today, and she didn't want to start now. She wanted to enjoy the occasion, not exploit it.

"Put the camera away, Lee. Today's not about us. It's about them."

"I knew better than to offer you a parfait so I brought you one of these." Spencer handed Amy a glass of champagne.

"Thank you." Amy accepted the glass and took a grateful sip. She still had tons of work to do today, but she felt semi-relaxed for the first time in hours. She was relieved the revised program had gone off without a hitch, but she suspected Spencer's calming presence might be partially responsible for her improved frame of mind.

"Was this your idea?"

"I would love to take credit, but Leanna proposed it, pardon the pun. All I did was help her dot the i's and cross the t's."

"If you say so. Whatever you did, Jordan and Tatum are over the moon right now so thank you for doing it. Are you really planning to come to the wedding if they send you an invitation?"

"The only parts of Georgia I've seen so far are the interstates in Atlanta and the inside of Hartsfield, which isn't called the world's busiest airport without reason. I hear the rest of the state is beautiful, though. Maybe I'll find a local tour guide to show me around one day."

"Maybe."

"What do you have on tap for today?"

"The girls and I were planning to watch Hannah and Maneet compete in the poker tournament upstairs, but I think this celebration is going to last a while. What about you? What's on your agenda?"

"I have to find creative ways to keep two thousand women from getting bored when there are no excursions to be taken, no exotic islands to explore, and no land in sight."

Days at sea were always difficult to plan. She wanted to give passengers as many entertainment options as possible, but she didn't want to overwhelm them, either. She wanted them to feel relaxed, not pressured.

"There are more than enough distractions on this ship to keep everyone occupied until we get to the Bahamas tomorrow," Spencer said. "After some of the adventures we've gotten into this week, I'm sure some of us could use some downtime, myself included."

"I hope you're right."

"I don't want to take up too much of your time. I just wanted to thank you for helping to make this happen."

Spencer looked like she wanted to say something else. Amy waited for her to decide whether she should say her piece or let whatever was bothering her remain unsaid. They stood in awkward silence for a moment or two before Spencer finally spoke.

"You don't have any hard feelings about the way we ended things yesterday, do you? About what I said?"

"Kissing you was a lapse in judgment. I won't call it a mistake." When was the last time a mistake had felt so good? "I will say, though, that I never should have done it. I should have found a way to extricate us from the situation without putting you on the spot. You spoke your mind about what happened and I respect that. How could I possibly hold it against you?"

"Some people find a way."

Amy remembered the story Spencer had told about making a drunken pass at a girl she had a crush on during a booze-fueled party on her senior trip. Her pass had been rebuffed in front of dozens of jeering witnesses. She'd been struggling to deal with the embarrassment—and the lingering disapproval—ever since.

"I'm not some people."

"So I've noticed." A brief but appreciative smile flickered across Spencer's lips before it quickly faded from view. "I'm glad we could clear the air."

"Me, too."

"Are you going to join me in Nassau tomorrow, or should I plan on going it alone?"

"The farewell dinner is tomorrow night. It's a formal event, so it's always one of the highlights of the trip. Everyone loves getting dressed up and taking pictures with all their friends. It takes a lot of planning."

"Sounds like it."

She would love to spend some time in Nassau—and with Spencer—but she didn't think it was in either of their best interest. There was a clear dividing line separating her and Spencer. She crossed that line yesterday. Now she needed to decide if she wanted to remain on her side of the line or rub it out for good.

"I've been shirking my duties long enough. I need to start pulling my weight again. I need to chain myself to my desk for the next couple of days to make sure everything goes off without a hitch."

If she was disappointed by Amy's answer, Spencer's expression didn't give her away. "Do you have any recommendations for me, at least?" she asked, sounding like a typical tourist on the hunt for one last grand adventure before her vacation came to an end.

"The pirate museum is fun if you want to learn about the history of the island. If you want to chill out, relax, and get some sun, spread a towel on Junkanoo Beach and watch the waves roll in. If you want a more fast-paced adventure, try one of the powerboat tours. Just make sure you're back here by three so I won't have to send a search party after you."

"Don't tempt me," Spencer said with a cheeky grin that offered a hint of the playful personality she normally kept hidden beneath her placid exterior. "I've never been involved in an international incident before. Tomorrow could be a good time to start."

"I'm responsible for you and the rest of the passengers on board until we drop anchor in Fort Lauderdale Saturday morning. Do I need to handcuff myself to you in order to keep you out of trouble?"

"Handcuffing yourself to me might get me *in* trouble."

"You and me both."

Spencer's lips parted slightly, reminding Amy of the kiss they had shared. Amy tried not to imagine all the sexy things she could do if she found herself shackled to Spencer for an hour or two. Preferably more.

"I'll let you get back to work," Spencer said.

"Right. Work." The look in Spencer's eyes had almost made her forget she had a job to do. "Will I see you at the dinner tomorrow night?"

"You can count on it."

Amy could count on something else, too. When Spencer returned home in two days' time, she would be taking part of her heart with her.

NIGHT SIX

The sixty contestants that had signed up for the poker tournament were competing for bragging rights instead of money. The "prize" that would be presented to the winner at the end of the event was a plastic replica of the coveted diamond-encrusted bracelet given out during the main event of the World Series of Poker, the high-stakes competition that drew thousands of entrants and fans to Las Vegas each year.

Hannah and Maneet were eliminated from the competition long before SOS' poker tournament reached its latter stages, but Bonnie, along with eight other players, managed to make it to the final table. The nearly four dozen women who had been eliminated along the way lingered on the sidelines to see which player would end up with the winning hand.

"I've always told Bonnie she has a better poker face than I do," Hannah said after Spencer joined her and Maneet in the casino. "Right now, you're reminding me of the old joke about a horse walking into a bar. Why the long face? You look more like you spent the afternoon drowning your sorrows instead of celebrating Jordan and Tatum's good news."

In a way, she had. Her attempt to clear the air with Amy that afternoon had worked all too well. During their conversation, Amy had let her know in no uncertain terms how she felt about yesterday's kiss. It hadn't been as mind-blowing for her as it had been for Spencer. For Amy, the kiss had been a mistake. A lapse in judgment. Something she regretted. Something, in other words, not meant to be repeated.

"I can't believe this week is practically over." Spencer had started the week with mixed emotions, and she was ending it the same way.

"Time passes differently when you're on vacation," Maneet said. "The first few days seem to take forever. The rest pass in the blink of an eye. Before you know it, you're back home dreaming about where you want to go next."

"I vote for Europe," Hannah said. "I haven't been in ages. Who's with me?"

"The riverboat cruise that Spencer won sounds nice," Maneet said. "I might sign up for it before we leave so I can receive the discounted rate."

"Someone hand me my credit card and show me where to sign," Hannah said. "I bet you thought you'd be done with us in a few days, didn't you, Spencer? No such luck."

"I guess I'll see you next year," Spencer said as Bonnie laid down a royal flush to win the poker tournament. "It seems like it was just yesterday that we arrived. Now it's almost time to leave. Tomorrow's our last stop before we make the turn for home."

"That's why you have to make the most of every minute." Hannah nuzzled the side of Maneet's neck. "I know I intend to."

Spencer was envious of Hannah and Maneet's uncomplicated relationship. What she and Amy had was much more complex.

She wanted to spend her last full day of vacation with Amy. Conversing with her. Getting to know her. Venturing into places tourists flocked to and finding out-of-the-way establishments only locals seemed to know about. Given the current state of their relationship, trying to do those things tomorrow would have been beyond awkward. This time, unlike in Grand Turk, San Juan, or Phillipsburg, Spencer would be better off going it alone.

What else was new?

❖

Jessica had taught so many classes over the years that most of the attendees' faces had blurred together. Yet another cruise had almost come to an end. One more day of classes remained before she could return home and prepare for the next round. She was scheduled to report to the Isaacsons' gym bright and early Monday morning. Her next cruise was supposed to start in three weeks, an eight-day trip to the Dominican Republic, Curacao, and Aruba. She hadn't traveled that route in a couple of years and had been looking forward to the change of scenery. If she truly meant to straighten up the mess she had made of her life, though, this trip had to be her last. She needed to turn in her notice and walk away from her old life so she could start a new one somewhere else. So she could be someone else. Someone Breanna could be proud of.

"Good job, everyone," she said after she led her group of power walkers back to their starting point and ran them through a series of light stretches to cool down. "I'll see you back here at the same time tomorrow. It'll be our last time together." The comment drew a chorus of disappointed groans as it always did. Each passenger was different, but none of them liked being reminded that their vacation was about to come to an end. "Let's make tomorrow a day to remember. Enjoy the rest of your afternoon."

Kendra Walsh, the assistant manager, was closing up tonight so Jessica was off the clock for the rest of the day. After her power walking class broke up, she tried to find something to help her wind down. She headed up to the lido deck to see if one of the masseuses could squeeze her into the schedule.

"No can do," the receptionist said as she studied the appointment book. "All the passengers are trying to get their last licks in before the trip ends. Everyone on staff is booked solid today and tomorrow."

"Fine. Since I can't get my kinks worked out, I'll spend some time sweating my ass off in the sauna instead."

"Have at it. You've got two to choose from. Since there aren't any male passengers, the men's sauna and locker room are both up for grabs this week."

The majority of the men's restrooms had been temporarily rebranded as well, alleviating the long bathroom lines that occasionally plagued straight cruises.

Jessica headed to the renamed locker room and stashed her clothes in one of the cubbyholes. She donned a complimentary pair of flip-flops provided by the salon, wrapped an oversized towel around her body, and headed to the sauna.

She felt the heat before she opened the door. The pebbled glass window was covered in steam and the brass doorknob was warm to the touch. Almost uncomfortably so. Once she was inside, she checked her palm to see if she had been burned. The skin was bright pink, but the heightened color was already starting to fade.

The three multi-level wooden seating areas were each large enough to accommodate four to six people. A four-foot-tall container filled with water and heated rocks stood in the center of the room.

The view alone was worth the price of admission. One wall was composed of thick glass, providing an unobstructed view of the crystal clear sky above and the similarly hued ocean below.

The room was empty, giving Jessica free rein. She positioned herself next to the window and peered out. Despite the soothing setting, she couldn't seem to relax. The ship was scheduled to arrive in Fort Lauderdale at eight a.m. on Saturday, giving her less than a day and a half to follow orders—or pay the price for refusing to comply.

"Plenty of time to choose between becoming a murderer or a drug dealer. No rush."

The thermostat on the far wall read one hundred seventy degrees, more than enough for Jessica to work up a sweat. She tossed her towel aside as drops of perspiration began to form on her face, arms, and shoulders. She poured water on the heated stones in the center of the room, sending a burst of steam into the dry air.

"Do you mind if we join you?" Raq asked as she and Luisa entered the sauna.

"Come on in. I hope you like it hot."

"That's the main reason we're here." Raq spread a towel on one of the seats opposite Jessica and draped her arms across the bench above her. "I had a few too many glasses of champagne celebrating some friends' engagement. I need to sweat out the alcohol if I don't want to spend the rest of the day passed out in my stateroom."

"Is that why I missed seeing you in the gym today? You were too busy barhopping to hit the weights?"

"Guilty as charged."

"Which friends got engaged? Have I met them?"

"You've met one of them. Tatum's a regular in your spin classes."

"She told me a little about her girlfriend the other day. They sound like they have a solid relationship. They must if they're planning to tie the knot. I'll have to take it easy on her tomorrow. If she looks anything like you two, chances are she won't be feeling too good."

"I can drink tequila like it's water," Luisa said, "but champagne always goes right to my head."

"Must be the bubbles."

"Must be."

"Have you been able to talk to your friend?" Raq asked.

"What's her name again?" Luisa asked. "I don't think you ever said."

"I didn't."

"Did you tell her about my offer, at least?" Raq asked.

"I haven't reached out to her yet." The sweat forming on Jessica's forehead had more to do with the increasing pressure she was under than the rising heat in the room. "I'll meet up with her when I get back to Fort Lauderdale. Some conversations are meant to be had face-to-face instead of from a distance."

Raq and Luisa shared a look. "That's the other reason why we're here." Raq leaned forward and placed her elbows on her knees. "You trust me, right?"

"Yeah." Jessica felt like Raq and Luisa were setting her up for something, but they couldn't be because it was plain to see neither was wearing a wire. "I trust you."

"Then why don't you tell us what's really going on? What are you mixed up in?"

"I'm not—"

Jessica's first instinct was to distance herself from what Raq was implying, but she didn't have the strength or the energy to do so. The time had finally come for her to face her problems instead of running from them.

She told Raq and Luisa everything. From the first run she had made to the one she hoped would be her last. Then she told them about the man she had met in Plaza las Americas. The man who had ordered her to become something she knew she could never be: a killer.

"You said he had a tattoo on his arm?" Luisa dragged her index finger through the condensation on the floor-to-ceiling window. "Did it look something like this?"

Jessica looked at the design Luisa had etched on the glass. A picture of a jaguar poised in mid-leap. "Yes, that's it." She joined Luisa by the window. "Brandon has one, too, but his looks more like this."

Luisa tapped the drawing she had made. "This tattoo is used to let people know the bearer is a hit man for the Jaguars cartel." She tapped the drawing Jessica had created. "We've spotted this one on a few low-level dealers. Insecure types who like to inflate their role in the organization."

"That description fits Brandon to a T." She examined Luisa's calm, determined face. "You seem awfully relaxed for someone who's just been told a cartel leader wants her dead."

"This isn't the first time I've heard this story."

"For your sake," Raq said, "I hope the story ends as well as it did the last time."

"It'd better," Luisa said. "Because if Pilar's men don't kill me, Finn will."

"I think it's time you found a new line of work, dog."

"So do I. Let's not plan the retirement party just yet, though. I've got a few more bad guys to catch first. Are you up for it, Raq?"

"I'm down for anything. You know that."

"What about you, Jessica? I've dealt with this organization before. Its leaders don't react well when someone turns on them. If things go sideways, they could come after you, too. I'm not trying to pressure you, but I need to know if you're in or out."

"I'm in." Jessica didn't need to hear what Luisa had in mind to know the mission would be dangerous. Given a chance to clear her conscience as well as her name, she had to take the risk.

"The ship's security team will search Brandon's room," Luisa said. "If they find his stash, they'll quietly take him into custody and turn him over to Interpol when we reach port tomorrow."

"What about me?" Jessica asked. "What do you want me to do?"

"Start by leaving a note for the maid to find. She'll deliver it to her contact, and that person will send word up the chain of command."

"What should the note say?"

"The truth. That you can't bring yourself to do what you were asked to do."

"Do you want me to return the gun, too?"

"No, hand it over to ship security," Raq said. "They'll tag it, bag it, and keep it as evidence. The serial number has probably been filed off, but maybe someone can *CSI* that shit and find out what it is so we can run a trace on where it was purchased and by who. Give them your burner phone, too, so they can read the texts and research the call history."

"While they're doing that, I'll call a few people to see if they can get their hands on the security footage from the mall," Luisa said. "Once they do, they can run our guy's image through facial recognition software and try to ID him."

"We should hook you up with a sketch artist, too," Raq said. "It's a low-tech way to go, but you'd be surprised how often it brings results."

"All the things you mentioned take time, don't they?" Jessica asked. "I was told to take care of you before the trip ends. That gives us less than two days."

"I know we're up against a deadline," Luisa said, "but some pieces of the puzzle won't fall into place overnight. The legal system simply doesn't work that fast. The Jaguars won't wait for us to get our ducks in a row before they make their move. The clock will start as soon as the maid picks up your note. I expect Pilar, or whoever's currently in charge of the cartel, will have someone in place by tomorrow."

"That means the three of us need to get our shit together by tonight," Raq said. "You didn't happen to pack your bulletproof vest, did you?"

"Hopefully, I won't need it," Luisa said. "As long as I remain in a crowd, the hit man won't have a clear shot at me. He'll have to get the job done up close. I like my chances if I have to resort to hand-to-hand combat, but I hope the situation doesn't get that hairy."

"Don't worry, dog," Raq said. "If shit pops off, I've got your back."

"That's all well and good," Jessica said, "but who's got mine?"

Day Seven

Amy walked through the ship's main dining room with Breanna, Gage Henderson, and Bobby Roberts at her side. Gage was the *Majestic Dream's* event coordinator and Bobby was SOS Tours' creative director. Breakfast service was well underway as they conducted their walkthrough, so they occasionally had to dodge waiters and passengers bearing plates of food.

Lunch service was scheduled to begin in less than three hours. Once lunch service ended, SOS' employees and members of the ship's crew would have less than four hours to prepare the vast space for that night's formal farewell dinner.

The theme Gage and Bobby had chosen for the event was Until We Meet Again. Their vision was ambitious with lots of moving parts. Decorations. Place cards. Party favors. The whole works. Amy didn't know if they would be able to pull it off in the allotted time. She didn't want the night—or the week—to end on a bad note.

"Prom committees take months to take their ideas from start to finish," she said. "Wedding planners, too. Final setup can take days. Are you guys sure four hours is going to provide us with enough of a turnaround? Maybe we should ask the kitchen to end lunch service early to give ourselves more time to get things ready."

Bobby placed his hands on his hips. "Girl, party planning is what I do. When have you ever known me to miss a deadline? Try never, okay? Bitches and queens get shit done. You should count your lucky stars you've got both."

"You're not the first cruise director who's worked herself into a panic over logistics," Gage said. "And rest assured you won't be the last. Sit back, relax, and let the experts do what they do best. Bobby and I won't let you down."

"I can guarantee the decorations will be on point," Bobby said. "What you need to do is check with the kitchen to make sure they'll have their act together. All the guests are going to be in a festive mood tonight because it's the last night of the cruise, but the good vibes won't last long if their food doesn't make it to the tables on time."

"Our kitchen staff is accustomed to serving much larger crowds than we'll be responsible for tonight," Gage said. "I'm confident food service will be fine. It's the other service areas I'm worried about."

Amy's heart sank. The trip had gone incredibly well so far. Even better than she had hoped for, to be honest. The praises SOS Tours and its staffers had received during the week had far outnumbered the complaints, a fact her bosses had been overjoyed to hear when she forwarded the information to them last night.

She was so close to accomplishing her goal of doing her part to get the company back on track. She couldn't afford for the final impression to be a negative one.

"What's your cause for concern, Gage?"

"We're down three people."

"Who?"

"A porter, a maid, and a fitness instructor. We have sufficient staffing to cover for a staff shortage in the gym. We'll need as many people as possible to ferry luggage from the ship to the dock on Saturday, and we're asking the other housekeepers to cover for the absent one. An efficient maid can clean fourteen to sixteen rooms during a shift. The rest of the staff will have to find a way to divvy up the affected rooms."

"Three people are missing at the same time?" This was the first Amy had heard about a staffing shortage. "Did they walk out or get fired?"

Gage lowered his voice to a conspiratorial whisper. "The security staff's trying to keep everything under wraps, but I hear drugs were involved. The porter was led away in handcuffs this morning, and the maid was taken in for questioning."

"What about the fitness instructor?" Breanna asked.

"She's been placed on house arrest 'for her protection.'" Bobby used air quotes to frame the words. "She allegedly brought the drugs on board. From what I heard, it isn't the first time. Just the first time she's gotten caught." He turned to Breanna. "Have you talked to Jessica today?"

"I haven't heard from her since last night. She said she'd be out of touch today but she hoped to see me tonight so she could explain some things she wasn't able to discuss a few days ago." Breanna's eyes widened. "Do you think she's involved in this?"

Amy fervently hoped the answer was no, but she was hesitant to commit one way or the other. "You know her better than I do. What is your gut telling you?"

"That we have more important things to worry about than planning a party."

That's what Amy was afraid of. Visions of Cancún were already running through her head. Was SOS about to have a repeat of what was initially considered a once-in-a-lifetime event?

"Try and get Jessica on the phone to see if she knows what's going on," she said, switching to crisis mode. "While you're doing that, I'll pay a visit to the security chief. He's in the best position to shed some light on things. Perhaps the situation isn't as dire as we're making it out to be."

"And if it is?" Bobby asked.

"We'll have to find a way to avert a disaster before it occurs."

❖

In the ship's security room, Jessica sat in front of a bank of monitors and peered at the images flickering across the rectangular screens. Dennis Shapalov, the *Majestic Dream*'s head of security, sat next to her. Two other members of Dennis's team crowded into the room, too, either to keep an eye on her, the monitors, or both.

She wasn't being treated like a criminal, but she was definitely starting to feel like one. Brandon's arrest had had a sobering effect on her. She had thought she would feel relieved once the crackdown began. Instead, all she felt was resigned to the fact that she might be taken in next. Just because she was cooperating with the authorities didn't mean she was off the hook. No one had offered her immunity yet, so her legal fate was still up in the air. If the people she was betraying vowed to exact revenge, as Luisa had warned they were prone to do, she might feel safer behind bars than on the streets.

"Our feed normally comes from the ship's numerous security cameras." Dennis fiddled with some of the controls on the complex security system. "Today, the Nassau police department was able to link us into its closed-circuit system. Let me know the instant you see someone you think you recognize so I can relay the information to the agents trailing Officer Moreno."

Jessica leaned in to get a closer look. Luisa's, Raq's, and Bathsheba's images appeared on all eight screens, each screen depicting them from a different angle. She watched them browse in one of the many stalls lining the dock. A large throng of tourists surrounded them, making it difficult to track their progress. The three of them were clearly visible one moment, and out of sight the next. Just like Luisa had planned.

Let's hope the bad guys have as much trouble keeping eyes on them as we are.

Nearly a dozen undercover officers from the Nassau police department and various international agencies were scattered throughout the market. They tried to look inconspicuous, but Jessica managed to spot one or two of them. Primarily because they seemed more interested in checking out the crowd than the souvenirs.

"Where's Finn?" she asked when she realized she didn't see her on any of the screens. "If I were her, I'd be hanging on to Luisa for dear life."

"She wanted to, but Officer Moreno and I convinced her to remain behind. Officer Morris and Miss Overstreet have received formal police training. Miss Chamberlain is a civilian. Neither Officer Moreno nor I wanted to put her at risk."

Jessica couldn't imagine what Finn was going through. Finn lived every day with the fear that Luisa might not make it home after her shift. Now she had to live with the fear that Luisa might not return from a shopping trip, an outing that was usually meant to be relaxing, not life-threatening.

"Is Finn on the ship or at the police station?"

"Miss Chamberlain is secure in her stateroom with a guard stationed at the door in case unauthorized personnel attempt to board the vessel while our attention is directed elsewhere. Though we believe the threat against Officer Moreno is real, any attempt on her life might be meant to serve as a diversion while they go after a bigger prize."

"Modern-day pirates attack pleasure boats and cargo vessels all the time. Do you honestly think the Jaguars would seriously consider hijacking a cruise ship?"

"One of the reasons cruise ships now conduct cashless transactions is to make them less attractive targets to the more nefarious members of society. No matter what the individuals we're looking for attempt to do, they won't succeed."

"How can you be sure? They successfully managed to infiltrate the staff of and take over an entire resort. What's to stop them from overwhelming us, too?"

"The resort was caught unawares during more innocent times. The staff didn't know what to look for. My team does.

We've been trained to prevent such occurrences. If we are challenged, we will put that training to use."

Jessica thought Dennis sounded more than a bit like Winston Churchill giving one of his many inspirational speeches during World War II. His confidence made her feel marginally better, but she wouldn't be able to breathe again until Luisa and everyone with her was safe. Maybe not even then. There was still the matter of the conversation she needed to have with Breanna. She had tried once before, but she had put off saying what needed to be said. This time, she wouldn't dodge the truth. She would face it head on, no matter what the consequences turned out to be.

Jessica's breath caught when she spotted a familiar face on the screen. The man who had sat across from her in Plaza las Americas was trailing Luisa, Bathsheba, and Raq through the market. He was about twenty feet behind them and closing fast.

"There! That's him!"

"Are you sure?"

Dennis selected one of the monitors and zoomed in on the image. Jessica instinctively retreated as the man's face and upper body filled the screen.

"Yes, I'm sure. I've had nightmares about that guy since the first time I laid eyes on him. As long as I live, I'll never be able to forget his face. Or that creepy smile of his."

She shuddered as she remembered him watching Breanna shopping in the lingerie store. The lascivious way he had looked at Breanna had made her skin crawl, but she had been powerless to do anything about it. Now the power was in her hands.

In the market, the man pushed unsuspecting shoppers aside with one hand and reached inside his jacket with the other. Jessica expected him to draw a gun at any second. The note she had left for the maid to find had apparently been effective. In it, she had let the powers-that-be know in no uncertain terms that she had no intention of obeying the order she had received to kill Luisa. Though they hadn't responded to her message, it hadn't taken them long to put a willing assassin in her place. If the man took Luisa out, he would undoubtedly come after her next. Her, along with everyone else she held dear. A betrayal like hers, she knew, wouldn't be allowed to go unpunished. She prayed the good guys would get to him first.

"Quick! Call it in. He's making his move! You've got to stop him before he gets to Luisa!"

Dennis hurriedly activated the microphone on his headset radio. "This is Dennis Shapalov from the *Majestic Dream*. We have a positive ID. Our subject is a Latino male with medium-length black hair. He's dressed in a white shirt and dark blue suit. He's approximately five meters behind Officer Moreno and her party. He appears to be armed. Proceed with caution. We don't want a bloodbath on our hands."

Half a dozen officers swarmed the man and ordered him to his knees. As panicked tourists ran for cover, the man held his hands up and slowly sank to the ground.

"It's over," Dennis said as the man was handcuffed and taken into custody.

As people began to abandon their hiding places, another face appeared on the screen. A face Jessica recognized but hadn't expected to see.

"It's not over. It's just beginning."

"Jessica's phone is going straight to voice mail and she isn't in her room or in the gym. Do you have any idea where she could be?"

Breanna sounded like she was on the verge of a full-scale panic attack. Amy couldn't blame her. She was close to losing it, too.

"Calm down, Bree. I'm heading to the security chief's office now. Hold on. Someone's hailing me on the walkie." She unclipped the two-way radio from her belt and held the receiver to her lips. "This is Amy. Go ahead. Over."

"We've got a problem in the atrium outside the excursion office," Bobby said.

"Can it wait?"

"No, we have an honest-to-God emergency. I've already called for a doctor. You'd better get down here fast. Over."

"This day is going from bad to worse," she said with a sigh. "I'll be there in a sec, Bobby. Over and out." She put the walkie-talkie away and returned to her phone call as she sprinted toward the elevator. "Change of plans, Bree. I need you to talk to the security chief. I've got to check in on one of the passengers."

"So I heard. I'm already on my way. And, Ames?"

Amy frantically pushed the down button on the elevator until the doors mercifully opened. "Yeah?"

"Be careful."

The elevator doors slid shut and the car began to descend. "You, too."

❖

Spencer was admiring the craftsmanship on a series of driftwood sculptures when she heard the screams. Petty thievery was a common occurrence in many port cities, according to some of the guidebooks she had read. She thought the disturbance was caused by someone who had been robbed by a pickpocket and was trying to draw attention to the incident before the bandit disappeared into the large crowd.

At least ten other cruise ships were anchored in the harbor, and most of their passengers had headed straight for the open-air market near the port as they searched for last-minute souvenirs on the penultimate day of their respective itineraries.

Spencer ignored the disruption, confident the security guards posted throughout the market were on top of the situation. Then she saw dozens of people running past her like thrill seekers trying to dodge a herd of bulls in Pamplona.

She walked out of the market stall so she could see what everyone was trying to get away from, but there was too much chaos for her to determine the cause. All she caught were flashes of color and snippets of what sounded like a dozen foreign languages. She was about to take a few more steps forward when the shopkeeper grabbed her arm and spun her around.

"Fifty dollars." The woman's thick Bahamian accent gave her statement the lilting quality of a lullaby.

"What?"

"You want the seahorse? You pay me fifty dollars first."

Spencer had forgotten she had the three-foot-tall driftwood replica of a seahorse in her hand. She had been trying to decide between it, an octopus, and a primitive peace sign when the commotion began. The stated price for the seahorse was higher than she wanted to pay, but it didn't seem like the right time or place to haggle. She pulled three twenties from her wallet and thrust the bills toward the woman. "Keep the change."

"Have a nice day. Try not to get run over. It's even crazier than usual out there."

The shopkeeper didn't seem too fazed about what was happening so Spencer didn't know if she should take it seriously or blow it off. Her internal debate ended when she saw a woman holding Luisa, Bathsheba, and Raq at gunpoint.

Spencer's Spanish was too limited for her to understand what the woman was saying, but her intent was obvious. She wasn't trying to rob them. She meant to kill one or all of them. Luisa drew most of the woman's focus, indicating she was the primary target. Raq and Bathsheba flanked her, shielding her from view. If the woman wanted Luisa, their positions made it clear she would have to go through them first.

Spencer slipped into a stall selling beach apparel and accessories. The stall's owner and four prospective customers were hiding under a folding table laden with an array of sandals, flip-flops, and knockoff designer sunglasses. Spencer crawled past racks filled with beach towels and cover-ups until she reached the stall's opening.

"This isn't a video game, you know," she reminded herself. "This is real life. This is no time to play hero."

But if she didn't assume the role, who would?

"Go big or go home."

Based on the sound of her voice, the woman had to be less than three feet away. Spencer took a deep breath, braced her back against one of the rack's metal supports, and pushed with all her might. The rack tipped over, spilling bikinis, T-shirts, board shorts, and rash guards on the woman's head. The woman yelped in surprise and spun toward her. Spencer raised the driftwood seahorse like it was an ax and brought it down hard on the woman's wrist.

The gun flew from the woman's hand. Spencer didn't wait to see where it went. She swung the sculpture again, aiming for the woman's head. The seahorse's curled tail caught her squarely on the chin.

The woman spun and went down, dazed but still conscious. Luisa and Raq took care of the rest. They rolled the woman onto her stomach and held her down until the police arrived a few seconds later.

Bathsheba secured the gun before she helped Spencer to her feet. "Are you out of your mind? She could have shot you."

Spencer dusted herself off and tucked the sculpture under her arm. The seahorse had seemed overpriced a few minutes ago. Now its worth was beyond measure. "They don't call me Kamikaze Collins for nothing."

"Yes!" Jessica thrust her arms in the air like she was helping a client celebrate the achievement of a hard-earned fitness goal. "Did you see that?"

"Who were those women?" Dennis asked.

"The woman with the gun was Pilar Obregon."

"The alleged head of the cartel targeting Officer Moreno?"

"Yep, that's her. She looks like a beauty queen because she used to be one. Don't let the pretty face fool you, though. She's as ruthless as they come. The woman who knocked her on her ass just now is one of our passengers."

"Why would someone who wields as much power as Miss Obregon does place herself at such risk? She could have sent anyone to do her bidding. It doesn't seem logical for her to perform the job herself."

"Luisa killed Pilar's lover a few months ago. Luisa was just doing her job, but Pilar wanted her to pay for her actions. After I refused to follow orders, she was obviously so hell-bent on revenge she decided to pull the trigger herself. She almost succeeded, too." Jessica watched as Luisa, Bathsheba, Raq, and Spencer exchanged a round of high fives. "Love makes you do crazy things."

"Is that the excuse you've decided to go with?"

Jessica turned to find Breanna standing behind her.

Breanna's eyes darted from Jessica's face to the bank of monitors and back again.

"What's going on, Jess? Why haven't you answered any of my calls? Bobby said you were under house arrest."

"Not quite. I've been in here helping the security team with something. I'm done now. With all of it."

Jessica reached for her, but Breanna backed away, rejecting her before she'd even had a chance to explain. No, that wasn't true. She'd had plenty of chances. She had simply chosen not to take any of them.

"I've done some things I'm not proud of, Bree, and I'm trying to make up for them."

Breanna's chin quivered as she tried not to cry. "So it's true? You smuggled drugs on the ship? You and Brandon were working together? You're the reason he got arrested?"

"I advise you not to answer any of those questions without a lawyer present," Dennis said.

"That means the answer to each of my questions is yes," Breanna said.

"Ah, well," Dennis stammered. "This is a conversation that needs to be had between the two of you. If you'll excuse me, I need to inform Miss Chamberlain that the threat against Officer Moreno has been successfully averted."

"How?" Breanna asked after Dennis left. "Why? For how long?"

Breanna sounded defeated. Jessica felt the same way.

"It started before I met you. Little things at first, then larger and larger favors."

"Why didn't you say no?"

"I wanted to, but the temptation was too great. I was offered a quick and easy way to earn enough money to open my own gym and I took it. Now my bank accounts are frozen and all my money's gone. If it isn't already, it soon will be. I would say I'm back at square one, but I'm actually worse off because I have even less now than I did when I started out."

"That's not true." Breanna took her hand. "You've still got me. *'Ohana* means family, remember?"

Jessica blinked back tears of gratitude. "How could I forget?"

The *Majestic Dream* featured three atriums: a small one on the lower promenade deck and larger ones on the two decks immediately above. The atrium on the promenade deck was so grand it looked like a set from a classic Hollywood movie. Each time she walked past it, Amy half-expected to see Cary Grant or Ingrid Bergman standing under the stained glass skylight at the top.

The ship's doctor had already arrived by the time she reached the promenade deck, and a large crowd of onlookers had gathered around him. She squeezed her way through the throng to see what had captured everyone's attention.

A woman lay on her back at the foot of the winding staircase. She was wearing an Evel Knievel T-shirt and a pair of board shorts emblazoned with illustrations of vintage motorcycles. Her right ankle was visibly swollen and already starting to bruise.

"It feels like a bad sprain rather than a break," the doctor said, "but I'll need to take a few X-rays to confirm."

Amy knelt next to them. She was glad to hear the woman was going to be okay, but she needed to make sure neither SOS Tours nor the ship's owners were about to have a lawsuit on their hands. "Did you fall? Were you pushed?"

"The banister looks like the one in my parents' house," the woman said. "I tried to slide down it like I used to when I was a kid. My feet got caught up in the railings before I made it halfway down and I ended up doing a header. Just like I used to when I as a kid. My mom always said I was going to break my neck one day. I'm starting to think she might be psychic." She grinned. "At least I'll have a great yarn to share at the farewell dinner tonight. Lesbians dig scars—and the stories behind them. If my ankle isn't broken, doc, do you think you can strap it up nice and tight? Bandages are almost as good as casts when it comes to garnering sympathy points."

"I'll see what I can do."

The doctor helped the woman into a wheelchair so he could ferry her to the infirmary three decks below and conduct a more thorough examination on her injured ankle.

"Let me know if the injury is too serious to be treated on the ship," Amy said. "If it is, I'll need to accompany you to the hospital."

"If I'd known I had a chance to spend the afternoon with you holding my hand," the woman said with a wink, "I would have done this days ago. Maybe I should give it another shot."

When the woman made a move to get out of the wheelchair, Amy pushed her back into it.

"Stay put. I don't think my heart could take much more drama today." She eagerly reached for her cell phone when she saw Breanna's name printed on the display. "Please tell me you have good news."

"That depends on your definition of *good.*"

Breanna began to weave a tale that seemed far-fetched but turned out to be all too true.

"Are you sure it was Spencer who took Pilar down?" Amy asked when Breanna had shared all the information she had gathered from Jessica and the security team. "She could have been seriously hurt. Maybe even killed."

"But she wasn't. No one else was, either. Spencer, Luisa, Raq, and Bathsheba have to wrap up a few things at the police station first, then they'll be free to explore Nassau or return to the ship." Breanna sighed. "Today was bad, Ames, but it could have been so much worse."

"I know the perfect way to make it better. I'll talk to you later, Bree. I have a dinner to plan."

And it could turn out to be the most important meal of her life.

NIGHT SEVEN

Spencer put on the tuxedo, pleated shirt, and dress shoes she had purchased from the boutique when she returned to the ship that afternoon. She wasn't going to like the looks of her credit card bill next month, but she loved the image that reflected back at her when she peered in the mirror: a woman who was confident and sure of herself, not an awkward loner who was afraid of her own shadow. A woman who was striding toward the future, not running from her past.

She headed downstairs to meet Hannah, Maneet, Bonnie, Raq, Bathsheba, Finn, Luisa, Jordan, and Tatum in the Reverie for a drink. Since most of them would be seated at different tables during dinner, this informal gathering would be their final chance to chat before they went their separate ways tomorrow morning.

"There she is," Raq said when Spencer walked into the bar. Raq beckoned her to join her and the rest of the group in the booth they had crowded into.

Spencer headed over to them and greeted everyone with a hug. The tight embrace Finn pulled her into was only slightly less crushing than the one Raq had doled out. "I don't know whether to applaud you for being brave or yell at you for being stupid," Finn said, "so I'll just thank you for helping to keep my girl safe."

"Hear, hear," Bathsheba said as everyone raised their glasses of champagne in a toast. "You slayed it out there today, Spencer.

Come through, diva." She snapped her fingers for emphasis. "Come through."

"I learned from the best." Spencer liked being the object of praise rather than the subject of ridicule. She could get used to this. "I was just trying to keep up with the rest of you."

"If you're trying to keep up with me, you've got some catching up to do. You're a few rounds behind." Raq handed Spencer a glass of champagne. "You look good, dog."

"Thanks. You guys do, too."

Everyone was wearing an attractive suit or gorgeous dress. Jordan won the accessories battle, however, thanks to the diamond engagement ring sparkling on her finger.

Raq brushed her hands over the lapels of her charcoal gray suit. The beaded dress Bathsheba was wearing was nearly the same shade. "Tell me something I don't know."

"This is the place where we met seven short days ago," Hannah said.

"Before you dumped me for Maneet?" Spencer asked.

Maneet chuckled. "I'm willing to share."

"That's what she said."

"Don't look now," Bonnie said, "but she might be changing her tune."

Hannah kissed Maneet's hand. "You're never too old to learn."

"Do you remember the offer you made me last week?" Spencer asked.

"At this point of the trip, she's lucky if she remembers her own name," Bonnie said. "You'd better refresh her memory."

"You said if I was in the market for a new place to stay, I should look you up."

Hannah's eyebrows shot up. "Are you considering a change of scenery?"

"I think it's time I took a look at what the West Coast has to offer."

"Excellent. Give me a call whenever you're ready to get the ball rolling. We can talk likes and dislikes and I'll get to work on finding something in your preferred style that's also within your budget."

"I'm happy for you," Maneet said.

"So am I."

"Does your decision to change zip codes have anything to do with a certain cruise director?"

"No. Well, maybe a little, but it has more to do with me. I'm ready to try something new."

Her brush with death that afternoon had given her a new appreciation for life. She had pledged to start living hers by her own rules instead of someone else's.

"It's been an honor to meet each and every one of you. Shall we do it again next year?"

"Sounds like a plan to me," Luisa said. "Without the gunplay next time."

"I'm down for that," Finn said.

Luisa leaned toward Finn and gave her a kiss. "I figured you might be."

"Be sure to give us your new address so we'll know where to send your wedding invitation," Tatum said.

"That's an event I wouldn't miss for the world," Spencer said.

"Unless you want me to hook you up with one of the bridesmaids," Jordan said, "you'll have to find your own date."

"I think I might be able to help with that."

Spencer turned at the sound of Amy's voice. What she saw took her breath away. Amy was dressed in a black silk chiffon cocktail dress with a plunging neckline. The sheer cape attached to the back of the dress gently wafted behind her as she moved. Her high heels made her long legs look even longer. A string of pearls circled her neck, and her long blond hair was gathered into an elegant chignon. Spencer had never seen anyone so beautiful. She rose to her feet even though she felt like bowing before her.

"Would you like to have dinner with me?" Amy asked.

"I'd love to. Shall we?" Spencer offered her arm. When Amy placed her hand in the crook of her elbow, Spencer felt ten feet tall. She had the privilege of squiring the hottest girl in the room.

The rest of the group joined them in the elevator. When they disembarked on the promenade deck, Spencer tried to follow suit, but Amy wouldn't let her.

"The main dining room is on this floor," Spencer said.

Amy punched a button for one of the lower decks. "But my room's not."

Spencer felt like she had died and gone to heaven.

Maybe Pilar got me after all. She pinched herself to see if she could still feel it. *Yep, still here.*

"Are you okay?" Amy asked as the elevator began to descend.

"I can honestly say I've never been better."

Amy unlocked her stateroom door and ushered Spencer inside. She had spent all afternoon decorating the room. She had felt like a passenger trying to win a prize for most creative door design, only on a larger scale. She didn't have as much square footage to work with as Bobby and Gage did, but she had done her best to transform the drab, utilitarian room into a more welcoming environment. Even though the final result paled in comparison to the dramatic makeover Bobby and Gage had given the main dining room, she was proud of her efforts. And even prouder to be sharing this night with Spencer.

The last night of a cruise was always bittersweet. Reliving fond memories was fun, but saying good-bye to newfound friends was difficult. This time, though, she felt like laughing instead of crying. Not only had her team met all the goals they had set for themselves before the cruise began, she had also accomplished something she hadn't expected. She had fallen for someone. Not just anyone. Spencer Collins. The most amazing woman she had ever met.

Since she was a passenger, Spencer was supposed to be off-limits. But Amy hadn't been able to abide by the rules. Not this time. Her heart wouldn't let her. Her bosses wouldn't be happy that she had allowed herself to become emotionally involved with a client, to put it mildly. She would deal with the expected fallout when it came. At the moment, however, her job was the last thing on her mind. Spencer had taught her many things over the past week, the most important being there were more important things to life than work.

"Room service takes a while on most nights," she said. "Tonight, the kitchen's especially overwhelmed, so I took the liberty of ordering ahead."

"How did you know I'd say yes?"

"I didn't, but I'm glad you did. Otherwise, I'd have to eat all this food myself."

Spencer examined the plates Amy had placed on a small candlelit table. She flashed a sly smile when she saw what Amy had chosen to serve for dessert. "Including the chocolate mousse?"

"Everything except for that." When Spencer didn't offer any comments on the main course, Amy began to worry Spencer might not like what was being served. Had she gotten something wrong? Had she been presumptuous? She chided herself for overthinking, then told herself to relax. Spencer wasn't like anyone she had ever been with. She didn't have to put on airs to impress her. She just had to be herself. "We have so many dining options I wasn't quite sure what to order. I was tempted to order barbecue to give you a taste of home, but I figured whatever the ship's chefs dished out couldn't compete with any of your favorite restaurants."

"Good call. When it comes to Southern barbecue, nothing beats a good hole-in-the-wall or a shack by the side of the road. If the food's really good, I usually end up dribbling most of the sauce on my shirt. I could probably find a bib if I had to, but that isn't the look I wanted to go for tonight."

"The James Bond thing definitely works for you. You should stick with it."

"I'll keep that in mind."

"Is surf and turf okay by you?"

"Let's see." Spencer regarded the table. "Candles, bone-in rib eye, grilled lobster tails, charred lime wedges, cauliflower puree, and a bottle of seriously expensive red wine to wash everything down? I think I can manage. The setup is amazing, and the menu is even better." She fingered the linen tablecloth Amy had borrowed for the night. "I do have one question for you, though."

"What might that be?"

"In case I haven't told you, you look amazing." Spencer twirled Amy in a slow circle like they were on a spacious dance floor rather than a cramped stateroom. "There are thousands of women on this ship who would love to catch even a fleeting glimpse of you in that outfit. Why am I the only one being treated to such an incredible view?"

"I've spent far too much time this week worrying about what everyone else thinks." Spencer looked so handsome in her tuxedo she was like a dream come true. Amy moved closer to her to make sure she was real. She rested her hands on Spencer's chest and looked deep into her eyes. "Tonight, the only opinion I care about is yours."

"What about the farewell dinner? Everyone's been talking about it for days. Isn't it supposed to be one of the highlights of the week?"

The farewell dinner, like the white party earlier in the week, were signature events on each trip. Amy had hoped to make her mark on both—until she had decided to take a chance on something long-term rather than temporary.

"The highlight of my week has been watching you come into your own. You seemed lost when you boarded the ship last week. When I looked into your eyes that first day, I was struck by what I saw: uncertainty and fear."

"What do you see when you look into my eyes now?"

Amy ran her palms over the lapels on Spencer's jacket. She could feel strength radiating from Spencer. Not just physical. Mental, too. She admired the courage Spencer had exhibited in pushing past the emotional roadblocks that had held her back for so long. "I see determination. Assurance. Fearlessness."

Spencer slipped her arms around Amy's waist. "Is that all you see?"

"No." Spencer's eyes burned with desire. Amy hoped Spencer saw the same emotion reflected in her eyes. She wanted Spencer. Here. Now. Forever. And she wanted her to know it. "A few days ago, you asked me not to kiss you again unless I meant it."

"I remember."

Amy leaned forward and captured Spencer's lips in a kiss. The previous kiss they had shared had felt wrong on some level because it hadn't been real. This one was as real as it got.

"Are you sure you want to repeat past mistakes?" Spencer asked when they finally came up for air.

"I used a poor choice of words when I tried to explain my actions that day. When I tried to convince myself I could ignore my feelings for you." Amy caressed her cheek. "The only mistake I made was trying to deny how deeply I've come to care for you. When I think about what could have happened to you today—"

Spencer silenced her with another kiss. "This afternoon is already over and done with. I'm through allowing the past to prevent me from having a future. If you can stop focusing on the future long enough to enjoy the present, maybe we can meet in the middle."

"I'm not thinking about the next trip, the one after that, or the one after that. Tonight, all I want to think about—all I *can* think about—is you. The rest of the staff can manage without me for a few hours. Will your friends be able to survive without you?"

Spencer grinned. "They're big girls. I think they'll be fine. Allow me." She pulled Amy's chair out for her, took the seat opposite her, and filled their glasses with wine. "I know this isn't the dinner party you originally intended to host tonight, but I must admit I like the change in plans. What should we drink to?"

Amy thought for a moment. Tonight didn't feel like the end of a trip. It felt like the start of a much different journey. "How about new beginnings?"

"To new beginnings. Speaking of which, I'm going to need your help with mine."

Amy listened as Spencer talked excitedly about picking up stakes and moving to the West Coast.

"Are you planning to move to Seattle to be closer to your job?" Amy pushed her empty plate away from her. The conversation had flowed so freely during dinner that the delicious main course had seemed more like an appetizer of things to come.

"It will be nice to be in the same time zone as the rest of my team for a change. I haven't decided which city I'll settle in, though. Seattle's beautiful, but it's cold and rainy most of the year. I'm a Georgia girl. I don't know if I can acclimate to such a drastic change in conditions."

"For what it's worth, the weather in southern California is gorgeous year-round." Amy felt like an unpaid spokesperson for the state tourism board.

"So I've heard. I'll make a deal with you," Spencer said as she refilled their glasses. "I'll show you around my neck of the woods if you do the same for me in yours."

"You've got a deal." They sealed their pact with a toast rather than a handshake. Amy cleared the dinner plates from the table and set a glass filled with whipped cream-topped chocolate mousse in the center. "Earlier this week, I promised I would spend the last night of the trip gorging on chocolate if you agreed to have dinner with me every night."

"Our dinner plans were broken a time or two, so I don't expect you to stick to the bargain we made."

"No, I insist. It was my idea, after all. I may have amended the terms a bit, but I never make a promise I don't intend to keep." Amy dipped her spoon into the sumptuous dessert. The mousse was rich, creamy, and surprisingly good. "What do you think?" she asked after she offered Spencer a sample.

Spencer licked her lips as she set her spoon down. "That the mousse is only the second sweetest thing I've tasted tonight."

"I aim to please."

"So do I. Right now, I'm making you a promise: I'm going to spend the rest of the night making love to you."

"Do you always keep your promises?"

Spencer held out her hand. "There's only one way to find out."

Much to Amy's delight, Spencer proved to be a woman of her word. Spencer was a gentle and attentive lover. She also didn't lack for enthusiasm. Their lovemaking wasn't a rush to the finish line, however. They took their time. Exploring each other's bodies. Discovering what gave the other pleasure. Then doing it all over again.

Amy felt like they were on another excursion. Slow, unhurried, and filled with new kinds of adventure. She couldn't wait to see what their next destination would be.

"I don't know about you," she said as she lay in Spencer's arms later, "but I could use a vacation."

"How does a trip to the south of France sound?"

"Like music to my ears."

"Good." Spencer slowly ran her hand along the length of Amy's bare back. Amy thrilled at her touch. "Now let's make a little more."

Amy's breath caught as Spencer kissed her way down her body. She closed her eyes when Spencer's mouth found her center.

"If this is your idea of a pleasure cruise, sign me up."

Anchors Aweigh

Spencer couldn't believe how much her life had changed. A year ago, she was a single loner with practically no friends. Now she was in a relationship and had been embraced by a band of women she could always count on to be there for her no matter what.

With Hannah's help, she was able to find a cool condo in West Hollywood that was in her price range. The spacious apartment was much too big for one person, but it was a cozy fit for two. She and Amy had been living together for almost seven months. Spencer wasn't planning to pop the question on this trip as Tatum had on the way to Nassau last year, but she was on the lookout for the perfect ring. Something elegant and understated. Just like Amy.

Amy had feared SOS Tours would fire her when she informed the members of senior management that she and Spencer were an item. Instead, they had given her their unconditional support, along with a promotion and a substantial raise.

"Maybe I should fall in love on every trip," Amy had said when she told Spencer the good news.

"You can, but only if it's with me."

Spencer held Amy's hand as they walked along Las Ramblas, the tree-lined pedestrian mall in central Barcelona that was popular with tourists and locals alike. Cafés and souvenir kiosks lined both sides of the nearly mile-long thoroughfare, which was composed of a series of shorter streets, each with its own set of attractions. One street featured a former monastery, one an arts center, and another a large open-air flower market.

Spencer reveled in the various sights and sounds. A year ago, she would have found the barrage of stimuli overwhelming. Now she couldn't get enough.

She and Amy had flown to Europe to board the long-awaited riverboat cruise from Montpellier to Monaco that Spencer had won the year before. The two-day trip to Barcelona was part of the vacation stretcher they had purchased to make the good times last even longer. Hannah, Maneet, Bathsheba, Raq, Jordan, Tatum, Luisa, and Finn had done the same. They were meeting for tapas later and had all purchased tickets on the same train from Barcelona to Montpellier tomorrow afternoon.

Spencer couldn't wait to see everyone again. She talked to each of them often, and she and Raq played video games against each other several times a week, but conversations held via FaceTime, Skype, or PlayStation weren't as satisfying as they were in person. Some women's personalities were too large to be contained by a small screen.

"Are you going to be able to handle being a passenger for the next eight days instead of an employee?" she asked.

Amy squeezed her hand. "As long as you're by my side, I can handle anything."

Spencer felt the same way. Amy was her partner in every sense of the word. Whether large or small, they made all their decisions together. They were a unit. A team. Spencer finally had something she never thought she'd have: a place to belong.

Amy stopped in front of the Font de Canaletes, an ornate fountain located on the upper part of Las Ramblas. "Should I?"

"That depends." According to the inscription on the bottom of the fountain, anyone who drank from it was destined to return to Barcelona. "Do you want to come back here one day?"

"Here and so many other places. I want to see the world with you."

"Then I guess I'd better drink up, too." Spencer dipped her hand into the water and took a sip. "Looks like you're stuck with me."

"Is that a promise?"

"You bet it is."

Like all the other promises she had made Amy, it was one she intended to keep.

About the Author

Yolanda Wallace is not a professional writer, but she plays one in her spare time. Her love of travel and adventure has helped her pen sixteen globe-spanning novels, including the Lambda Award-winning *Month of Sundays* and the Lambda Award finalist *Date with Destiny*, written as Mason Dixon. Her short stories have appeared in multiple anthologies including *Romantic Interludes 2: Secrets* and *Women of the Dark Streets*. She and her wife live in beautiful coastal Georgia, where they are parents to two children of the four-legged variety.

Books Available from Bold Strokes Books

Exposed by MJ Williamz. The closet is no place to live if you want to find true love. (978-1-62639-989-1)

Force of Fire: Toujours a Vous by Ali Vali. Immortals Kendal and Piper welcome their new child and celebrate the defeat of an old enemy, but another ancient evil is about to awaken deep in the jungles of Costa Rica. (978-1-63555-047-4)

Holding Their Place by Kelly A. Wacker. Together Dr. Helen Connery and ambulance driver Julia March, discover that goodness, love, and passion can be found in the most unlikely and even dangerous places during WWI. (978-1-63555-338-3)

Landing Zone by Erin Dutton. Can a career veteran finally discover a love stronger than even her pride? (978-1-63555-199-0)

Love at Last Call by M. Ullrich. Is balancing business, friendship, and love more than any willing woman can handle? (978-1-63555-197-6)

Pleasure Cruise by Yolanda Wallace. Spencer Collins and Amy Donovan have few things in common, but a Caribbean cruise offers both women an unexpected chance to face one of their greatest fears: falling in love. (978-1-63555-219-5)

Running Off Radar by MB Austin. Maji's plans to win Rose back are interrupted when work intrudes and duty calls her to help a SEAL team stop a Russian mobster from harvesting gold from the bottom of Sitka Sound. (978-1-63555-152-5)

Shadow of the Phoenix by Rebecca Harwell. In the final battle for the fate of Storm's Quarry, even Nadya's and Shay's powers may not be enough. (978-1-63555-181-5)

Shadow of the Phoenix by Rebecca Harwell. In the final battle for the fate of Storm's Quarry, even Nadya's and Shay's powers may not be enough. (978-1-63555-181-5)

Take a Chance by D. Jackson Leigh. There's hardly a woman within fifty miles of Pine Cone that veterinarian Trip Beaumont can't charm, except for the irritating new cop, Jamie Grant, who keeps leaving parking tickets on her truck. (978-1-63555-118-1)

The Outcasts by Alexa Black. Spacebus driver Sue Jones is running from her past. When she crash-lands on a faraway world, the Outcast Kara might be her chance for redemption. (978-1-63555-242-3)

Alias by Cari Hunter. A car crash leaves a woman with no memory and no identity. Together with Detective Bronwen Pryce, she fights to uncover a truth that might just kill them both. (978-1-63555-221-8)

Death in Time by Robyn Nyx. Working in the past is hell on your future. (978-1-63555-053-5)

Hers to Protect by Nicole Disney. High school sweethearts Kaia and Adrienne will have to see past their differences and survive the vengeance of a brutal gang if they want to be together. (978-1-63555-229-4)

Of Echoes Born by 'Nathan Burgoine. A collection of queer fantasy short stories set in Canada from Lambda Literary Award finalist 'Nathan Burgoine. (978-1-63555-096-2)

Perfect Little Worlds by Clifford Mae Henderson. Lucy can't hold the secret any longer. Twenty-six years ago, her sister did the unthinkable. (978-1-63555-164-8)

Room Service by Fiona Riley. Interior designer Olivia likes stability, but when work brings footloose Savannah into her world and into a new city every month, Olivia must decide if what makes her comfortable is what makes her happy. (978-1-63555-120-4)

Sparks Like Ours by Melissa Brayden. Professional surfers Gia Malone and Elle Britton can't deny their chemistry on and off the beach. But only one can win... (978-1-63555-016-0)

Take My Hand by Missouri Vaun. River Hemsworth arrives in Georgia intent on escaping quickly, but when she crashes her Mercedes into the Clip 'n Curl, sexy Clay Cahill ends up rescuing more than her car. (978-1-63555-104-4)

The Last Time I Saw Her by Kathleen Knowles. Lane Hudson only has twelve days to win back Alison's heart. That is if she can gather the courage to try. (978-1-63555-067-2)

Wayworn Lovers by Gun Brooke. Will agoraphobic composer Giselle Bonnaire and Tierney Edwards, a wandering soul who can't remain in one place for long, trust in the passionate love destiny hands them? (978-1-62639-995-2)

Breakthrough by Kris Bryant. Falling for a sexy ranger is one thing, but is the possibility of love worth giving up the career Kennedy Wells has always dreamed of? (978-1-63555-179-2)

Certain Requirements by Elinor Zimmerman. Phoenix has always kept her love of kinky submission strictly behind the bedroom door and inside the bounds of romantic relationships, until she meets Kris Andersen. (978-1-63555-195-2)

Dark Euphoria by Ronica Black. When a high-profile case drops in Detective Maria Diaz's lap, she forges ahead only to discover this case, and her main suspect, aren't like any other. (978-1-63555-141-9)

Fore Play by Julie Cannon. Executive Leigh Marshall falls hard for Peyton Broader, her golf pro…and an ex-con. Will she risk sabotaging her career for love? (978-1-63555-102-0)

Love Came Calling by CA Popovich. Can a romantic looking for a long-term, committed relationship and a jaded cynic too busy for love conquer life's struggles and find their way to what matters most? (978-1-63555-205-8)

Outside the Law by Carsen Taite. Former sweethearts Tanner Cohen and Sydney Braswell must work together on a federal task force to see justice served, but will they choose to embrace their second chance at love? (978-1-63555-039-9)

The Princess Deception by Nell Stark. When journalist Missy Duke realizes Prince Sebastian is really his twin sister Viola in disguise, she plays along, but when sparks flare between them, will the double deception doom their fairy-tale romance? (978-1-62639-979-2)

The Smell of Rain by Cameron MacElvee. Reyha Arslan, a wise and elegant woman with a tragic past, shows Chrys that there's still beauty to embrace and reason to hope despite the world's cruelty. (978-1-63555-166-2)

The Talebearer by Sheri Lewis Wohl. Liz's visions show her the faces of the lost and the killers who took their lives. As one by one, the murdered are found, a stranger works to stop Liz before the serial killer is brought to justice. (978-1-635550-126-6)

White Wings Weeping by Lesley Davis. The world is full of discord and hatred, but how much of it is just human nature when an evil with sinister intent is invading people's hearts? (978-1-63555-191-4)

A Call Away by KC Richardson. Can a businesswoman from a big city find the answers she's looking for, and possibly love, on a small-town farm? (978-1-63555-025-2)

Berlin Hungers by Justine Saracen. Can the love between an RAF woman and the wife of a Luftwaffe pilot, former enemies, survive in besieged Berlin during the aftermath of World War II? (978-1-63555-116-7)

Blend by Georgia Beers. Lindsay and Piper are like night and day. Working together won't be easy, but not falling in love might prove the hardest job of all. (978-1-63555-189-1)

Hunger for You by Jenny Frame. Principe of an ancient vampire clan Byron Debrek must save her one true love from falling into the hands of her enemies and into the middle of a vampire war. (978-1-63555-168-6)

Mercy by Michelle Larkin. FBI Special Agent Mercy Parker and psychic ex-profiler Piper Vasey learn to love again as they race to stop a man with supernatural gifts who's bent on annihilating humankind. (978-1-63555-202-7)

Pride and Porters by Charlotte Greene. Will pride and prejudice prevent these modern-day lovers from living happily ever after? (978-1-63555-158-7)

Rocks and Stars by Sam Ledel. Kyle's struggle to own who she is and what she really wants may end up landing her on the bench and without the woman of her dreams. (978-1-63555-156-3)

The Boss of Her: Office Romance Novellas by Julie Cannon, Aurora Rey, and M. Ullrich. Going to work never felt so good. Three office romance novellas from talented writers Julie Cannon, Aurora Rey, and M. Ullrich. (978-1-63555-145-7)

The Deep End by Ellie Hart. When family ties become entangled in murder and deception, it's time to find a way out... (978-1-63555-288-1)

A Country Girl's Heart by Dena Blake. When Kat Jackson gets a second chance at love, following her heart will prove the hardest decision of all. (978-1-63555-134-1)

Dangerous Waters by Radclyffe. Life, death, and war on the home front. Two women join forces against a powerful opponent, nature itself. (978-1-63555-233-1)

Fury's Death by Brey Willows. When all we hold sacred fails, who will be there to save us? (978-1-63555-063-4)

It's Not a Date by Heather Blackmore. Kade's desire to keep things with Jen on a professional level is in Jen's best interest. Yet what's in Kade's best interest...is Jen. (978-1-63555-149-5)

Killer Winter by Kay Bigelow. Just when she thought things could get no worse, homicide Lieutenant Leah Samuels learns the woman she loves has betrayed her in devastating ways. (978-1-63555-177-8)

Score by MJ Williamz. Will an addiction to pain pills destroy Ronda's chance with the woman she loves or will she come out on top and score a happily ever after? (978-1-62639-807-8)

Spring's Wake by Aurora Rey. When wanderer Willa Lange falls for Provincetown B&B owner Nora Calhoun, will past hurts and a fifteen-year age gap keep them from finding love? (978-1-63555-035-1)

The Northwoods by Jane Hoppen. When Evelyn Bauer, disguised as her dead husband, George, travels to a Northwoods logging camp to work, she and the camp cook Sarah Bell forge a friendship fraught with both tenderness and turmoil. (978-1-63555-143-3)

Truth or Dare by C. Spencer. For a group of six lesbian friends, life changes course after one long snow-filled weekend. (978-1-63555-148-8)